EVERYMAN, I will go with thee,
and be thy guide,
In thy most need to go by thy side

THOMAS HARDY

Stories and Poems

SELECTED AND EDITED BY
DONALD J. MORRISON
BIOGRAPHICAL NOTE BY
JAMES GIBSON
INTRODUCTION BY
J. I. M. STEWART

DENT: LONDON
EVERYMAN'S LIBRARY

NO. 1708

ISBN: 0 460 01708 x

Contents

Contents

POEMS

Contents

Contents

Contents

Contents

Contents

Contents

The particulars identifying the medium and date of first publication are followed, as appropriate, by the title of the collection in which the story or poem was later included, or that of a longer work of which it formed part before ultimate publication in the *Collected Works*.

Thomas Hardy

A BIOGRAPHICAL NOTE

Hardy was fascinated by the relationship of time and place, and part of his greatness as a writer results from his strong sense of the transience of time and the permanence of place. When he was born in the village of Bockhampton on 2nd June 1840 there were many alive who could well remember the Napoleonic War. When he died on 11th January 1928 those early Victorian years of his youth must have seemed several lifetimes away. Bockhampton in 1840 was a remote hamlet, three miles out of the small country town of Dorchester. Hardy's father had an old-established building business, but the great love of his life was music, and his son grew up in a rural setting to the accompaniment of music both in the parish church of Stinsford and at local festivities. These early years of his life, the Wessex people and the Wessex country-side, were to be immortalized in the finest of his novels and in some of his greatest poems.

It is wrong to regard Hardy as an uneducated countryman and a clumsy literary craftsman. He went to the village school, and at nine moved on to a day-school in Dorchester. Here he stayed until he was sixteen, when he was apprenticed to a local architect. He himself des-cribes how, for the next six years, he lived:

a triple existence unusual for a young man . . . a life twisted of three strands—the professional life, the scholar's life, and the rustic life, combined in the twenty-four hours of one day. . . . He would be reading the 'Iliad', the 'Aeneid', or the Greek Testament from six to eight in the morning, would work at Gothic architecture all day, and then in the evening rush off with his fiddle . . . to play country dances.

He read widely and deeply at a time when Christian beliefs were under severe attack from the new scientific and philosophic knowledge, and he became painfully aware of the dynamic new forces which were to destroy the Wessex of that time. He lost his own belief in the simple Faith of his people, became an unwilling agnostic, and was deeply disturbed by his consciousness of the tensions that existed between the old way of life and the new.

In 1862 he left Dorchester for London and spent five important years there, not only practising as an architect but furthering his education by partaking of the cultural activities of the capital. He saw

Thomas Hardy

Shakespeare being acted, visited the opera, heard Dickens reading, and studied art at the National Gallery. But the pull of Wessex was strong and, tiring of London, he returned in 1867 to his former employer in Dorchester. It was now that he began to think seriously of being a writer. In London he had written poetry but had failed to get it published. In 1868 he sent his first novel to Macmillan's, who rejected it while recognizing that it showed promise. Hardy tried again and his next novel, *Desperate Remedies*, was published by Tinsley's in 1871. It had a mixed reception and he tried yet again. *Under the Greenwood Tree* was published in 1872 and did rather better. *A Pair of Blue Eyes* followed in 1873, but it was not until 1874 that he achieved a solid success with *Far from the Madding Crowd* and was able to regard himself as a writer rather than an architect. In the next twenty-two years he was to write a further ten novels and more than forty short stories, and to establish himself as one of England's great masters of fiction. The best of his novels are deeply rooted in his native Wessex and in his own life, for he was an intensely personal writer. Memories of his youth, his love for the old rural way of life, his interest in architecture and music, his knowledge of Shakespeare and of the great writers of the world, his religious and philosophical doubts—all these appear again and again in his stories. But there was another major influence.

Hardy was a passionate and emotional person with a deep need for a happy relationship with a woman. But this was not to be. In the late 1860's he had an unhappy affair with his cousin, Tryphena Sparks. Not long after this he met the most powerful influence in his life, Emma Gifford, at St Juliot in Cornwall, on a day he was never to forget—7th March 1870. He had journeyed to Cornwall to restore St Juliot church, and his meeting with Emma, the rector's sister-in-law, was the beginning of an idyllic courtship which led to their marriage in 1874. It should have been a marriage of great happiness, but it turned out to be as much of a failure as his career was a success. It was childless—and it became loveless, but it did provide the material and emotional pressure which resulted in some of his finest stories. His constant preoccupation with the marriage relationship came straight out of his own experience.

Tess of the d'Urbervilles (1891) and *Jude the Obscure* (1896) are his last great novels. Both were well received, but there was some strident criticism by the more puritanical reviewers, who accused Hardy of corrupting morals by attacking the institution of marriage. Hardy, always a very sensitive man, was distressed by the fury of some of the attacks on him and announced that he would never write another novel. He would return to his first love, poetry, and so, in 1898, when almost sixty, he published *Wessex Poems*, his first book of verse. In the next thirty years he was to publish a further seven books of verse, the last, *Winter Words*, appearing shortly after his death in 1928.

A Biographical Note

Altogether he published over nine hundred poems in those thirty years, a remarkable achievement for someone of his age.

In 1912 Emma died and her death provided him with yet another source of inspiration. Shortly before her death she had written an account of her childhood and of her romantic meeting with Hardy in Cornwall. She called these reminiscences *Some Recollections*. Immediately after her death Hardy found the exercise-book containing these memories and it helped to increase his sense of loss and his realization of the tragedy of his married life and of its lost opportunities. He poured out his feeling of remorse and his still vivid memories of the happy early days in Cornwall in the 'Vestigia' poems which are to be found in *Satires of Circumstance* (1914); nine are here printed. These have been judged to be the peak of his poetic achievement. Although he married Florence Dugdale in 1914 and she looked after him devotedly for the rest of his life, he never forgot Emma, and poems about her appeared in volume after volume of the verse which with such remarkable energy he continued to produce in his seventies and eighties.

During these years he lived at his house, Max Gate, on the outskirts of Dorchester, the Grand Old Man of English Literature, visited by other great writers, respected by the famous, and yet still very much that young boy who had grown up in the Bockhampton cottage so many lifetimes ago, still sensitively aware of the sadnesses and injustices of the world, the greatness of man's spirit, and of the ironies of man's existence. Ironically enough, even his wish that he should be buried in Stinsford churchyard, the heart of his Wessex and the burial place of his family, was partly ignored. A proud nation demanded that this humble man should be buried with the great in Westminster Abbey, and a typical English compromise was agreed over his dead body. His heart was buried at Stinsford—the rest of him was cremated and the ashes buried in the Abbey, shrine of a religion in which he could not believe. 'What a subject for a poem!' his spirit must have thought!

1970   JAMES GIBSON.

Select Bibliography

WORKS. *Collected Editions.* The best text is that of the Wessex Edition (1912–1931), reprinted in the Greenwood Edition. *The Short Stories of Thomas Hardy* (1928). *The Collected Poems of Thomas Hardy* (1930).

Individual Works

1. Novels. *Desperate Remedies* (1871). *Under the Greenwood Tree* (1872). *A Pair of Blue Eyes* (1873). *Far from the Madding Crowd* (1874). *The Hand of Ethelberta* (1876). *The Return of the Native* (1878). *The Trumpet-Major* (1880). *A Laodicean* (1881). *Two on a Tower* (1882). *The Mayor of Casterbridge* (1886). *The Woodlanders* (1887). *Tess of the d'Urbervilles* (1891). *Jude the Obscure* (1896). *The Well-Beloved* (1897).

2. Short Stories. *Wessex Tales* (1888). *A Group of Noble Dames* (1891). *Life's Little Ironies* (1894). *A Changed Man and other Tales* (1913).

3. Poetry. *Wessex Poems* (1898): early editions included the thirty-one illustrations by the author. *Poems of the Past and the Present* (1902). *The Dynasts* (three parts, 1904, 1906, 1908). *Time's Laughing-stocks* (1909). *Satires of Circumstance* (1914). *Moments of Vision* (1917). *Late Lyrics and Earlier* (1922). *The Famous Tragedy of the Queen of Cornwall* (1923). *Human Shows, Far Phantasies* (1925). *Winter Words* (1928).

4. The essays and prefaces are collected in H. Orel's *Hardy's Personal Writings* (1967). As Hardy was largely responsible for the shaping of *The Early Life of Thomas Hardy, 1840–1891* and *The Later Years of Thomas Hardy, 1892–1928* issued under Florence Emily Hardy's name (1928 and 1930: one-volume edition 1962, *The Life of Thomas Hardy*), this work may be regarded as autobiography. Although Hardy's first novel, *The Poor Man and the Lady* (1867), was not published, some part of it was reworked and appeared in 1878 as *An Indiscretion in the Life of an Heiress* (first book publication 1934).

BIOGRAPHY AND CRITICISM. Lionel Johnson, *The Art of Thomas Hardy* (1894); Lascelles Abercrombie, *Thomas Hardy: A Critical Study* (1912); H. C. Duffin, *Thomas Hardy* (1916); E. Brennecke, *Thomas Hardy's Universe: A Study of a Poet's Mind* (1924) and *The Life of Thomas Hardy* (1925); A. S. McDowall, *Thomas Hardy: A Critical Study* (1931). W. R. Rutland, *Thomas Hardy: A Study of his writings and their Background* (1938); A. Chakravarty, '*The Dynasts*' *and the Post-War Age in Poetry* (1938); C. Weber, *Hardy of Wessex* (1940); Edmund Blunden, *Thomas Hardy* (1941); Lord David Cecil,

Select Bibliography

Hardy the Novelist (1943); H. C. Webster, *On a Darkling Plain: The Art and Thought of Thomas Hardy* (1947); J. G. Southworth, *The Poetry of Thomas Hardy* (1947); A. J. Guerard, *Thomas Hardy: The Novels and Stories* (1949); Evelyn Hardy, *Thomas Hardy, A Critical Biography* (1954); D. Brown, *Thomas Hardy* (1954); J. Paterson, *The Making of 'The Return of the Native'* (1960); S. Hynes, *The Pattern of Hardy's Poetry* (1961); J. I. M. Stewart, *Eight Modern Writers* (1963); G. Wing, *Hardy* (1963); R. Carpenter, *Thomas Hardy* (1964); L. Deacon and T. Coleman, *Providence and Mr. Hardy* (1966); W. Wright, *The Shaping of 'The Dynasts': A Study in Thomas Hardy* (1967); K. Marsden, *The Poems of Thomas Hardy: A Critical Introduction* (1969).

CRITICAL ESSAYS. The Thomas Hardy Centenary Issue of *The Southern Review*, VI (Summer, 1940). A. Guerard (ed.), *Hardy: A Collection of Critical Essays* (1963). L. Lerner and J. Holmstrom, *Thomas Hardy and his Readers: A Selection of Contemporary Reviews* (1968).

MISCELLANEOUS. *Thomas Hardy's Notebooks* have been edited by Evelyn Hardy (1955) and *The Architectural Notebook of Thomas Hardy* has been reproduced in facsimile, with notes by C. Beatty (1966). Many visitors to Max Gate have recorded their conversations, among them W. Archer, in *Real Conversations* (1901), and V. H. G. Collins, in *Talks with Thomas Hardy at Max Gate, 1920–1922* (1928); R. A. Firor's *Folk-ways in Thomas Hardy* (1931), examines Hardy's knowledge of folk-lore. J. Stevens Cox's pamphlet by various authors, *Monographs on the Life of Thomas Hardy*, is still in progress. The largest Hardy manuscript collection is that of the Dorset County Museum, Dorchester.

BIBLIOGRAPHIES. Richard L. Purdy, *Thomas Hardy: A Bibliographical Study* (1954). L. Stevenson, 'Thomas Hardy', in *The Victorian Poets: A Guide to Research*, ed. F. Faverty (1956). M. Beebe, B. Culotta and E. Marcus, 'Criticism of Thomas Hardy: A Selected Check List', in *Modern Fiction Studies* VI (1960). G. Fayen, 'Thomas Hardy', in *Victorian Fiction: A Guide to Research*, ed. L. Stevenson (1964). K. Carter, *Dorset County Library: Thomas Hardy Catalogue* (1968): includes an account of the microfilm collection.

The publishers thank Macmillan and Company Limited for their permission to print the present selection from volumes of the Wessex Edition of Hardy's works and the *Collected Poems*, *The Dynasts* and *The Three Wayfarers*; and from Florence Emily Hardy's *Life of Thomas Hardy* (1962), and *Hardy's Personal Writings* (1967) edited by Harold Orel. The frontispiece map is based on Hardy's own pen and ink drawing. 'The Wessex of the Novels and Poems', and is reproduced with permission from the Greenwood Edition.

Introduction

THOMAS HARDY was born in 1840, twelve years after George Meredith. It is interesting that these are the only major English writers to defy classification in one important regard: neither can confidently be called a novelist who also wrote poetry (like James Joyce and D. H. Lawrence) or a poet who also wrote novels (like Robert Graves or Cecil Day Lewis). Long after their death, critical opinion is divided as to where the chief importance of Meredith and Hardy lies. Is it in verse, or in prose?

Something more than coincidence was at work in producing so close a balance of achievement twice within a single period of literature. For it was the period during which, in England, the novel was aspiring to a parity of esteem with poetry and the drama. People were ceasing to feel, as hitherto, slightly ashamed of giving more than the idlest leisure-time to what they would call 'taking up', 'turning over', or 'glancing through' romances. It had begun to be realized—particularly before the grave and intellectual art of George Eliot—that the novel was coming of age as a major literary form. So it was possible for a poet to feel that he might explore the craft of fiction without, as it were, letting himself down; and, correspondingly, a novelist could write regularly for the circulating libraries without fearing that he was thereby impairing the chances of his serious reception as a poet. These facts clearly have a bearing on the unique careers of Meredith and Hardy.

But Hardy's attitude here was odder than Meredith's—or at least it was more old-fashioned. He published his first volume of verse in his fifty-ninth year, and with one small exception published only verse during the remaining twenty-nine years of his life. But he had written verse throughout his career; he declared, more or less on his deathbed, that his only ambition had been 'to have some poem or poems in a good anthology like the Golden Treasury'; and he steadily insisted that the large body of his novels and short stories represented an activity of inferior worth and interest, undertaken merely for the sake of a livelihood. It pained him to hear of serious people reading novels. He was distressed when told that Tennyson had taken to them in old age.

If we are thus inclined to conclude that Hardy's attitude to the novel was essentially disparaging, we shall not have much difficulty in assembling what has the appearance of substantial supporting evidence. He was willing to maim and bowdlerize his stories in order to secure their profitable serial publication in 'family' magazines. 'The truth is', he once wrote, 'that I am willing, and indeed anxious, to give up any points which may be desirable in a story when read as a whole, for the sake of others which shall please those who read it in numbers.' His plots are often of a melodramatic and sensational sort which seems to aim at a merely popular readership; and once or twice they conclude, even in their definitive 'volume form', with an ending which Hardy confesses he doesn't like but leaves untouched all the same. He may thus seem not to be in at all the same position as Meredtih, who perceived the arrival of an equal scope for high literary ambition in poetry and prose fiction alike.

But first appearances are deceptive here, and we soon discover a certain disingenuousness in Hardy's professed attitude. Although he could declare that his novel-writing career had been 'a hand-to-mouth matter', and give Virginia Woolf the impression that he regarded the activity as 'scarcely to be taken seriously', there are many indications that he really brought the same pitch of artistic aspiration to his prose as to his poetry. When Coventry Patmore—who particularly delighted in the early *A Pair of Blue Eyes*—paid him some compliment on his fiction as a whole. Hardy replied: 'It is what I might have deserved if my novels had been exact transcripts of their original irradiated conception, before any attempt at working out that glorious dream had been made.' An artist does not speak in these terms of work in what he believes to be a second-rate medium.

And there is another pointer here. Hardy believed, whether rightly or wrongly, that the work of the great Greek tragedians represents the very acme of all literary achievement, and that only Shakespeare comes near to it. It is significant, therefore, how often references to Shakespeare, Aeschylus, Sophocles creep into his novels. 'It is pleasant to dream'—we are told in the preface to *The Return of the Native*—'that some spot in the extensive tract whose southwestern quarter is here described, may be the heath of that traditional King of Wessex— Lear.' And at the end of *Tess of the d'Urbervilles*, in words as famous as any their author ever wrote, we read that 'the President of the Immortals, in Aeschylean phrase, had ended his sport with Tess.' We come to recognize in such allusions the presence of a challenge, and are not surprised to learn that Hardy sometimes prepared himself for a new novel by reading Greek tragedies. If we are to judge by the yard-stick he thus brought to his work, the author of *The Woodlanders* and *Jude the Obscure* did not really esteem the craft of fiction less than did the authors of, say, *Nostromo* and *The Golden Bowl*.

Although as a writer of fiction Hardy cannot, of course, be fairly assessed merely on the basis of his short stories, these do afford, even in a brief view, a conspectus alike of many of his powers and of all that strong idiosyncrasy of attitude and manner with which we must come to terms if we are to read the body of his work with enjoyment. His sense of what he called 'the general grimness of the human situation' frequently expressed itself through tales in which dreadful calamities are brought about through the mere chance operation of converging and fatally synchronized events. 'A strange concurrence of phenomena now confronts us,' he says somewhere. It does so, for example, in 'The Withered Arm'. In this finely Gothic tale we are told of the principal character, Rhoda Brook, that 'she did not reason on the freaks of coincidence'. Neither must we, if we are to accept this kind of story. And so with the little play called *The Three Way-farers* and the story 'The Three Strangers' of which it is a dramatiza-tion. That the hangman, the hangman's destined victim, and that victim's brother should find themselves all present at a christening-party is not probable—but grant the possibility, and a superb tale results. 'The Melancholy Hussar of the German Legion' similarly presents circumstances which strain credulity. Phyllis Grove's truant fiancé turns up too pat, and his overheard talk is too neatly ambiguous; nor is it likely that an English girl, glancing over her garden wall, will be greeted with the spectacle of a solemn military execution. Others of Hardy's stories are so macabre as to be wholly disconcerting. Thus in 'Barbara of the House of Grebe', which will be found in *Wessex Tales*, a married woman still has fond thoughts of a former lover who has been hideously disfigured in a fire; her husband, discovering this, causes a statue of the lover to be similarly disfigured, and exposes it nightly to her gaze until her spirit is broken. It was this story that T. S. Eliot denounced as introducing us 'into a world of pure Evil' and as 'written solely to provide a satisfaction for some morbid emotion'. The charge is exaggerated. Yet the short stories do often afford a naked exhibition of human suffering in a pitiless universe, whereas in the majority of the novels this theme, so central to Hardy's imagination, is to some extent clothed in the softening garments of humour and of a deeply loved and keenly observed rural world.

There are, of course, some short stories in which these materials of Hardy's art themselves appear in near-isolation. 'A Tryst at an Ancient Earthwork' is simply a topographical sketch of Wessex in one of its immemorial faces, that of the vast prehistoric earthwork of Maiden Castle outside Dorchester; if we read this along with the essay 'The Dorsetshire Labourer' we are at once in contact with the two main regions of his feeling as a countryman: the historical background and the present condition of agricultural England. 'Absentmindedness in a Parish Choir' and 'Tony Kytes, The Arch-Deceiver' represent, correspondingly, Hardy's feeling for rustic society at its warmest, its most human, and its most amusing. It is perhaps true that what Eliot, again, disparagingly calls 'the period peasants pleasing to the metropolitan imagination' are at their best when disengaged in this way and, so to speak, left to their own devices. They delight us in the novels as well, but there we at times feel a slight disparity between their sustained quaintness and the sombre events to which they act as chorus.

When we turn from Hardy's prose fiction to his verse, it is by no means to enter a different world. The contention that he wrote novels and short stories to please an undiscriminating public and poems to please himself breaks down before the strong continuities of theme and attitude to be found throughout his writing in both kinds. For a start, the dynamic is the same. As a novelist Hardy relies largely upon feeling, upon a power of emotional response to his material which intermittently raises his prose itself to the pitch of poetry What he chiefly gained when he published *Wessex Poems* in 1898 may be defined as new and varied units of utterance. We realize as we read that the novels and stories have been filled with lyrics, ballads, threnodies, meditations, monologues all awaiting disengagement and the disciplining and condensing power of verse form.

'If way to the Better there be, it exacts a full look at the Worst.' This favourite aphorism of Hardy's could no doubt be employed with some appropriateness as epigraph to his entire poetical works. And what he meant by the 'Worst' was the brute regardlessness of the cosmos as it has been expressed by James Thomson:

> *I find no hint throughout the Universe*
> *Of good or ill, of blessing or of curse;*
> *I find alone Necessity supreme.*

One of the earliest of his own surviving poems, 'Hap', asserts that a sadistic deity would be easier to take than the mere 'crass Casualty' and 'purblind Doomsters' who deal out bliss and pain at random. A great deal of his verse embodies reflections of this kind. What a later age has called the death of God is a cardinal conception of Hardy's; God has been at best 'a forced device', and is now fading out altogether 'beneath the Deicide eyes of seers'; to the challenge 'Who or what shall fill his place?' the poet can only respond 'No answerer I'. And his 'full look at the Worst' has to be confessed a lingering one. There is an oppressive amount of bad luck in the verse, just as there is in the prose, and an oppressive amount, too, of what may be called mortuary meditation. Man is

> *but a thing of flesh and bone*
> *Speeding on to its cleft in the clay*

and his destiny and home is simply the churchyard, 'where the worms waggle under the grass'.

Yet Hardy professed to be not without hope of the 'Better'. A philosophy of 'evolutionary meliorism' is conceivably just tenable. In our universe 'the disease of feeling germed' prematurely or in the wrong place, and when we are gloomy we can only pray that soon 'nescience shall be reaffirmed'—perhaps through some astronomical calamity blotting out all trace of life. But there is at least another possibility:

> By some still close-cowled mystery
> We have reached feeling faster than he,
> But he will overtake us anon,
>   If the world goes on.

To the extent that Hardy is the poet of late-nineteenth-century pessimism, this last speculation may be described as a mere occasional euphoria, a comforting notion such as might please Robert Browning and other unreflectingly cheerful persons. Hardy himself does not, really and truly, see any road that way. His more authentic sense of the 'Better' is something that commonly steals upon him unawares, but that also finds explicit statement in the first poem to figure in the present selection:

> Let me enjoy the earth no less
> Because the all-enacting Might
> That fashioned forth its loveliness
> Had other aims than my delight.

Such enjoyment must be ephemeral and poignant, as another poem here printed, 'Proud Songsters', tells us. Yet it is immensely important, since it witnesses to something intuitive and spontaneous in our nature which prompts us to challenge life, to discern and assert immutable values which men have, after all, found for themselves: those values of fidelity, tenderness and pity that give dignity and meaning to the human lot. Above all, it is as a love-poet that Hardy is most affirmative. As a man, his experience of love had brought him, it seems, keen and enduring pain. As an artist, he was sensitively aware of the blindness of passion, the fatality of women, the helplessness of the individual before one or another deep biological drive. Yet he knows that there is more than magic, more than enchantment and disenchantment, on this perilous terrain. In poems such as 'Beeny Cliff', 'At Castle Boterel', and 'The Phantom Horsewoman' the worms no longer waggle, and it is an austere triumph of the spirit that he wrests from the grave.

Such poems as these so powerfully suggest a basis in intimate personal experience that we are not surprised to hear of Hardy's declaring (when questioned by a correspondent about the extent to which his own history was reflected in *Jude the Obscure*) that there was 'more autobiography' in a hundred lines of his poetry than in all his novels. Yet factual curiosity has to tread warily here. We know, for example, that some of the most poignant poems of frustration and regret (including, perhaps, 'The Division' here printed) are to be associated with a sentimental attachment which Hardy, in his fifties, formed for a married lady of his acquaintance. But the poetic imagination is an intricate thing, and may endow an occasion in itself of no deep significance with a colouring of emotion drawn from some other experience quite remote in time. We do best to accept Hardy's poetry not as material for a biography but as constituting—in a definition of his own—'a particular man's artistic interpretation of life'.

Among the English poets who were his near-contemporaries, it was chiefly Browning who interested and puzzled Hardy. How could a great writer, fully aware of that 'general grimness' which science has revealed to modern man, assert so confident, so optimistic, an attitude? Sometimes Hardy felt that he must answer Browning—as when, in his eightieth year, the memory of 'Abt Vogler' prompted him to write 'The Chapel-Organist'. In a sense he answered him, too, simply by equalling him as a love-poet. And it is possible that his largest-scale and most ambitious work, *The Dynasts*, was in part prompted by the sheer mass of *The Ring and the Book*. It is, of course, a totally different kind of achievement, and in all literature nothing much with which to compare it exists. Tolstoy's *War and Peace* is also an epic of Napoleonic Europe, and Tolstoy's theory of history has at least some common ground with Hardy's. But whereas against the tremendous backdrop of dynastic struggle Tolstoy's figures remain fully life-size, Hardy's are with a deliberate craft distanced and shrunk to the dimensions of a sort of bizarrely populous puppet-show. That his 'one hundred and thirty scenes' of battle and political debate and palace-history are uniformly successful, or constitute the same sort of artistic unity as does Tolstoy's masterpiece, must be held doubtful. The strange overworld of 'Phantom Intelligences' who hover above and comment upon the action fall short of providing any sort of controlling myth, and in general it is the *genre* pieces rather than the more elevated historical tableaux that have life in them. But better than these again are the purely descriptive passages given in the form of dumb shows and extended stage directions. These confirm something that Hardy's prose and verse have alike long ago declared: the quite exceptional power of his visual imagination.

J. I. M. STEWART

Christ Church, Oxford, 1970

THE DORSETSHIRE LABOURER

STORIES

THE DESERTERS: A SCENE

THE THREE WAYFARERS

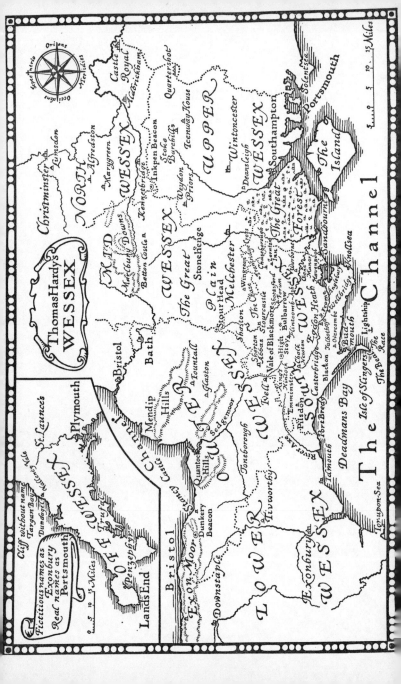

The Dorsetshire Labourer

It seldom happens that a nickname which affects to portray a class is honestly indicative of the individuals composing that class. The few features distinguishing them from other bodies of men have been seized on and exaggerated, while the incomparably more numerous features common to all humanity have been ignored. In the great world this wild colouring of so-called typical portraits is clearly enough recognized. Nationalities, the aristocracy, the plutocracy, the citizen class, and many others have their allegorical representatives, which are received with due allowance for flights of imagination in the direction of burlesque.

But when the class lies somewhat out of the ken of ordinary society the caricature begins to be taken as truth. Moreover, the original is held to be an actual unit of the multitude signified. He ceases to be an abstract figure and becomes a sample. Thus when we arrive at the farm-labouring community we find it to be seriously personified by the pitiable picture known as Hodge; not only so, but the community is assumed to be a uniform collection of concrete Hodges.

This supposed real but highly conventional Hodge is a degraded being of uncouth manner and aspect, stolid understanding, and snail-like movement. His speech is such a chaotic corruption of regular language that few persons of progressive aims consider it worth while to inquire what views, if any, of life, of nature, or of society are conveyed in these utterances. Hodge hangs his head or looks sheepish when spoken to, and thinks Lunnon a place paved with gold. Misery and fever lurk in his cottage, while, to paraphrase the words of a recent writer on the labouring classes, in his future there are only the workhouse and the grave. He hardly dares to think at all. He has few thoughts of joy, and little hope of rest. His life slopes into a darkness not 'quieted by hope'.

If one of the many thoughtful persons who hold this view were to go by rail to Dorset, where Hodge in his most unmitigated form is supposed to reside, and seek out a retired district, he might by and by certainly meet a man who, at first contact with an intelligence fresh from the contrasting world of London, would seem to exhibit some of the above-mentioned qualities.

3

The latter items in the list, the mental miseries, the visitor might hardly look for in their fullness, since it would have become perceptible to him as an explorer, and to any but the chamber theorist, that no uneducated community, rich or poor, bond or free, possessing average health and personal liberty, could exist in an unchangeable slough of despond, or that it would for many months if it could. Its members, like the accursed swine, would rush down a steep place and be choked in the waters. He would have learnt that wherever a mode of supporting life is neither noxious nor absolutely inadequate, there springs up happiness, and will spring up happiness, of some sort or other. Indeed, it is among such communities as these that happiness will find her last refuge on earth, since it is among them that a perfect insight into the conditions of existence will be longest postponed.

That in their future there are only the workhouse and the grave is no more and no less true than that in the future of the average well-to-do householder there are only the invalid chair and the brick vault.

Waiving these points, however, the investigator would insist that the man he had encountered exhibited a suspicious blankness of gaze, a great uncouthness and inactivity; and he might truly approach the unintelligible if addressed by a stranger on any but the commonest subject. But suppose that, by some accident, the visitor were obliged to go home with this man, take pot-luck with him and his, as one of the family. For the nonce the very sitting down would seem an undignified performance, and at first, the ideas, the modes, and the surroundings generally, would be puzzling—even impenetrable; or if in a measurable penetrable, would seem to have but little meaning. But living on there for a few days the sojourner would become conscious of a new aspect in the life around him. He would find that, without any objective change whatever, variety had taken the place of monotony; that the man who had brought him home—the typical Hodge, as he conjectured—was somehow not typical of anyone but himself. His host's brothers, uncles, and neighbours, as they became personally known, would appear as different from his host himself as one member of a club, or inhabitant of a city street, from another. As, to the eye of a diver, contrasting colours shine out by degrees from what has originally painted itself of an unrelieved earthy hue, so would shine out the characters, capacities, and interests of these people to him. He would, for one thing, find that the language, instead of being a vile corruption of cultivated speech, was a tongue with grammatical inflection rarely disregarded by his entertainer, though his entertainer's children would occasionally make a sad hash of their talk. Having attended

4

the National School they would mix the printed tongue as taught therein with the unwritten, dying, Wessex English that they had learnt of their parents, the result of this transitional state of theirs being a composite language without rule or harmony.

Six months pass, and our gentleman leaves the cottage, bidding his friends good-bye with genuine regret. The great change in his perception is that Hodge, the dull, unvarying, joyless one, has ceased to exist for him. He has become disintegrated into a number of dissimilar fellow-creatures, men of many minds, infinite in difference; some happy, many serene, a few depressed; some clever, even to genius, some stupid, some wanton, some austere; some mutely Miltonic, some Cromwellian, into men who have private views of each other, as he has of his friends; who applaud or condemn each other; amuse or sadden themselves by the contemplation of each other's foibles or vices; and each of whom walks in his own way the road to dusty death. Dick the carter, Bob the shepherd, and Sam the ploughman, are, it is true, alike in the narrowness of their means and their general open-air life; but they cannot be rolled together again into such a Hodge as he dreamt of, by any possible enchantment. And should time and distance render an abstract being, representing the field labourer, possible again to the mind of the inquirer (a questionable possibility) he will find that the Hodge of current conception no longer sums up the capacities of the class so defined.

The pleasures enjoyed by the Dorset labourer may be far from pleasures of the highest kind desirable for him. They may be pleasures of the wrong shade. And the inevitable glooms of a straitened hard-working life occasionally enwrap him from such pleasures as he has; and in times of special storm and stress the 'Complaint of Piers the Ploughman' is still echoed in his heart. But even Piers had his flights of merriment and humour; and ploughmen as a rule do not give sufficient thought to the morrow to be miserable when not in physical pain. Drudgery in the slums and alleys of a city, too long pursued, and accompanied as it too often is by indifferent health, may induce a mood of despondency which is wellnigh permanent; but the same degree of drudgery in the fields results at worst in a mood of painless passivity. A pure atmosphere and a pastoral environment are a very appreciable portion of the sustenance which tends to produce the sound mind and body, and thus much sustenance is, at least, the labourer's birthright.

If it were possible to gauge the average sufferings of classes, the probability is that in Dorsetshire the figure would be lower with the regular farmer's labourers—'workfolk' as they call themselves—than with the adjoining class, the unattached labourers, approximating to the free labourers of the middle ages, who are to be found in the larger villages and small towns of the county—many of them, no doubt, descendants of the old copy-holders who were ousted from their little plots when the system of leasing large farms grew general. They are, what the regular labourer is not, out of sight of patronage; and to be out of sight is to be out of mind when misfortune arises, and pride or sensitiveness leads them to conceal their privations.

The happiness of a class can rarely be estimated aright by philosophers who look down upon that class from the Olympian heights of society. Nothing, for instance, is more common than for some philanthropic lady to burst in upon a family, be struck by the apparent squalor of the scene, and to straightway mark down that household in her note-book as a frightful example of the misery of the labouring classes. There are two distinct probabilities of error in forming any such estimate. The first is that the apparent squalor is no squalor at all. I am credibly informed that the conclusion is nearly always based on *colour*. A cottage in which the walls, the furniture, and the dress of the inmates reflect the brighter rays of the solar spectrum is read by these amiable visitors as a cleanly, happy home, while one whose prevailing hue happens to be dingy russet, or a quaint old leather tint, or any of the numerous varieties of mud colour, is thought necessarily the abode of filth and Giant Despair. 'I always kip a white apron behind the door to slip on when the gentlefolk knock, for if so be they see a white apron they think ye be clane,' said an honest woman one day, whose bedroom floors could have been scraped with as much advantage as a pigeon-loft; but who, by a judicious use of high lights, shone as a pattern of neatness in her patrons' eyes.

There was another woman who had long nourished an un-reasoning passion for burnt umber, and at last acquired a pot of the same from a friendly young carpenter. With this pigment she covered every surface in her residence to which paint is usually applied, and having more left, and feeling that to waste it would be a pity as times go, she went on to cover other surfaces till the whole was consumed. Her dress and that of the children were mostly of faded snuff-colour, her natural thrift inducing her to cut up and re-make a quantity of old stuffs that had been her mother's; and to add to the misery the floor of her cottage was of Mayne brick—a material which has the complexion of gravy mottled with cinders. Notwithstanding that the bed-linen and underclothes of this unfortunate woman's family were like the driven snow, and that the insides of her cooking utensils were concave mirrors, she was used with great effect as the frightful example of slovenliness for many years in that neighbourhood.

The second probability arises from the error of supposing that actual slovenliness is always accompanied by unhappiness. If it were so, a windfall of any kind would be utilized in most cases in improving the surroundings. But the money always goes in the acquisition of something new, and not in the removal of what there is already too much of, dirt. And most frequently the grimiest families are not the poorest; nay, paradoxical as it may seem, external neglect in a household implies something above the lowest level of poverty. Copyholders, cottage freeholders, and the like, are as a rule less trim and neat, more muddling in their ways, than the dependent labourer; and yet there is no more comfortable or serene being than the cottager who is sure of his roof. An instance of probable error through inability to see below the surface of things occurred the other day in an article by a lady on the peasant proprietors of Auvergne. She states that she discovered these persons living on an earth floor, mixed up with onions, dirty clothes, and the 'indescribable remnants of never stirred rubbish'; while one of the houses had no staircase, the owners of the premises reaching their bedrooms by climbing up a bank, and stepping in at the higher level. This was an inconvenient way of getting upstairs; but we must guard against the inference that because these peasant proprietors are in a slovenly condition, and certain English peasants who are not proprietors live in model cottages copied out of a book by the squire, the latter are so much happier than the former as the dignity of their architecture is greater. It were idle to deny that, other things being equal, the family which dwells in a cleanly and spacious cottage has the probability of a more cheerful existence than a family narrowly housed and draggletailed. It has guarantees for health which the other has not. But it must be remembered that melancholy among the rural poor arises primarily from a sense of incertitude and precariousness of their position. Like Burns's field mouse, they are overawed and timorous lest those who can wrong them should be inclined to exercise their power. When we know that the Damocles' sword of the poor is the fear of being turned out of their houses by the farmer or squire, we may wonder how many scrupulously clean English labourers would not be glad with half-an-acre of the complaint that afflicts these unhappy freeholders of Auvergne.

It is not at all uncommon to find among the workfolk philosophers who recognize, as clearly as Lord Palmerston did, that dirt is only matter in the wrong place. A worthy man holding these wide views had put his clean shirt on a gooseberry bush one Sunday morning, to be aired in the sun, whence it blew off into the mud, and was much soiled. His wife would have got him another, but 'No,' he said, 'the shirt shall wear his week. 'Tis fresh dirt, anyhow, and starch is no more.'

On the other hand, true poverty—that is, the actual want of necessaries—is constantly trying to be decent, and one of the clearest signs of deserving poverty is the effort it makes to appear otherwise by scrupulous neatness.

To see the Dorset labourer at his worst and saddest time, he should be viewed when attending a wet hiring-fair at Candlemas, in search of a new master. His natural cheerfulness bravely struggles against the weather and the incertitude; but as the day passes on, and his clothes get wet through, and he is still unhired, there does appear a factitiousness in the smile which, with a self-repressing mannerliness hardly to be found among any other class, he yet has ready when he encounters and talks with friends who have been more fortunate. In youth and manhood, this disappointment occurs but seldom; but at threescore and over, it is frequently the lot of those who have no sons and daughters to fall back upon, or whose children are ingrates, or far away.

Here, at the corner of the street, in this aforesaid wet hiring-fair, stands an old shepherd. He is evidently a lonely man. The battle of life has always been a sharp one with him, for, to begin with, he is a man of small frame. He is now so bowed by hard work and years that, approaching from behind, you can scarcely see his head. He has planted the stem of his crook in the gutter, and rests upon the bow, which is polished to silver brightness by the long friction of his hands. He has quite forgotten where he is and what he has come for, his eyes being bent on the ground. 'There's work in en,' says one farmer to another, as they look dubiously across; 'there's work left in en still; but not so much as I want for my acreage.' 'You'd get en cheap,' says the other. The shepherd does not hear them, and there seem to be passing through his mind pleasant visions of the hiring successes of his prime—when his skill in ovine surgery laid open any farm to him for the asking, and his employer would say uneasily in the early days of February, 'You don't mean to leave us this year?'

But the hale and strong have not to wait thus, and having secured places in the morning, the day passes merrily enough with them.

The hiring-fair of recent years presents an appearance unlike that of former times. A glance up the high street of the town on a Candlemas-fair day twenty or thirty years ago revealed a crowd whose general colour was whity-brown flecked with white. Black was almost absent, the few farmers who wore that shade hardly discernible. Now the crowd is as dark as a London crowd. This change is owing to the rage for cloth clothes which possesses the labourers of today. Formerly they came in smock-frocks and gaiters, the shepherds with their crooks, the carters with a zone of whipcord round their hats, thatchers with a straw tucked into the brim, and so on. Now, with the exception of the crook in the hands of an occasional old shepherd, there is no mark of speciality in the groups, who might be tailors or undertakers' men, for what they exhibit externally. Out of a group of eight, for example, who talk together in the middle of the road, only one wears corduroy trousers. Two wear cloth pilot-coats and black trousers, two patterned tweed suits with black canvas overalls, the remaining four suits being of faded broadcloth. To a great extent these are their Sunday suits; but the genuine white smock-frock of Russia duck and the whity-brown one of drabbet, are rarely seen now afield, except on the shoulders of old men. Where smocks are worn by the young and middle-aged, they are of blue material. The mechanic's 'slop' has also been adopted; but a mangy old cloth coat is preferred; so that often a group of these honest fellows on the arable has the aspect of a body of tramps up to some mischief in the field, rather than its natural tillers at work there.

That pecularity of the English urban poor (which M. Taine ridicules, and unfavourably contrasts with the taste of the Continental working-people)—their preference for the cast-off clothes of a richer class to a special attire of their own—has, in fact, reached the Dorset farm folk. Like the men, the women are, pictorially, less interesting than they used to be. Instead of the wing bonnet like the tilt of a waggon, cotton gown, bright-hued neckerchief, and strong flat boots and shoes, they (the younger ones at least) wear shabby millinery bonnets and hats with beads and feathers, 'material' dresses, and boot-heels almost as foolishly shaped as those of ladies of highest education.

Having 'agreed for a place', as it is called, either at the fair, or (occasionally) by private intelligence, or (with growing frequency) by advertisement in the penny local papers, the terms are usually reduced to writing: though formerly a written agreement was unknown, and is now, as a rule, avoided by the farmer if the labourer does not insist upon one. It is signed by both, and a shilling is passed to bind the bargain. The business is then settled, and the man returns to his place of work, to do no more in the matter till Lady Day, Old Style—April 6.

Of all the days in the year, people who love the rural poor of the south-west should pray for a fine day then. Dwellers near the highways of the country are reminded of the anniversary surely enough. They are conscious of a disturbance of their night's rest by noises beginning in the small hours of darkness, and intermittently continuing till daylight—noises as certain to recur on that particular night of the month as the voice of the cuckoo on the third or fourth week of the same. The day of fulfilment has come, and the labourers are on the point of being fetched from the old farm by the carters of the new. For it is always by the waggon and horses of the farmer who requires his services that the hired man is conveyed to his destination; and that this may be accomplished within the day is the reason that the noises begin so soon after midnight. Suppose the distance to be an ordinary one of a dozen or fifteen miles. The carter at the prospective place rises 'when Charles's Wain is over the new chimney', harnesses his team of three horses by lantern light, and proceeds to the present home of his coming comrade. It is the passing of these empty waggons in all directions that is heard breaking the stillness of the hours before dawn. The aim is usually to be at the door of the removing household by six o'clock, when the loading of goods at once begins; and at nine or ten the start to the new home is made. From this hour till one or two in the day, when the other family arrives at the old house, the cottage is empty, and it is only in that short interval that the interior can be in any way cleaned and lime-whitened for the new comers, however dirty it may have become, or whatever sickness may have prevailed among members of the departed family.

Should the migrant himself be a carter there is a slight modification in the arrangement, for carters do not fetch carters, as they fetch shepherds and general hands. In this case the man has to transfer himself. He relinquishes charge of the horses of the old farm in the afternoon of April 5, and starts on foot the same afternoon for the new place. There he makes the acquaintance of the horses which are to be under his care for the ensuing year, and passes the night sometimes on a bundle of clean straw in the stable, for he is as yet a stranger here, and too indifferent to the comforts of a bed on this particular evening to take much trouble to secure one. From this couch he uncurls himself about two o'clock, a.m. (for the distance we have assumed), and, harnessing his new charges, moves off with them to his old home, where, on his arrival, the packing is already advanced by the wife, and loading goes on as before mentioned.

The goods are built up on the waggon to a well-nigh unvarying pattern, which is probably as peculiar to the country labourer as the hexagon to the bee. The dresser, with its finger-marks and domestic evidences thick upon it, stands importantly in front, over the backs of the shaft horses, in its erect and natural position, like some Ark of the Covenant, which must not be handled slightingly or overturned. The hive of bees is slung up to the axle of the waggon, and alongside it the cooking pot or crock, within which are stowed the roots of garden flowers. Barrels are largely used for crockery, and budding gooseberry bushes are suspended by the roots; while on the top of the furniture a circular nest is made of the bed and bedding for the matron and children, who sit there through the journey. If there is no infant in arms, the woman holds the head of the clock, which at any exceptional lurch of the waggon strikes one, in thin tones. The other object of solicitude is the looking-glass, usually held in the lap of the eldest girl. It is emphatically spoken of as *the* looking-glass, there being but one in the house, except possibly a small shaving-glass for the husband. But labouring men are not much dependent upon mirrors for a clean chin. I have seen many men shaving in the chimney corner, looking into the fire; or, in summer, in the garden, with their eyes fixed upon a gooseberry-bush, gazing as steadfastly as if there were a perfect reflection of their image— from which it would seem that the concentrated look of shavers in general was originally demanded rather by the mind than by the eye. On the other hand, I knew a man who used to walk about the room all the time he was engaged in the operation, and how he escaped cutting himself was a marvel. Certain luxurious dandies of the furrow, who could not do without a reflected image of themselves when using the razor, obtained it till quite recently by placing the crown of an old hat outside the window-pane, then confronting it inside the room and falling to —a contrivance which formed a very clear reflection of a face in high light.

The day of removal, if fine, wears an aspect of jollity, and the whole proceeding is a blithe one. A bundle of provisions for the journey is usually hung up at the side of the vehicle, together with a three-pint stone jar of extra strong ale; for it is as impossible to move house without beer as without horses. Roadside inns, too, are patronized, where, during the halt, a mug is seen ascending and descending through the air to and from the feminine portion of the household at the top of the waggon. The drinking at these times is, however, moderate, the beer supplied to travelling labourers being of a preternaturally small brew; as was illustrated by a dialogue which took place on such an occasion quite recently. The liquor was not quite to the taste of the male travellers, and they complained. But the landlady upheld its merits. ''Tis our own brewing, and there is nothing in it but malt and hops,' she said, with rectitude. 'Yes, there is,' said the traveller. 'There's water.' 'Oh! I forgot the water,' the landlady replied. 'I'm d——d if you did, mis'ess,' replied the man; 'for there's hardly anything else in the cup.'

Ten or a dozen of these families, with their goods, may be seen halting simultaneously at an out-of-the-way inn, and it is not possible to walk a mile on any of the high roads this day without meeting several. This annual migration from farm to farm is much in excess of what it was formerly. For example, on a particular farm where, a generation ago, not more than one cottage on an average changed occupants yearly, and where the majority remained all their lifetime, the whole number of tenants were changed at Lady Day just past, and this though nearly all of them had been new arrivals on the previous Lady Day. Dorset labourers now look upon an annual removal as the most natural thing in the world, and it becomes with the younger families a pleasant excitement. Change is also a certain sort of education. Many advantages accrue to the labourers from the varied experience it brings, apart from the discovery of the best market for their abilities. They have become shrewder and sharper men of the world, and have learnt how to hold their own with firmness and judgment. Whenever the habitually-removing man comes into contact with one of the old-fashioned stationary sort, who are still to be found, it is impossible not to perceive that the former is much more wide awake than his fellow-worker, astonishing him with stories of the wide world comprised in a twenty-mile radius from their homes.

They are also losing their peculiarities as a class; hence the humorous simplicity which formerly characterized the men and the unsophisticated modesty of the women are rapidly disappearing or lessening, under the constant attrition of lives mildly approximating to those of workers in a manufacturing town. It is the common remark of villagers above the labouring class, who know the latter well as personal acquaintances, that 'there are no nice homely workfolk now as there used to be.' There may be, and is, some exaggeration in this, but it is only natural that, now different districts of them are shaken together once a year and redistributed, like a shuffled pack of cards, they have ceased to be so local in feeling or manner as formerly, and have entered on the condition of inter-social citizens, 'whose city stretches the whole county over'. Their brains are less frequently than they once were 'as dry as the remainder biscuit after a voyage', and they vent less often the result of their own observations than what they have heard to be the current ideas of smart chaps in towns. The women have, in many districts, acquired the rollicking air of factory hands. That seclusion and immutability, which was so bad for their pockets, was an unrivalled fosterer of their personal charm in the eyes of those whose experiences had been less limited. But the artistic merit of their old condition is scarcely a reason why they should have continued in it when other communities were marching on so vigorously towards uniformity and mental equality. It is only the old story that progress and picturesqueness do not harmonize. They are losing their individuality, but they are widening the range of their ideas, and gaining in freedom. It is too much to expect them to remain stagnant and old-fashioned for the pleasure of romantic spectators.

But, picturesqueness apart, a result of this increasing nomadic habit of the labourer is naturally a less intimate and kindly relation with the land he tills than existed before enlightenment enabled him to rise above the condition of a serf who lived and died on a particular plot, like a tree. During the centuries of serfdom, of copyholding tenants, and down to twenty or thirty years ago, before the power of unlimited migration had been clearly realized, the husbandman of either class had the interest of long personal association with his farm. The fields were those he had ploughed and sown from boyhood, and it was impossible for him, in such circumstances, to sink altogether the character of natural guardian in that of hireling. Not so very many years ago, the landowner, if he were good for anything, stood as a court of final appeal in cases of the harsh dismissal of a man by the farmer. 'I'll go to my lord' was a threat which overbearing farmers respected, for 'my lord' had often personally known the labourer long before he knew the labourer's master. But such arbitrament is rarely practicable now. The landlord does not know by sight, if even by name, half the men who preserve his acres from the curse of Eden. They come and go yearly, like birds of passage, nobody thinks whence or whither. This dissociation is favoured by the customary system of letting the cottages with the land, so that, far from having a guarantee of a holding to keep him fixed, the labourer has not even the stability of a landlord's tenant; he is only tenant of a tenant, the latter possibly a new comer, who takes strictly commercial views of his man and cannot afford to waste a penny on sentimental considerations.

Thus, while their pecuniary condition in the prime of life is bettered, and their freedom enlarged, they have lost touch with their environment, and that sense of long local participancy which is one of the pleasures of age. The old *casus conscientiae* of those in power—whether the weak tillage of an enfeebled hand ought not to be put up with in fields which have had the benefit of that hand's strength—arises less frequently now that the strength has often been expended elsewhere. The sojourning existence of the town masses is more and more the existence of the rural masses, with its corresponding benefits and disadvantages. With uncertainty of residence often comes a laxer morality, and more cynical views of the duties of life. Domestic stability is a factor in conduct which nothing else can equal. On the other hand, new varieties of happiness evolve themselves like new varieties of plants, and new charms may have arisen among the classes who have been driven to adopt the remedy of locomotion for the evils of oppression and poverty—charms which compensate in some measure for the lost sense of home.

A practical injury which this wandering entails on the children of the labourers should be mentioned here. In shifting from school to school, their education cannot possibly progress with that regularity which is essential to their getting the best knowledge in the short time available to them. It is the remark of village schoolteachers of experience, that the children of the vagrant workfolk form the mass of those who fail to reach the ordinary standard of knowledge expected of their age. The rural schoolmaster or mistress enters the schoolroom on the morning of the sixth of April, and finds that a whole flock of the brightest young people has suddenly flown away. In a village school which may be taken as a fair average specimen, containing seventy-five scholars, thirty-three vanished thus on the Lady Day of the present year. Some weeks elapse before the new comers drop in, and a longer time passes before they take root in the school, their dazed, unaccustomed mood rendering immediate progress impossible; while the original bright ones have by this time themselves degenerated into the dazed strangers of other districts.

That the labourers of the country are more independent since their awakening to the sense of an outer world cannot be disputed. It was once common enough on inferior farms to hear a farmer, as he sat on horseback amid a field of workers, address them with a contemptuousness which could not have been greatly exceeded in the days when the thralls of Cedric wore their collars of brass. Usually no answer was returned to these tirades; they were received as an accident of the land on which the listeners had happened to be born, calling for no more resentment than the blows of the wind and rain. But now, no longer fearing to avail himself of his privilege of flitting, these acts of contumely have ceased to be regarded as inevitable by the peasant. And while men do not of their own accord leave a farm without a grievance, very little fault-finding is often deemed a sufficient one among the younger and stronger. Such ticklish relations are the natural result of generations of unfairness on one side, and on the other

14

an increase of knowledge, which has been kindled into activity by the exertions of Mr. Joseph Arch.

Nobody who saw and heard Mr. Arch in his early tours through Dorsetshire will ever forget him and the influence his presence exercised over the crowds he drew. He hailed from Shakespeare's county, where the humours of the peasantry have a marked family relationship with those of Dorset men; and it was this touch of nature, as much as his logic, which afforded him such ready access to the minds and hearts of the labourers here. It was impossible to hear and observe the speaker for more than a few minutes without perceiving that he was a humorist—moreover, a man by no means carried away by an idea beyond the bounds of common sense. Like his renowned fellow-dalesman Corin, he virtually confessed that he was never in court, and might, with that eminent shepherd, have truly described himself as a 'natural philosopher', who had discovered that 'he that wants money, means, and content, is without three good friends'.

'Content' may for a moment seem a word not exactly explanatory of Mr. Arch's views; but on the single occasion, several years ago, on which the present writer numbered himself among those who assembled to listen to that agitator, there was a remarkable moderation in his tone, and an exhortation to contentment with a reasonable amelioration, which, to an impartial auditor, went a long way in the argument. His views showed him to be rather the social evolutionist—what M. Émile de Laveleye would call a 'Possibilist'—than the anarchic irreconcilable. The picture he drew of a comfortable cottage life as it should be, was so cosy, so well within the grasp of his listeners' imagination, that an old labourer in the crowd held up a coin between his finger and thumb exclaiming, 'Here's zixpence towards that, please God!' 'Towards what?' said a bystander. 'Faith, I don't know that I can spak the name o't, but I know 'tis a good thing,' he replied.

The result of the agitation, so far, upon the income of the labourers, has been testified by independent witnesses with a unanimity which leaves no reasonable doubt of its accuracy. It amounts to an average rise of three shillings a week in wages nearly all over the county. The absolute number of added shillings seems small; but the increase is considerable when we remember that it is three shillings on eight or nine—*i.e.*, between thirty and forty per cent. And the reflection is forced upon everyone who thinks of the matter, that if a farmer can afford to pay thirty per cent. more wages in times of agricultural depression that he paid in times of agricultural prosperity, and yet live, and keep a carriage, while the landlord still thrives on the reduced rent which has resulted, the labourer must have been greatly wronged in those prosperous times. That the maximum of wage has been reached for the present is, however, pretty clear; and indeed it should be added that on several farms the labourers have submitted to a slight reduction during the past year, under stress of representations which have appeared reasonable.

It is hardly necessary to observe that the quoted wages never represent the labourer's actual income. Beyond the weekly payment—now standing at eleven or twelve shillings—he invariably receives a lump sum of 2*l*. or 3*l*. for harvest work. A cottage and garden is almost as invariably provided, free of rent, with, sometimes, an extra piece of ground for potatoes in some field near at hand. Fuel, too, is frequently furnished, in the form of wood faggots. At springtime, on good farms, the shepherd receives a shilling for every twin reared, while a carter gets what is called journey-money, that is, a small sum, mostly a shilling, for every journey taken beyond the bounds of the farm. Where all these supplementary trifles are enjoyed together, the weekly wage in no case exceeds eleven shillings at the present time.

The question of enough or not enough often depends less upon the difference of two or three shillings a week in the earnings of the head of a family than upon the nature of his household. With a family of half a dozen children, the eldest of them delicate girls, nothing that he can hope to receive for the labour of his one pair of hands can save him from many hardships during a few years. But with a family of strong boys, of ages from twelve to seventeen or eighteen, he enjoys a season of prosperity. The very manner of the farmer towards him is deferential; for home-living boys, who in many cases can do men's work at half the wages, and without requiring the perquisites of house, garden-land, and so on, are treasures to the employer of agricultural labour. These precious lads are, according to the testimony of several respectable labourers, a more frequent cause of contention between employer and man than any other item in their reckonings. As the boys grow, the father asks for a like growth in their earnings; and disputes arise which frequently end in the proprietor of the valuables taking himself off to a farm where he and his will be better appreciated. The mother of the same goodly row of sons can afford to despise the farmer's request for female labour; she stays genteelly at home, and looks with some superciliousness upon wives who, having no useful children, are obliged to work in the fields like their husbands. A triumphant family of the former class, which recently came under notice, may be instanced. The father and eldest son were paid eleven shillings a week each, the younger son ten shillings, three nearly grown-up daughters four shillings a week each, the mother the same when she chose to go out, and all the women two shillings a week additional at harvest; the men, of course, receiving their additional harvest-money as previously stated, with house, garden, and allotment free of charge. And since '*sine prole*' would not frequently be written of the Dorset labourer if his pedigree were recorded in the local history like that of the other county families, such cases as the above are not uncommon.

Women's labour, too, is highly in request, for a woman who, like a boy, fills the place of a man at half the wages, can be better depended on for steadiness. Thus where a boy is useful in driving a cart or a plough, a woman is invaluable in work which, though somewhat lighter, demands thought. In winter and spring a farmwoman's occupation is often 'turnip-hacking'—that is, picking out from the land the stumps of turnips which have been eaten off by the sheep—or feeding the threshing-machine, clearing away straw from the same, and standing on the rick to hand forward the sheaves. In mid-spring and early summer her services are required for weeding wheat and barley (cutting up thistles and other noxious plants with a spud), and clearing weeds from pasture-land in like manner. In later summer her time is entirely engrossed by haymaking—quite a science, though it appears the easiest thing in the world to toss hay about in the sun. The length to which a skilful raker will work and retain command over her rake without moving her feet is dependent largely upon practice, and quite astonishing to the uninitiated.

Haymaking is no sooner over than the women are hurried off to the harvest-field. This is a lively time. The bonus in wages during these few weeks, the cleanliness of the occupation, the heat, the cider and ale, influence to facetiousness and vocal strains. Quite the reverse do these lively women feel in the occupation which may be said to stand, emotionally, at the opposite pole to gathering in corn: that is, threshing it. Not a woman in the county but hates the threshing machine. The dust, the din, the sustained exertion demanded to keep up with the steam tyrant, are distasteful to all women but the coarsest. I am not sure whether, at the present time, women are employed to feed the machine, but some years ago a woman had frequently to stand just above the whizzing wire drum, and feed from morning to night—a performance for which she was quite unfitted, and many were the manœuvres to escape that responsible position. A thin saucer-eyed woman of fifty-five, who had been feeding the machine all day, declared on one occasion that in crossing a field on her way home in the fog after dusk, she was so dizzy from the work as to be unable to find the opposite gate, and there she walked round and round the field, bewildered and terrified, till three o'clock in the morning, before she could get out. The farmer said that the ale had got into her head, but she maintained that it was the spinning of the machine. The point was never clearly settled between them; and the poor woman is now dead and buried.

To be just, however, to the farmers, they do not enforce the letter of the Candlemas agreement in relation to the woman, if she makes any reasonable excuse for breaking it; and indeed, many a nervous farmer is put to flight by a matron who has a tongue with a tang, and who chooses to assert, without giving any reason whatever, that, though she had made fifty agreements, 'be cust if she will come out unless she is minded'—possibly terrifying him with accusations of brutality at asking her, when he knows 'how she is just now'. A farmer of the present essayist's acquaintance, who has a tendency to blush in the presence of beauty, and is in other respects a bashful man for his years, says that when the ladies of his farm are all together in the field, and he is the single one of the male sex present, he would as soon put his head into a hornet's nest as utter a word of complaint, or even a request beyond the commonest.

The changes which are so increasingly discernible in village life by no means originate entirely with the agricultural unrest. A depopulation is going on which in some quarters is truly alarming. Villages used to contain, in addition to the agricultural inhabitants, an interesting and better-informed class, ranking distinctly above those—the blacksmith, the carpenter, the shoemaker, the small higgler, the shopkeeper (whose stock-in-trade consisted of a couple of loaves, a pound of candles, a bottle of brandy-balls and lumps of delight, three or four scrubbing-brushes, and a frying-pan), together with nondescript-workers other than farm-labourers, who had remained in the houses where they were born for no especial reason beyond an instinct of association with the spot. Many of these families had been life-holders, who built at their own expense the cottages they occupied, and as the lives dropped, and the property fell in they would have been glad to remain as weekly or monthly tenants of the owner. But the policy of all but some few philanthropic land-owners is to disapprove of these petty tenants who are not in the estate's employ, and to pull down each cottage as it falls in, leaving standing a sufficient number for the use of the farmer's men and no more. The occupants who formed the backbone of the village life have to seek refuge in the boroughs. This process, which is designated by statisticians as 'the tendency of the rural population towards the large towns', is really the tendency of water to flow uphill when forced. The poignant regret of those who are thus obliged to forsake the old nest can only be realized by people who have witnessed it—concealed as it often is under a mask of indifference. It is anomalous that landowners who are showing unprecedented activity in the erection of comfortable cottages for their farm labourers, should see no reason for benefiting in the same way these unattached natives of the village who are nobody's care. They might often expostulate in the words addressed to King Henry the Fourth by his fallen subject:

> *Our house, my sovereign liege, little deserves*
> *The scourge of greatness to be used on it;*
> *And that same greatness, too, which our own hands*
> *Have holp to make so portly.*

The system is much to be deplored, for every one of these banished people imbibes a sworn enmity to the existing order of things, and not a few of them, far from becoming merely honest Radicals, degenerate into Anarchists, waiters on chance, to whom danger to the State, the town—nay, the street they live in, is a welcomed opportunity.

A reason frequently advanced for dismissing these families from the villages where they have lived for centuries is that it is done in the interests of morality; and it is quite true that some of the 'liviers' (as these half-independent villagers used to be called) were not always shining examples of churchgoing, temperance, and quiet walking. But a natural tendency to evil, which develops to unlawful action when excited by contact with others like-minded, would often have remained latent amid the simple isolated experiences of a village life. The cause of morality cannot be served by compelling a population hitherto evenly distributed over the country to concentrate in a few towns, with the inevitable results of overcrowding and want of regular employment. But the question of the Dorset cottager here merges in that of all the houseless and landless poor, and the vast topic of the Rights of Man, to consider which is beyond the scope of a merely descriptive article.

The Withered Arm

I A LORN MILKMAID

IT was an eighty-cow diary, and the troop of milkers, regular and supernumerary, were all at work; for, though the time of year was as yet but early April, the feed lay entirely in water-meadows, and the cows were 'in full pail'. The hour was about six in the evening, and three-fourths of the large, red, rectangular animals having been finished off, there was opportunity for a little conversation.

'He do bring home his bride to-morrow, I hear. They've come as far as Anglebury to-day.'

The voice seemed to proceed from the belly of the cow called Cherry, but the speaker was a milking-woman, whose face was buried in the flank of that motionless beast.

'Hav' anybody seen her?' said another.

There was a negative response from the first. 'Though they say she's a rosy-cheeked, tisty-tosty little body enough,' she added; and as the milkmaid spoke she turned her face so that she could glance past her cow's tail to the other side of the barton, where a thin, fading woman of thirty milked somewhat apart from the rest.

'Years younger than he, they say,' continued the second, with also a glance of reflectiveness in the same direction.

'How old do you call him, then?'

'Thirty or so.'

'More like forty,' broke in an old milkman near, in a long white pinafore or 'wropper', and with the brim of his hat tied down, so that he looked like a woman. ''A was born before our Great Weir was builded, and I hadn't man's wages when I laved water there.'

The discussion waxed so warm that the purr of the milk-streams became jerky, till a voice from another cow's belly cried with authority, 'Now then, what the Turk do it matter to us about Farmer Lodge's age, or Farmer Lodge's new mis'ess? I shall have to pay him nine pound a year for the rent of every one of these milchers, whatever his age or hers. Get on with your work, or 'twill be dark afore we have done. The evening is pinking in a'ready.' This speaker was the dairyman himself, by whom the milkmaids and men were employed.

Nothing more was said publicly about Farmer Lodge's wedding, but the first woman murmured under her cow to her next neighbour, ''Tis hard for *she*,' signifying the thin worn milkmaid aforesaid.

'O no,' said the second. 'He ha'n't spoke to Rhoda Brook for years.'

When the milking was done they washed their pails and hung them on a many-forked stand made as usual of the peeled limb of an oak-tree, set upright in the earth, and resembling a colossal antlered horn. The majority then dispersed in various directions homeward. The thin woman who had not spoken was joined by a boy of twelve or thereabout, and the twain went away up the field also.

Their course lay apart from that of the others, to a lonely spot high above the water-meads, and not far from the border of Egdon Heath, whose dark countenance was visible in the distance as they drew nigh to their home.

'They've just been saying down in barton that your father brings his young wife home from Anglebury to-morrow,' the woman observed. 'I shall want to send you for a few things to market, and you'll be pretty sure to meet 'em.'

'Yes, mother,' said the boy. 'Is father married then?'

'Yes. . . . You can give her a look, and tell me what's she's like, if you do see her.'

'Yes, mother.'

'If she's dark or fair, and if she's tall—as tall as I. And if she seems like a woman who has ever worked for a living, or one that has been always well off, and has never done anything, and shows marks of the lady on her, as I expect she do.'

'Yes.'

They crept up the hill in the twilight, and entered the cottage. It was built of mud-walls, the surface of which had been washed by many rains into channels and depressions that left none of the original flat face visible; while here and there in the thatch above a rafter showed like a bone protruding through the skin.

She was kneeling down in the chimney-corner, before two pieces of turf laid together with the heather inwards, blowing at the red-hot ashes with her breath till the turves flamed. The radiance lit her pale cheek, and made her dark eyes, that had once been handsome, seem handsome anew. 'Yes,' she resumed, 'see if she is dark or fair, and if you can, notice if her hands be white; if not, see if they look as though she had ever done houeswork, or are milker's hands like mine.'

The boy again promised, inattentively this time, his mother not observing that he was cutting a notch with his pocket-knife in the beech-backed chair.

II THE YOUNG WIFE

THE road from Anglebury to Holmstoke is in general level; but there is one place where a sharp ascent breaks its monotony. Farmers homeward-bound from the former market-town, who trot all the rest of the way, walk their horses up this short incline.

The next evening, while the sun was yet bright, a handsome new gig, with a lemon-coloured body and red wheels, was spinning westward along the level highway at the heels of a powerful mare. The driver was a yeoman in the prime of life, cleanly shaven like an actor, his face being toned to that bluish-vermilion hue which so often graces a thriving farmer's features when returning home after successful dealings in the town. Beside him sat a woman, many years his junior—almost, indeed, a girl. Her face too was fresh in colour, but it was of a totally different quality—soft and evanescent, like the light under a heap of rose-petals.

Few people travelled this way, for it was not a main road; and the long white riband of gravel that stretched before them was empty, save of one small scarce-moving speck, which presently resolved itself into the figure of a boy, who was creeping on at a snail's pace, and continually looking behind him—the heavy bundle he carried being some excuse for, if not the reason of, his dilatoriness. When the bouncing gig-party slowed at the bottom of the incline above mentioned, the pedestrian was only a few yards in front. Supporting the large bundle by putting one hand on his hip, he turned and looked straight at the farmer's wife as though he would read her through and through, pacing along abreast of the horse.

The low sun was full in her face, rendering every feature, shade, and contour distinct, from the curve of her little nostril to the colour of her eyes. The farmer, though he seemed annoyed at the boy's persistent presence, did not order him to get out of the way; and thus the lad preceded them, his hard gaze never leaving her, till they reached the top of the ascent, when the farmer trotted on with relief in his lineaments—having taken no outward notice of the boy whatever.

'How that poor lad stared at me!' said the young wife.

'Yes, dear; I saw that he did.'

'He is one of the village, I suppose?'

'One of the neighbourhood. I think he lives with his mother a mile or two off.'

'He knows who we are, no doubt?'

'O yes. You must expect to be stared at just at first, my pretty Gertrude.'

'I do—though I think the poor boy may have looked at us in the hope we might relieve him of his heavy load, rather than from curiosity.'

'O no,' said her husband off-handedly. 'These country lads will carry a hundredweight once they get it on their backs; besides his pack had more size than weight in it. Now, then, another mile and I shall be able to show you our house in the distance—if it is not too dark before we get there.' The wheels spun round, and particles flew from their periphery as before, till a white house of ample dimensions revealed itself, with farm-buildings and ricks at the back.

Meanwhile the boy had quickened his pace, and turning up a by-lane some mile and half short of the white farmstead, ascended towards the leaner pastures, and so on to the cottage of his mother.

She had reached home after her day's milking at the outlying dairy, and was washing cabbage at the doorway in the declining light. 'Hold up the net a moment,' she said, without preface, as the boy came up.

He flung down his bundle, held the edge of the cabbage-net, and as she filled its meshes with the dripping leaves she went on, 'Well, did you see her?'

'Yes; quite plain.'

'Is she ladylike?'

'Yes; and more. A lady complete.'

'Is she young?'

'Well, she's growed up, and her ways be quite a woman's.'

'Of course. What colour is her hair and face?'

'Her hair is lightish, and her face as comely as a live doll's.'

'Her eyes, then, are not dark like mine?'

'No—of a bluish turn, and her mouth is very nice and red; and when she smiles, her teeth show white.'

'Is she tall?' said the woman sharply.

'I couldn't see. She was sitting down.'

'Then do you go to Holmstoke church to-morrow morning: she's sure to be there. Go early and notice her walking in, and come home and tell me if she's taller than I.'

'Very well, mother. But why don't you go and see for yourself?'

'*I* go to see her! I wouldn't look up at her if she were to pass my window this instant. She was with Mr. Lodge, of course. What did he say or do?'

'Just the same as usual.'

'Took no notice of you?'

'None.'

Next day the mother put a clean shirt on the boy, and started him off for Holmstoke church. He reached the ancient little pile when the door was just being opened, and he was the first to enter. Taking his seat by the font, he watched all the parishioners file in. The well-to-do Farmer Lodge came nearly last; and his young wife, who accompanied him, walked up the aisle with the shyness natural to a modest woman who had appeared thus for the first time. As all other eyes were fixed upon her, the youth's stare was not noticed now.

When he reached home his mother said, 'Well?' before he had entered the room.

'She is not tall. She is rather short,' he replied.

'Ah!' said his mother, with satisfaction.

'But she's very pretty—very. In fact, she's lovely.' The youthful freshness of the yeoman's wife had evidently made an impression even on the somewhat hard nature of the boy.

'That's all I want to hear,' said his mother quickly. 'Now, spread the table-cloth. The hare you wired is very tender; but mind that nobody catches you.—You've never told me what sort of hands she had.'

'I have never seen 'em. She never took off her gloves.'

'What did she wear this morning?'

'A white bonnet and a silver-coloured gownd. It whewed and whistled so loud when it rubbed against the pews that the lady coloured up more than ever for very shame at the noise, and pulled it in to keep it from touching; but when she pushed into her seat, it whewed more than ever. Mr. Lodge, he seemed pleased, and his waistcoat stuck out, and his great golden seals hung like a lord's; but she seemed to wish her noisy gownd anywhere but on her.'

'Not she! However, that will do now.'

These descriptions of the newly married couple were continued from time to time by the boy at his mother's request, after any chance encounter he had had with them. But Rhoda Brook, though she might easily have seen young Mrs. Lodge for herself by walking a couple of miles, would never attempt an excursion towards the quarter where the farmhouse lay. Neither did she, at the daily milking in the dairyman's yard on Lodge's outlying second farm, ever speak on the subject of the recent marriage. The dairyman, who rented the cows of Lodge, and knew perfectly the tall milkmaid's history, with manly kindliness always kept the gossip in the cow-barton from annoying Rhoda. But the atmosphere thereabout was full of the subject during the first days of Mrs. Lodge's arrival; and from her boy's description and the casual words of the other milkers, Rhoda Brook could raise a mental image of the unconscious Mrs. Lodge that was realistic as a photograph.

III A VISION

ONE night, two or three weeks after the bridal return, when the boy was gone to bed, Rhoda sat a long time over the turf ashes that she had raked out in front of her to extinguish them. She contemplated so intently the new wife, as presented to her in her mind's eye over the embers, that she forgot the lapse of time. At last, wearied with her day's work, she too retired.

But the figure which had occupied her so much during this and the previous days was not to be banished at night. For the first time Gertrude Lodge visited the supplanted woman in her dreams. Rhoda Brook dreamed—since her assertion that she really saw, before falling asleep, was not to be believed—that the young wife, in the pale silk dress and white bonnet, but with features shockingly distorted, and wrinkled as by age, was sitting upon her chest as she lay. The pressure of Mrs. Lodge's person grew heavier; the blue eyes peered cruelly into her face; and then the figure thrust forward its left hand mockingly, so as to make the wedding-ring it wore glitter in Rhoda's eyes. Maddened mentally, and nearly suffocated by pressure, the sleeper struggled; the incubus, still regarding her, withdrew to the foot of the bed, only, however, to come forward by degrees, resume her seat, and flash her left hand as before.

Gasping for breath, Rhoda, in a last desperate effort, swung out her right hand, seized the confronting spectre by its obtrusive left arm, and whirled it backward to the floor, starting up herself as she did so with a low cry.

'O, merciful heaven!' she cried, sitting on the edge of the bed in a cold sweat; 'that was not a dream—she was here!'

She could feel her antagonist's arm within her grasp even now —the very flesh and bone of it, as it seemed. She looked on the floor whither she had whirled the spectre, but there was nothing to be seen.

Rhoda Brook slept no more that night, and when she went milking at the next dawn they noticed how pale and haggard she looked. The milk that she drew quivered into the pail; her hand had not calmed even yet, and still retained the feel of the arm. She came home to breakfast as wearily as if it had been supper-time.

'What was that noise in your chimmer, mother, last night?' said her son. 'You fell off the bed, surely?'

'Did you hear anything fall? At what time?'

'Just when the clock struck two.'

She could not explain, and when the meal was done went silently about her household work, the boy assisting her, for he hated going afield on the farms, and she indulged his reluctance. Between eleven and twelve the garden-gate clicked, and she lifted her eyes to the window. At the bottom of the garden, within the gate, stood the woman of her vision. Rhoda seemed trans-fixed.

'Ah, she said she would come!' exclaimed the boy, also observing her.

'Said so—when? How does she know us?'

'I have seen and spoken to her. I talked to her yesterday.'

'I told you', said the mother, flushing indignantly, 'never to speak to anybody in that house, or go near the place.'

'I did not speak to her till she spoke to me. And I did not go near the place. I met her in the road.'

'What did you tell her?'

'Nothing. She said, "Are you the poor boy who had to bring the heavy load from market?" And she looked at my boots, and said they would not keep my feet dry if it came on wet, because they were so cracked. I told her I lived with my mother, and we had enough to do to keep ourselves, and that's how it was; and she said then, "I'll come and bring you some better boots, and see your mother." She gives away things to other folks in the meads besides us.'

Mrs. Lodge was by this time close to the door—not in her silk, as Rhoda had dreamt of in the bed-chamber, but in a morning hat, and gown of common light material, which became her better than silk. On her arm she carried a basket.

The impression remaining from the night's experience was still strong. Brook had almost expected to see the wrinkles, the scorn, and the cruelty on her visitor's face. She would have escaped an interview, had escape been possible. There was, however, no backdoor to the cottage, and in an instant the boy had lifted the latch to Mrs. Lodge's gentle knock.

'I see I have come to the right house,' said she, glancing at the lad, and smiling. 'But I was not sure till you opened the door.'

The figure and action were those of the phantom; but her voice was so indescribably sweet, her glance so winning, her smile so tender, so unlike that of Rhoda's midnight visitant, that the latter could hardly believe the evidence of her senses. She was truly glad that she had not hidden away in sheer aversion, as she had been inclined to do. In her basket Mrs. Lodge brought the pair of boots that she had promised to the boy, and other useful articles.

At these proofs of a kindly feeling towards her and hers Rhoda's heart reproached her bitterly. This innocent young thing should have her blessing and not her curse. When she left them a light seemed gone from the dwelling. Two days later she came again to know if the boots fitted; and less than a fortnight after that paid Rhoda another call. On this occasion the boy was absent.

'I walk a good deal,' said Mrs. Lodge, 'and your house is the nearest outside our own parish. I hope you are well. You don't look quite well.'

Rhoda said she was well enough; and, indeed, though the paler of the two, there was more of the strength that endures in her well-defined features and large frame, than in the soft-cheeked young woman before her. The conversation became quite confidential as regarded their powers and weaknesses; and when Mrs. Lodge was leaving, Rhoda said, 'I hope you will find this air agree with you, ma'am, and not suffer from the damp of the water meads.'

The younger one replied that there was not much doubt of it, her general health being usually good. 'Though, now you remind me,' she added, 'I have one little ailment which puzzles me. It is nothing serious, but I cannot make it out.'

She uncovered her left hand and arm; and their outline confronted Rhoda's gaze as the exact original of the limb she had beheld and seized in her dream. Upon the pink round surface of the arm were faint marks of an unhealthy colour, as if produced by a rough grasp. Rhoda's eyes became riveted on the discolorations; she fancied that she discerned in them the shape of her own four fingers.

'How did it happen?' she said mechanically.

'I cannot tell,' replied Mrs. Lodge, shaking her head. 'One night when I was sound asleep, dreaming I was away in some strange place, a pain suddenly shot into my arm there, and was so keen as to awaken me. I must have struck it in the daytime, I suppose, though I don't remember doing so.' She added, laughing, 'I tell my dear husband that it looks just as if he had flown into a rage and struck me there. O, I daresay it will soon disappear.'

'Ha, ha! Yes. . . . On what night did it come?'

Mrs. Lodge considered, and said it would be a fortnight ago on the morrow. 'When I awoke I could not remember where I was,' she added, 'till the clock striking two reminded me.'

She had named the night and the hour of Rhoda's spectral encounter, and Brook felt like a guilty thing. The artless disclosure startled her; she did not reason on the freaks of coincidence; and all the scenery of that ghastly night returned with double vividness to her mind.

'O, can it be,' she said to herself, when her visitor had departed, 'that I exercise a malignant power over people against my own will?' She knew that she had been slyly called a witch since her fall; but never having understood why that particular stigma had been attached to her, it had passed disregarded. Could this be the explanation, and had such things as this ever happened before?

IV A SUGGESTION

THE summer drew on, and Rhoda Brook almost dreaded to meet Mrs. Lodge again, notwithstanding that her feeling for the young wife amounted wellnigh to affection. Something in her own individuality seemed to convict Rhoda of crime. Yet a fatality sometimes would direct the steps of the latter to the outskirts of Holmstoke whenever she left her house for any other purpose than her daily work; and hence it happened that their next encounter was out of doors. Rhoda could not avoid the subject which had so mystified her, and after the first few words she stammered, 'I hope your—arm is well again, ma'am?' She had perceived with consternation that Gertrude Lodge carried her left arm stiffly.

'No; it is not quite well. Indeed it is no better at all; it is rather worse. It pains me dreadfully sometimes.'

'Perhaps you had better go to a doctor, ma'am.'

She replied that she had already seen a doctor. Her husband had insisted upon her going to one. But the surgeon had not seemed to understand the afflicted limb at all; he had told her to bathe it in hot water, and she had bathed it, but the treatment had done no good.

'Will you let me see it?' said the milkwoman.

Mrs. Lodge pushed up her sleeve and disclosed the place, which was a few inches above the wrist. As soon as Rhoda Brook saw it, she could hardly preserve her composure. There was nothing of the nature of a wound, but the arm at that point had a shrivelled look, and the outline of the four fingers appeared more distinct than at the former time. Moreover, she fancied that they were imprinted in precisely the relative position of her clutch upon the arm in the trance; the first finger towards Gertrude's wrist, and the fourth towards her elbow.

What the impress resembled seemed to have struck Gertrude herself since their last meeting. 'It looks almost like finger-marks,' she said; adding with a faint laugh, 'my husband says it is as if some witch, or the devil himself, had taken hold of me there, and blasted the flesh.'

Rhoda shivered. 'That's fancy,' she said hurriedly. 'I wouldn't mind it, if I were you.'

'I shouldn't so much mind it,' said the younger, with hesitation, 'if—if I hadn't a notion that it makes my husband—dislike me —no, love me less. Men think so much of personal appearance.'

'Some do—he for one.'

'Yes; and he was very proud of mine, at first.'

'Keep your arm covered from his sight.'

'Ah—he knows the disfigurement is there!' She tried to hide the tears that filled her eyes.

'Well, ma'am, I earnestly hope it will go away soon.'

And so the milkwoman's mind was chained anew to the subject by a horrid sort of spell as she returned home. The sense of having been guilty of an act of malignity increased, affect as she might to ridicule her superstition. In her secret heart Rhoda did not altogether object to a slight diminution of her successor's beauty, by whatever means it had come about; but she did not wish to inflict upon her physical pain. For though this pretty young woman had rendered impossible any reparation which Lodge might have made Rhoda for his past conduct, everything like resentment at the unconscious usurpation had quite passed away from the elder's mind.

If the sweet and kindly Gertrude Lodge only knew of the dream-scene in the bed-chamber, what would she think? Not to inform her of it seemed treachery in the presence of her friendliness; but tell she could not of her own accord—neither could she devise a remedy.

She mused upon the matter the greater part of the night; and the next day, after the morning milking, set out to obtain another glimpse of Gertrude Lodge if she could, being held to her by a gruesome fascination. By watching the house from a distance the milkmaid was presently able to discern the farmer's wife in a ride she was taking alone—probably to join her husband in some distant field. Mrs. Lodge perceived her, and cantered in her direction.

'Good morning, Rhoda!' Gertrude said, when she had come up. 'I was going to call.'

Rhoda noticed that Mrs. Lodge held the reins with some difficulty.

'I hope—the bad arm,' said Rhoda.

'They tell me there is possibly one way by which I might be able to find out the cause, and so perhaps the cure, of it,' replied the other anxiously. 'It is by going to some clever man over in Egdon Heath. They did not know if he was still alive—and I cannot remember his name at this moment; but they said that you knew more of his movements than anybody else hereabout, and could tell me if he were still to be consulted. Dear me—what was his name? But you know.'

'Not Conjuror Trendle?' said her thin companion, turning pale.

'Trendle—yes. Is he alive?'

'I believe so,' said Rhoda, with reluctance.

'Why do you call him conjuror?'

'Well—they say—they used to say he was a—he had powers other folks have not.'

'O, how could my people be so superstitious as to recommend a man of that sort! I thought they meant some medical man. I shall think no more of him.'

Rhoda looked relieved, and Mrs. Lodge rode on. The milk-woman had inwardly seen, from the moment she heard of her having been mentioned as a reference for this man, that there must exist a sarcastic feeling among the workfolk that a sorceress would know the whereabouts of the exorcist. They suspected her, then. A short time ago this would have given no concern to a woman of her common-sense. But she had a haunting reason to be superstitious now; and she had been seized with sudden dread that this Conjuror Trendle might name her as the malignant influence which was blasting the fair person of Gertrude, and so lead her friend to hate her for ever, and to treat her as some fiend in human shape.

But all was not over. Two days after, a shadow intruded into the window-pattern thrown on Rhoda Brook's floor by the afternoon sun. The woman opened the door at once, almost breathlessly.

'Are you alone?' said Gertrude. She seemed to be no less harassed and anxious than Brook herself.

'Yes,' said Rhoda.

'The place on my arm seems worse, and troubles me!' the

young farmer's wife went on. 'It is so mysterious! I do hope it
will not be an incurable wound. I have again been thinking of
what they said about Conjuror Trendle. I don't really believe in
such men, but I should not mind just visiting him, from curiosity
—though on no account must my husband know. Is it far to
where he lives?'

'Yes—five miles,' said Rhoda backwardly. 'In the heart of
Egdon.'

'Well, I should have to walk. Could not you go with me to
show me the way—say to-morrow afternoon?'

'O, not I—that is——' the milkwoman murmured, with a
start of dismay. Again the dread seized her that something to do
with her fierce act in the dream might be revealed, and her
character in the eyes of the most useful friend she had ever had
be ruined irretrievably.

Mrs. Lodge urged, and Rhoda finally assented, though with
much misgiving. Sad as the journey would be to her, she could
not conscientiously stand in the way of a possible remedy for her
patron's strange affliction. It was agreed that, to escape suspicion
of their mystic intent, they should meet at the edge of the heath
at the corner of a plantation which was visible from the spot
where they now stood.

V CONJUROR TRENDLE

By the next afternoon Rhoda would have done anything to
escape this inquiry. But she had promised to go. Moreover, there
was a horrid fascination at times in becoming instrumental in
throwing such possible light on her own character as would
reveal her to be something greater in the occult world than she
had ever herself suspected.

She started just before the time of day mentioned between
them, and half-an-hour's brisk walking brought her to the south-
eastern extension of the Egdon tract of country, where the fir
plantation was. A slight figure, cloaked and veiled, was already
there. Rhoda recognized, almost with a shudder, that Mrs.
Lodge bore her left arm in a sling.

They hardly spoke to each other, and immediately set out on
their climb into the interior of this solemn country, which stood
high above the rich alluvial soil they had left half an hour before.
It was a long walk; thick clouds made the atmosphere dark,
though it was as yet only early afternoon; and the wind howled
dismally over the slopes of the heath—not improbably the same

heath which had witnessed the agony of the Wessex King Ina, presented to after-ages as Lear. Gertrude Lodge talked most, Rhoda replying with monosyllabic preoccupation. She had a strange dislike to walking on the side of her companion where hung the afflicted arm, moving round to the other when inadvertently near it. Much heather had been brushed by their feet when they descended upon a cart-track, beside which stood the house of the man they sought.

He did not profess his remedial practices openly, or care anything about their continuance, his direct interests being those of a dealer in furze, turf, 'sharp sand', and other local products. Indeed, he affected not to believe largely in his own powers, and when warts that had been shown him for cure miraculously disappeared—which it must be owned they infallibly did—he would say lightly, 'O, I only drink a glass of grog upon 'em at your expense—perhaps it's all chance,' and immediately turn the subject.

He was at home when they arrived, having in fact seen them descending into his valley. He was a grey-bearded man, with a reddish face, and he looked singularly at Rhoda the first moment he beheld her. Mrs. Lodge told him her errand; and then with words of self-disparagement he examined her arm.

'Medicine can't cure it,' he said promptly. ''Tis the work of an enemy.'

Rhoda shrank into herself, and drew back.

'An enemy? What enemy?' asked Mrs. Lodge.

He shook his head. 'That's best known to yourself,' he said. 'If you like, I can show the person to you, though I shall not myself know who it is. I can do no more; and don't wish to do that.'

She pressed him; on which he told Rhoda to wait outside where she stood, and took Mrs. Lodge into the room. It opened immediately from the door; and, as the latter remained ajar, Rhoda Brook could see the proceedings without taking part in them. He brought a tumbler from the dresser, nearly filled it with water, and fetching an egg, prepared it in some private way; after which he broke it on the edge of the glass, so that the white went in and the yolk remained. As it was getting gloomy, he took the glass and its contents to the window, and told Gertrude to watch the mixture closely. They leant over the table together, and the milkwoman could see the opaline hue of the egg-fluid changing form as it sank in the water, but she was not near enough to define the shape that it assumed.

'Do you catch the likeness of any face or figure as you look?' demanded the conjuror of the young woman.

She murmured a reply, in tones so low as to be inaudible to Rhoda, and continued to gaze intently into the glass. Rhoda turned, and walked a few steps away.

When Mrs. Lodge came out, and her face was met by the light, it appeared exceedingly pale—as pale as Rhoda's—against the sad dun shades of the upland's garniture. Trendle shut the door behind her, and they at once started homeward together. But Rhoda perceived that her companion had quite changed.

'Did he charge much?' she asked tentatively.

'O no—nothing. He would not take a farthing,' said Gertrude.

'And what did you see?' inquired Rhoda.

'Nothing I—care to speak of.' The constraint in her manner was remarkable; her face was so rigid as to wear an oldened aspect, faintly suggestive of the face in Rhoda's bed-chamber.

'Was it you who first proposed coming here?' Mrs. Lodge suddenly inquired, after a long pause. 'How very odd, if you did!'

'No. But I am not sorry we have come, all things considered,' she replied. For the first time a sense of triumph possessed her, and she did not altogether deplore that the young thing at her side should learn that their lives had been antagonized by other influences than their own.

The subject was no more alluded to during the long and dreary walk home. But in some way or other a story was whispered about the many-dairied lowland that winter that Mrs. Lodge's gradual loss of the use of her left arm was owing to her being 'overlooked' by Rhoda Brook. The latter kept her own counsel about the incubus, but her face grew sadder and thinner; and in the spring she and her boy disappeared from the neighbourhood of Holmstoke.

VI   A SECOND ATTEMPT

HALF-a-dozen years passed away, and Mr. and Mrs. Lodge's married experience sank into prosiness, and worse. The farmer was usually gloomy and silent: the woman whom he had wooed for her grace and beauty was contorted and disfigured in the left limb; moreover, she had brought him no child, which rendered it likely that he would be the last of a family who had occupied that valley for some two hundred years. He thought of Rhoda Brook and her son; and feared this might be a judgment from heaven upon him.

The once blithe-hearted and enlightened Gertrude was changing into an irritable, superstitious woman, whose whole time was given to experimenting upon her ailment with every quack remedy she came across. She was honestly attached to her husband, and was ever secretly hoping against hope to win back his heart against by regaining some at least of her personal beauty. Hence it arose that her closet was lined with bottles, packets, and ointment-pots of every description—nay, bunches of mystic herbs, charms, and books of necromancy, which in her schoolgirl time she would have ridiculed as folly.

'Damned if you won't poison yourself with these apothecary messes and witch mixtures some time or other,' said her husband, when his eye chanced to fall upon the multitudinous array.

She did not reply, but turned her sad, soft glance upon him in such heart-swollen reproach that he looked sorry for his words, and added, 'I only meant it for your good, you know, Gertrude.'

'I'll clear out the whole lot, and destroy them,' said she huskily, 'and try such remedies no more!'

'You want somebody to cheer you,' he observed. 'I once thought of adopting a boy; but he is too old now. And he is gone away I don't know where.'

She guessed to whom he alluded; for Rhoda Brook's story had in the course of years become known to her; though not a word had ever passed between her husband and herself on the subject. Neither had she ever spoken to him of her visit to Conjuror Trendle, and of what was revealed to her, or she thought was revealed to her, by that solitary heath-man.

She was now five-and-twenty; but she seemed older. 'Six years of marriage, and only a few months of love,' she sometimes whispered to herself. And then she thought of the apparent cause, and said, with a tragic glance at her withering limb, 'If I could only again be as I was when he first saw me!'

She obediently destroyed her nostrums and charms; but there remained a hankering wish to try something else—some other sort of cure altogether. She had never revisited Trendle since she had been conducted to the house of the solitary by Rhoda against her will; but it now suddenly occurred to Gertrude that she would, in a last desperate effort at deliverance from this seeming curse, again seek out the man, if he yet lived. He was entitled to a certain credence, for the indistinct form he had raised in the glass had undoubtedly resembled the only woman in the world who—as she now knew, though not then—could have a reason for bearing her ill-will. The visit should be paid.

This time she went alone, though she nearly got lost on the heath, and roamed a considerable distance out of her way.

Trendle's house was reached at last, however: he was not indoors, and instead of waiting at the cottage, she went to where his bent figure was pointed out to her at work a long way off. Trendle remembered her, and laying down the handful of furze-roots which he was gathering and throwing into a heap, he offered to accompany her in her homeward direction, as the distance was considerable and the days were short. So they walked together, his head bowed nearly to the earth, and his form of a colour with it.

'You can send away warts and other excrescences, I know,' she said; 'why can't you send away this?' And the arm was uncovered.

'You think too much of my powers!' said Trendle; 'and I am old and weak now, too. No, no; it is too much for me to attempt in my own person. What have ye tried?'

She named to him some of the hundred medicaments and counterspells which she had adopted from time to time. He shook his head.

'Some were good enough,' he said approvingly; 'but not many of them for such as this. This is of the nature of a blight, not of the nature of a wound; and if you ever do throw it off, it will be all at once.'

'If I only could!'

'There is only one chance of doing it known to me. It has never failed in kindred afflictions—that I can declare. But it is hard to carry out, and especially for a woman.'

'Tell me!' said she.

'You must touch with the limb the neck of a man who's been hanged.'

She started a little at the image he had raised.

'Before he's cold—just after he's cut down,' continued the conjuror impassively.

'How can that do good?'

'It will turn the blood and change the constitution. But, as I say, to do it is hard. You must go to the jail when there's a hanging, and wait for him when he's brought off the gallows. Lots have done it, though perhaps not such pretty women as you. I used to send dozens for skin complaints. But that was in former times. The last I sent was in '13—near twelve years ago.'

He had no more to tell her; and, when he had put her into a straight track homeward, turned and left her, refusing all money as at first.

35

VII A RIDE

THE communication sank deep into Gertrude's mind. Her nature was rather a timid one; and probably of all remedies that the white wizard could have suggested there was not one which would have filled her with so much aversion as this, not to speak of the immense obstacles in the way of its adoption.

Casterbridge, the county-town, was a dozen or fifteen miles off; and though in those days, when men were executed for horse-stealing, arson, and burglary, an assize seldom passed without a hanging, it was not likely that she could get access to the body of the criminal unaided. And the fear of her husband's anger made her reluctant to breathe a word of Trendle's suggestion to him or to anybody about him.

She did nothing for months, and patiently bore her disfigure-ment as before. But her woman's nature, craving for renewed love, through the medium of renewed beauty (she was but twenty-five), was ever stimulating her to try what, at any rate, could hardly do her any harm. 'What came by a spell will go by a spell surely,' she would say. Whenever her imagination pictured the act she shrank in terror from the possibility of it: then the words of the conjuror, 'It will turn your blood,' were seen to be capable of a scientific no less than a ghastly interpretation; the mastering desire returned, and urged her on again.

There was at this time but one county paper, and that her husband only occasionally borrowed. But old-fashioned days had old-fashioned means, and news was extensively conveyed by word of mouth from market to market, or from fair to fair, so that, whenever such an event as an execution was about to take place, few within a radius of twenty miles were ignorant of the coming sight; and, so far as Holmstoke was concerned, some enthusiasts had been known to walk all the way to Casterbridge and back in one day, solely to witness the spectacle. The next assizes were in March; and when Gertrude Lodge heard that they had been held, she inquired stealthily at the inn as to the result, as soon as she could find opportunity.

She was, however, too late. The time at which the sentences were to be carried out had arrived, and to make the journey and obtain admission at such short notice required at least her husband's assistance. She dared not tell him, for she had found by delicate experiment that these smouldering village beliefs made him furious if mentioned, partly because he half entertained them himself. It was therefore necessary to wait for another opportunity.

Her determination received a fillip from learning that two

epileptic children had attended from this very village of Holmstoke many years before with beneficial results, though the experiment had been strongly condemned by the neighbouring clergy. April, May, June, passed; and it is no overstatement to say that by the end of the last-named month Gertrude wellnigh longed for the death of a fellow-creature. Instead of her formal prayers each night, her unconscious prayer was, 'O Lord, hang some guilty or innocent person soon!'

This time she made earlier inquiries, and was altogether more systematic in her proceedings. Moreover, the season was summer, between the haymaking and the harvest, and in the leisure thus afforded him her husband had been holiday-taking away from home.

The assizes were in July, and she went to the inn as before. There was to be one execution—only one—for arson.

Her greatest problem was not how to get to Casterbridge, but what means she should adopt for obtaining admission to the jail. Though access for such purposes had formerly never been denied, the custom had fallen into desuetude; and in contemplating her possible difficulties, she was again almost driven to fall back upon her husband. But, on sounding him about the assizes, he was so uncommunicative, so more than usually cold, that she did not proceed, and decided that whatever she did she would do alone.

Fortune, obdurate hitherto, showed her unexpected favour. On the Thursday before the Saturday fixed for the execution, Lodge remarked to her that he was going away from home for another day or two on business at a fair, and that he was sorry he could not take her with him.

She exhibited on this occasion so much readiness to stay at home that he looked at her in surprise. Time had been when she would have shown deep disappointment at the loss of such a jaunt. However, he lapsed into his usual taciturnity, and on the day named left Holmstoke.

It was now her turn. She at first had thought of driving, but on reflection held that driving would not do, since it would necessitate her keeping to the turnpike-road, and so increase by tenfold the risk of her ghastly errand being found out. She decided to ride, and avoid the beaten track, notwithstanding that in her husband's stables there was no animal just at present which by any stretch of imagination could be considered a lady's mount, in spite of his promise before marriage to always keep a mare for her. He had, however, many cart-horses, fine ones of their kind; and among the rest was a serviceable creature, an equine Amazon, with a back as broad as a sofa, on which Gertrude had occasionally taken an airing when unwell. This horse she chose.

On Friday afternoon one of the men brought it round. She was dressed, and before going down looked at her shrivelled arm. 'Ah!' she said to it, 'if it had not been for you this terrible ordeal would have been saved me!'

When strapping up the bundle in which she carried a few articles of clothing, she took occasion to say to the servant, 'I take these in case I should not get back to-night from the person I am going to visit. Don't be alarmed if I am not in by ten, and close up the house as usual. I shall be at home to-morrow for certain.' She meant then to tell her husband privately: the deed accomplished was not like the deed projected. He would almost certainly forgive her.

And then the pretty palpitating Gertrude Lodge went from her husband's homestead; but though her goal was Casterbridge she did not take the direct route thither through Stickleford. Her cunning course at first was in precisely the opposite direction. As soon as she was out of sight, however, she turned to the left, by a road which led into Egdon, and on entering the heath wheeled round, and set out in the true course, due westerly. A more private way down the county could not be imagined; and as to direction, she had merely to keep her horse's head to a point a little to the right of the sun. She knew that she would light upon a furze-cutter or cottager of some sort from time to time, from whom she might correct her bearing.

Though the date was comparatively recent, Egdon was much less fragmentary in character than now. The attempts—successful and otherwise—at cultivation on the lower slopes, which intrude and break up the original heath into small detached heaths, had not been carried far; Enclosure Acts had not taken effect, and the banks and fences which now exclude the cattle of those villagers who formerly enjoyed rights of commonage thereon, and the carts of those who had turbary privileges which kept them in firing all the year round, were not erected. Gertrude, therefore, rode along with no other obstacles than the prickly furze-bushes, the mats of heather, the white water-courses, and the natural steeps and declivities of the ground.

Her horse was sure, if heavy-footed and slow, and though a draught animal, was easy-paced; had it been otherwise, she was not a woman who could have ventured to ride over such a bit of country with a half-dead arm. It was therefore nearly eight o'clock when she drew rein to breathe her bearer on the last outlying high point of heath-land towards Casterbridge, previous to leaving Egdon for the cultivated valleys.

She halted before a pool called Rushy-pond, flanked by the

ends of two hedges; a railing ran through the centre of the pond, dividing it in half. Over the railing she saw the low green country; over the green trees the roofs of the town; over the roofs a white flat façade, denoting the entrance to the county jail. On the roof of this front specks were moving about; they seemed to be workmen erecting something. Her flesh crept. She descended slowly, and was soon amid corn-fields and pastures. In another half-hour, when it was almost dusk, Gertrude reached the White Hart, the first inn of the town on that side.

Little surprise was excited by her arrival; farmers' wives rode on horseback then more than they do now; though, for that matter, Mrs. Lodge was not imagined to be a wife at all; the innkeeper supposed her some harum-skarum young woman who had come to attend 'hang-fair' next day. Neither her husband nor herself ever dealt in Casterbridge market, so that she was unknown. While dismounting she beheld a crowd of boys standing at the door of a harness-maker's shop just above the inn, looking inside it with deep interest.

'What is going on there?' she asked of the ostler.

'Making the rope for to-morrow.'

She throbbed responsively, and contracted her arm.

''Tis sold by the inch afterwards,' the man continued. 'I could get you a bit, miss, for nothing, if you'd like?'

She hastily repudiated any such wish, all the more from a curious creeping feeling that the condemned wretch's destiny was becoming interwoven with her own; and having engaged a room for the night, sat down to think.

Up to this time she had formed but the vaguest notions about her means of obtaining access to the prison. The words of the cunning-man returned to her mind. He had implied that she should use her beauty, impaired though it was, as a pass-key. In her inexperience she knew little about jail functionaries; she had heard of a high-sheriff and an under-sheriff, but dimly only. She knew, however, that there must be a hangman, and to the hang-man she determined to apply.

VIII A WATER-SIDE HERMIT

AT this date, and for several years after, there was a hangman to almost every jail. Gertrude found, on inquiry, that the Caster-bridge official dwelt in a lonely cottage by a deep slow river flowing under the cliff on which the prison buildings were situate —the stream being the self-same one, though she did not know it, which watered the Stickleford and Holmstoke meads lower down in its course.

Having changed her dress, and before she had eaten or drunk —for she could not take her ease till she had ascertained some particulars—Gertrude pursued her way by a path along the water-side to the cottage indicated. Passing thus the outskirts of the jail, she discerned on the level roof over the gateway three rectangular lines against the sky, where the specks had been moving in her distant view; she recognized what the erection was, and passed quickly on. Another hundred yards brought her to the executioner's house, which a boy pointed out. It stood close to the same stream, and was hard by a weir, the waters of which emitted a steady roar.

While she stood hesitating the door opened, and an old man came forth shading a candle with one hand. Locking the door on the outside, he turned to a flight of wooden steps fixed against the end of the cottage, and began to ascend them, this being evidently the staircase to his bedroom. Gertrude hastened forward, but by the time she reached the foot of the ladder he was at the top. She called to him loudly enough to be heard above the roar of the weir; he looked down and said, 'What d'ye want here?'

'To speak to you a minute.'

The candle-light, such as it was, fell upon her imploring, pale, upturned face, and Davies (as the hangman was called) backed down the ladder. 'I was just going to bed,' he said; '"Early to bed and early to rise," but I don't mind stopping a minute for such a one as you. Come into house.' He reopened the door, and preceded her to the room within.

The implements of his daily work, which was that of a jobbing gardener, stood in a corner, and seeing probably that she looked rural, he said, 'If you want me to undertake country work I can't come, for I never leave Casterbridge for gentle nor simple—not I. My real calling is officer of justice,' he added formally.

'Yes, yes! That's it. To-morrow!'

'Ah! I thought so. Well, what's the matter about that? 'Tis no use to come here about the knot—folks do come continually, but I tell 'em one knot is as merciful as another if ye keep it under the ear. Is the unfortunate man a relation; or, I should say, perhaps' (looking at her dress) 'a person who's been in your employ?'

'No. What time is the execution?'

'The same as usual—twelve o'clock, or as soon after as the London mail coach gets in. We always wait for that, in case of a reprieve.'

'O—a reprieve—I hope not!' she said involuntarily.

'Well,—hee, hee!—as a matter of business, so do I! But still, if ever a young fellow deserved to be let off, this one does; only just turned eighteen, and only present by chance when the rick was fired. Howsomever, there's not much risk of it, as they are obliged to make an example of him, there having been so much destruction of property that way lately.'

'I mean,' she explained, 'that I want to touch him for a charm, a cure of an affliction, by the advice of a man who has proved the virtue of the remedy.'

'O yes, miss! Now I understand. I've had such people come in past years. But it didn't strike me that you looked of a sort to require blood-turning. What's the complaint? The wrong kind for this, I'll be bound.'

'My arm.' She reluctantly showed the withered skin.

'Ah!—'tis all a-scram!' said the hangman, examining it.

'Yes,' said she.

'Well,' he continued, with interest, 'that *is* the class o' subject, I'm bound to admit! I like the look of the wownd; it is truly as suitable for the cure as any I ever saw. 'Twas a knowing-man that sent 'ee, whoever he was.'

'You can contrive for me all that's necessary?' she said breathlessly.

'You should really have gone to the governor of the jail, and your doctor with 'ee, and given your name and address—that's how it used to be done, if I recollect. Still, perhaps, I can manage it for a trifling fee.'

'O, thank you! I would rather do it this way, as I should like it kept private.'

'Lover not to know, eh?'

'No—husband.'

'Aha! Very well. I'll get ee' a touch of the corpse.'

'Where is it now?' she said, shuddering.

'It?—*he*, you mean; he's living yet. Just inside that little small winder up there in the glum.' He signified the jail on the cliff above.

She thought of her husband and her friends. 'Yes, of course,' she said; 'and how am I to proceed?'

He took her to the door. 'Now, do you be waiting at the little wicket in the wall, that you'll find up there in the lane, not later than one o'clock. I will open it from the inside, as I shan't come home to dinner till he's cut down. Good-night. Be punctual; and if you don't want anybody to know 'ee, wear a veil. Ah—once I had such a daughter as you!'

She went away, and climbed the path above, to assure herself that she would be able to find the wicket next day. Its outline was soon visible to her—a narrow opening in the outer wall of the prison precincts. The steep was so great that, having reached the wicket, she stopped a moment to breathe; and, looking back upon the water-side cot, saw the hangman again ascending his outdoor staircase. He entered the loft or chamber to which it led, and in a few minutes extinguished his light.

The town clock struck ten, and she returned to the White Hart as she had come.

IX   A RENCOUNTER

IT was one o'clock on Saturday. Gertrude Lodge, having been admitted to the jail as above described, was sitting in a waiting-room within the second gate, which stood under a classic arch-way of ashlar, then comparatively modern, and bearing the inscription, 'COVNTY JAIL: 1793.' This had been the façade she saw from the heath the day before. Near at hand was a passage to the roof on which the gallows stood.

The town was thronged, and the market suspended; but Gertrude had seen scarcely a soul. Having kept her room till the hour of the appointment, she had proceeded to the spot by a way which avoided the open space below the cliff where the spectators had gathered; but she could, even now, hear the multitudinous babble of their voices, out of which rose at intervals the hoarse croak of a single voice uttering the words, 'Last dying speech and confession.' There had been no reprieve, and the execution was over; but the crowd still waited to see the body taken down.

Soon the persistent woman heard a trampling overhead, then a hand beckoned to her, and, following directions, she went out and crossed the inner paved court beyond the gatehouse, her knees trembling so that she could scarcely walk. One of her arms was out of its sleeve, and only covered by her shawl.

On the spot at which she had now arrived were two trestles, and before she could think of their purpose she heard heavy feet descending stairs somewhere at her back. Turn her head she would not, or could not, and, rigid in this position, she was conscious of a rough coffin passing her shoulder, borne by four men. It was open, and in it lay the body of a young man, wearing the smock-frock of a rustic, and fustian breeches. The corpse had been thrown into the coffin so hastily that the skirt of the smock-frock was hanging over. The burden was temporarily deposited on the trestles.

By this time the young woman's state was such that a grey mist seemed to float before her eyes, on account of which, and the veil she wore, she could scarcely discern anything: it was as though she had nearly died, but was held up by a sort of galvanism.

'Now!' said a voice close at hand, and she was just conscious that the word had been addressed to her.

By a last strenuous effort she advanced, at the same time hearing persons approaching behind her. She bared her poor curst arm; and Davies, uncovering the face of the corpse, took Gertrude's hand, and held it so that her arm lay across the dead man's neck, upon a line the colour of an unripe blackberry, which surrounded it.

Gertrude shrieked: 'the turn o' the blood', predicted by the conjuror, had taken place. But at that moment a second shriek rent the air of the enclosure: it was not Gertrude's, and its effect upon her was to make her start round.

Immediately behind her stood Rhoda Brook, her face drawn, and her eyes red with weeping. Behind Rhoda stood Gertrude's own husband; his countenance lined, his eyes dim, but without a tear.

'D—n you! what are you doing here?' he said hoarsely.

'Hussy—to come between us and our child now!' cried Rhoda. 'This is the meaning of what Satan showed me in the vision! You are like her at last!' And clutching the bare arm of the younger woman, she pulled her unresistingly back against the wall. Immediately Brook had loosened her hold the fragile young Gertrude slid down against the feet of her husband. When he lifted her up she was unconscious.

The mere sight of the twain had been enough to suggest to her that the dead young man was Rhoda's son. At that time the relatives of an executed convict had the privilege of claiming the body for burial, if they chose to do so; and it was for this purpose that Lodge was awaiting the inquest with Rhoda. He had been summoned by her as soon as the young man was taken in the crime, and at different times since; and he had attended in court during the trial. This was the 'holiday' he had been indulging in of late. The two wretched parents had wished to avoid exposure; and hence had come themselves for the body, a waggon and sheet for its conveyance and covering being in waiting outside.

Gertrude's case was so serious that it was deemed advisable to call to her the surgeon who was at hand. She was taken out of the jail into the town; but she never reached home alive. Her delicate vitality, sapped perhaps by the paralysed arm, collapsed under the double shock that followed the severe strain, physical and mental, to which she had subjected herself during the previous twenty-four hours. Her blood had been 'turned' indeed—too far. Her death took place in the town three days after.

Her husband was never seen in Casterbridge again; once only in the old market-place at Anglebury, which he had so much frequented, and very seldom in public anywhere. Burdened at first with moodiness and remorse, he eventually changed for the better, and appeared as a chastened and thoughtful man. Soon after attending the funeral of his poor young wife he took steps towards giving up the farms in Holmstoke and the adjoining parish, and, having sold every head of his stock, he went away to Port-Bredy, at the other end of the county, living there in solitary lodgings till his death two years later of a painless decline. It was then found that he had bequeathed the whole of his not inconsiderable property to a reformatory for boys, subject to the payment of a small annuity to Rhoda Brook, if she could be found to claim it.

For some time she could not be found; but eventually she reappeared in her old parish—absolutely refusing, however, to have anything to do with the provision made for her. Her monotonous milking at the dairy was resumed. and followed for many long years, till her form became bent, and her once abundant dark hair white and worn away at the forehead—perhaps by long pressure against the cows. Here, sometimes, those who knew her experiences would stand and observe her, and wonder what sombre thoughts were beating inside that impassive, wrinkled brow, to the rhythm of the alternating milk-streams.

The Melancholy Hussar Of The German Legion

I

HERE stretch the downs, high and breezy and green, absolutely unchanged since those eventful days. A plough has never disturbed the turf, and the sod that was uppermost then is uppermost now. Here stood the camp; here are distinct traces of the banks thrown up for the horses of the cavalry, and spots where the midden-heaps lay are still to be observed. At night, when I walk across the lonely place, it is impossible to avoid hearing, amid the scourings of the wind over the grass-bents and thistles, the old trumpet and bugle calls, the rattle of the halters; to help seeing rows of spectral tents and the *impedimenta* of the soldiery. From within the canvases come guttural syllables of foreign tongues, and broken songs of the fatherland; for they were mainly regiments of the King's German Legion that slept round the tent-poles hereabout at that time.

It was nearly ninety years ago. The British uniform of the period, with its immense epaulettes, queer cocked-hat, breeches, gaiters, ponderous cartridge-box, buckled shoes, and what not, would look strange and barbarous now. Ideas have changed; invention has followed invention. Soldiers were monumental objects then. A divinity still hedged kings here and there; and war was considered a glorious thing.

Secluded old manor-houses and hamlets lie in the ravines and hollows among these hills, where a stranger had hardly ever been seen till the King chose to take the baths yearly at the sea-side watering-place a few miles to the south; as a consequence of which battalions descended in a cloud upon the open country around. Is it necessary to add that the echoes of many characteristic tales, dating from that picturesque time, still linger about here in more or less fragmentary form, to be caught by the attentive ear? Some of them I have repeated; most of them I have forgotten; one I have never repeated, and assuredly can never forget.

Phyllis told me the story with her own lips. She was then an old lady of seventy-five, and her auditor a lad of fifteen. She enjoined silence as to her share in the incident, till she should be 'dead, buried, and forgotten'. Her life was prolonged twelve years after the day of her narration, and she has now been dead nearly twenty. The oblivion which in her modesty and humility she courted for herself has only partially fallen on her, with the unfortunate result of inflicting an injustice upon her memory; since such fragments of her story as got abroad at the time, and have been kept alive ever since, are precisely those which are most unfavourable to her character.

It all began with the arrival of the York Hussars, one of the foreign regiments above alluded to. Before that day scarcely a soul had been seen near her father's house for weeks. When a noise like the brushing skirt of a visitor was heard on the doorstep, it proved to be a scudding leaf; when a carriage seemed to be nearing the door, it was her father grinding his sickle on the stone in the garden for his favourite relaxation of trimming the box-tree borders to the plots. A sound like luggage thrown down from the coach was a gun far away at sea; and what looked like a tall man by the gate at dusk was a yew bush cut into a quaint and attenuated shape. There is no such solitude in country places now as there was in those old days.

Yet all the while King George and his court were at his favourite sea-side resort, not more than five miles off.

The daughter's seclusion was great, but beyond the seclusion of the girl lay the seclusion of the father. If her social condition was twilight, his was darkness. Yet he enjoyed his darkness, while her twilight oppressed her. Dr. Grove had been a professional man whose taste for lonely meditation over metaphysical questions had diminished his practice till it no longer paid him to keep it going; after which he had relinquished it and hired at a nominal rent the small, dilapidated, half farm half manor-house of this obscure inland nook, to make a sufficiency of an income which in a town would have been inadequate for their maintenance. He stayed in his garden the greater part of the day, growing more and more irritable with the lapse of time, and the increasing perception that he had wasted his life in the pursuit of illusions. He saw his friends less and less frequently. Phyllis became so shy that if she met a stranger anywhere in her short rambles she felt ashamed at his gaze, walked awkwardly, and blushed to her shoulders.

Yet Phyllis was discovered even here by an admirer, and her hand most unexpectedly asked in marriage.

The King, as aforesaid, was at the neighbouring town, where he had taken up his abode at Gloucester Lodge; and his presence in the town naturally brought many county people thither. Among these idlers—many of whom professed to have connections and interests with the Court—was one Humphrey Gould, a bachelor; a personage neither young nor old; neither good-looking nor positively plain. Too steady-going to be 'a buck' (as fast and unmarried men were then called), he was an approximately fashionable man of a mild type. This bachelor of thirty found his way to the village on the down: beheld Phyllis; made her father's acquaintance in order to make hers; and by some means or other she sufficiently inflamed his heart to lead him in that direction almost daily; till he became engaged to marry her.

As he was of an old local family, some of whose members were held in respect in the county, Phyllis, in bringing him to her feet, had accomplished what was considered a brilliant move for one in her constrained position. How she had done it was not quite known to Phyllis herself. In those days unequal marriages were regarded rather as a violation of the laws of nature than as a mere infringement of convention, the more modern view, and hence when Phyllis, of the watering-place *bourgeoisie*, was chosen by such a gentlemanly fellow, it was as if she were going to be taken to heaven, though perhaps the uninformed would have seen no great difference in the respective positions of the pair, the said Gould being as poor as a crow.

This pecuniary condition was his excuse—probably a true one—for postponing their union, and as the winter drew nearer, and the King departed for the season, Mr. Humphrey Gould set out for Bath, promising to return to Phyllis in a few weeks. The winter arrived, the date of his promise passed, yet Gould postponed his coming, on the ground that he could not very easily leave his father in the city of their sojourn, the elder having no other relative near him. Phyllis, though lonely in the extreme, was content. The man who had asked her in marriage was a desirable husband for her in many ways; her father highly approved of his suit; but this neglect of her was awkward, if not painful, for Phyllis. Love him in the true sense of the word she assured me she never did, but she had a genuine regard for him; admired a certain methodical and dogged way in which he sometimes took his pleasure; valued his knowledge of what the Court was doing, had done, or was about to do; and she was not without a feeling of pride that he had chosen her when he might have exercised a more ambitious choice.

But he did not come; and the spring developed. His letters were regular though formal; and it is not to be wondered that the uncertainty of his position, linked with the fact that there was not much passion in her thoughts of Humphrey, bred an indescribable dreariness in the heart of Phyllis Grove. The spring was soon summer, and the summer brought the King; but still no Humphrey Gould. All this while the engagement by letter was maintained intact.

At this point of time a golden radiance flashed in upon the lives of people here, and charged all youthful thought with emotional interest. This radiance was the aforesaid York Hussars.

II

The present generation has probably but a very dim notion of the celebrated York Hussars of ninety years ago. They were one of the regiments of the King's German Legion, and (though they somewhat degenerated later on) their brilliant uniform, their splendid horses, and above all, their foreign air and mustachios (rare appendages then), drew crowds of admirers of both sexes wherever they went. These with other regiments had come to encamp on the downs and pastures, because of the presence of the King in the neighbouring town.

The spot was high and airy, and the view extensive, commanding the Isle of Portland in front, and reaching to St. Aldhelm's Head eastward, and almost to the Start on the west.

Phyllis, though not precisely a girl of the village, was as interested as any of them in this military investment. Her father's home stood somewhat apart, and on the highest point of ground to which the lane ascended, so that it was almost level with the top of the church tower in the lower part of the parish. Immediately from the outside of the garden-wall the grass spread away to a great distance, and it was crossed by a path which came close to the wall. Ever since her childhood it had been Phyllis's pleasure to clamber up this fence and sit on the top—a feat not so difficult as it may seem, the walls in this district being built of rubble, without mortar, so that there were plenty of crevices for small toes.

She was sitting up here one day, listlessly surveying the pasture without, when her attention was arrested by a solitary figure walking along the path. It was one of the renowned German Hussars, and he moved onward with his eyes on the ground, and with the manner of one who wished to escape company. His head would probably have been bent like his eyes but for his stiff neck-gear. On nearer view she perceived that his face was marked with deep sadness. Without observing her, he advanced by the footpath till it brought him almost immediately under the wall.

Phyllis was much surprised to see a fine, tall soldier in such a mood as this. Her theory of the military, and of the York

Hussars in particular (derived entirely from hearsay, for she had never talked to a soldier in her life), was that their hearts were as gay as their accoutrements.

At this moment the Hussar lifted his eyes and noticed her on her perch, the white muslin neckerchief which covered her shoulders and neck where left bare by her low gown, and her white raiment in general, showing conspicuously in the bright sunlight of this summer day. He blushed a little at the suddenness of the encounter, and without halting a moment from his pace passed on.

All that day the foreigner's face haunted Phyllis; its aspect was so striking, so handsome, and his eyes were so blue, and sad, and abstracted. It was perhaps only natural that on some following day at the same hour she should look over that wall again, and wait till he had passed a second time. On this occasion he was reading a letter, and at the sight of her his manner was that of one who had half expected or hoped to discover her. He almost stopped, smiled, and made a courteous salute. The end of the meeting was that they exchanged a few words. She asked him what he was reading, and he readily informed her that he was re-perusing letters from his mother in Germany; he did not get them often, he said, and was forced to read the old ones a great many times. This was all that passed at the present interview, but others of the same kind followed.

Phyllis used to say that his English, though not good, was quite intelligible to her, so that their acquaintance was never hindered by difficulties of speech. Whenever the subject became too delicate, subtle, or tender, for such words of English as were at his command, the eyes no doubt helped out the tongue, and—though this was later on—the lips helped out the eyes. In short this acquaintance, unguardedly made, and rash enough on her part, developed and ripened. Like Desdemona, she pitied him, and learnt his history.

His name was Matthäus Tina, and Saarbrück his native town, where his mother was still living. His age was twenty-two, and he had already risen to the grade of corporal, though he had not long been in the army. Phyllis used to assert that no such refined or well-educated young man could have been found in the ranks of the purely English regiments, some of these foreign soldiers having rather the graceful manner and presence of our native officers than of our rank and file.

She by degrees learnt from her foreign friend a circumstance about himself and his comrades which Phyllis would least have expected of the York Hussars. So far from being as gay as its uniform, the regiment was pervaded by a dreadful melancholy, a

49

chronic home-sickness, which depressed many of the men to such an extent that they could hardly attend to their drill. The worst sufferers were the younger soldiers who had not been over here long. They hated England and English life; they took no interest whatever in King George and his island kingdom, and they only wished to be out of it and never to see it any more. Their bodies were here, but their hearts and minds were always far away in their dear fatherland, of which—brave men and stoical as they were in many ways—they would speak with tears in their eyes. One of the worst of the sufferers from this home-woe, as he called it in his own tongue, was Matthäus Tina, whose dreamy musing nature felt the gloom of exile still more intensely from the fact that he had left a lonely mother at home with nobody to cheer her.

Though Phyllis, touched by all this, and interested in his history, did not disdain her soldier's acquaintance, she declined (according to her own account, at least) to permit the young man to overstep the line of mere friendship for a long while—as long, indeed, as she considered herself likely to become the possession of another; though it is probable that she had lost her heart to Matthäus before she was herself aware. The stone wall of necessity made anything like intimacy difficult; and he had never ventured to come, or to ask to come, inside the garden, so that all their conversation had been overtly conducted across this boundary.

III

But news reached the village from a friend of Phyllis's father concerning Mr. Humphrey Gould, her remarkably cool and patient betrothed. This gentleman had been heard to say in Bath that he considered his overtures to Miss Phyllis Grove to have reached only the stage of a half-understanding; and in view of his enforced absence on his father's account, who was too great an invalid now to attend to his affairs, he thought it best that there should be no definite promise as yet on either side. He was not sure, indeed, that he might not cast his eyes elsewhere.

This account—though only a piece of hearsay, and as such entitled to no absolute credit—tallied so well with the infrequency of his letters and their lack of warmth, that Phyllis did not doubt its truth for one moment; and from that hour she felt herself free to bestow her heart as she should choose. Not so her father; he declared the whole story to be a fabrication. He had known Mr.

Gould's family from his boyhood; and if there was one proverb which expressed the matrimonial aspect of that family well, it was 'Love me little, love me long.' Humphrey was an honourable man, who would not think of treating his engagement so lightly. 'Do you wait in patience,' he said; 'all will be right enough in time.'

From these words Phyllis at first imagined that her father was in correspondence with Mr. Gould; and her heart sank within her; for in spite of her original intentions she had been relieved to hear that her engagement had come to nothing. But she presently learnt that her father had heard no more of Humphrey Gould than she herself had done; while he would not write and address her affianced directly on the subject, lest it should be deemed an imputation on that bachelor's honour.

'You want an excuse for encouraging one or other of those foreign fellows to flatter you with his unmeaning attentions,' her father exclaimed, his mood having of late been a very unkind one towards her. 'I see more than I say. Don't you ever set foot outside that garden-fence without my permission. If you want to see the camp I'll take you myself some Sunday afternoon.'

Phyllis had not the smallest intention of disobeying him in her actions, but she assumed herself to be independent with respect to her feelings. She no longer checked her fancy for the Hussar, though she was far from regarding him as her lover in the serious sense in which an Englishman might have been regarded as such. The young foreign soldier was almost an ideal being to her, with none of the appurtenances of an ordinary house-dweller; one who had descended she knew not whence, and would disappear she knew not whither; the subject of a fascinating dream—no more.

They met continually now—mostly at dusk—during the brief interval between the going down of the sun and the minute at which the last trumpet-call summoned him to his tent. Perhaps her manner had become less restrained latterly; at any rate that of the Hussar was so; he had grown more tender every day, and at parting after these hurried interviews she reached down her hand from the top of the wall that he might press it. One evening he held it so long that she exclaimed, 'The wall is white, and somebody in the field may see your shape against it!'

He lingered so long that night that it was with the greatest difficulty that he could run across the intervening stretch of ground and enter the camp in time. On the next occasion of his awaiting her she did not appear in her usual place at the usual hour. His disappointment was unspeakably keen; he remained staring blankly at the spot, like a man in a trance. The trumpets and tattoo sounded, and still he did not go.

She had been delayed purely by an accident. When she arrived she was anxious because of the lateness of the hour, having heard as well as he the sounds denoting the closing of the camp. She implored him to leave immediately.

'No,' he said gloomily. 'I shall not go in yet—the moment you come—I have thought of your coming all day.'

'But you may be disgraced at being after time?'

'I don't mind that. I should have disappeared from the world some time ago if it had not been for two persons—my beloved, here, and my mother in Saarbrück. I hate the army. I care more for a minute of your company than for all the promotion in the world.'

Thus he stayed and talked to her, and told her interesting details of his native place, and incidents of his childhood, till she was in a simmer of distress at his recklessness in remaining. It was only because she insisted on bidding him good-night and leaving the wall that he returned to his quarters.

The next time that she saw him he was without the stripes that had adorned his sleeve. He had been broken to the level of private for his lateness that night; and as Phyllis considered herself to be the cause of his disgrace her sorrow was great. But the position was now reversed; it was his turn to cheer her.

'Don't grieve, meine Liebliche!' he said. 'I have got a remedy for whatever comes. First, even supposing I regain my stripes, would your father allow you to marry a non-commissioned officer in the York Hussars?'

She flushed. This practical step had not been in her mind in relation to such an unrealistic person as he was; and a moment's reflection was enough for it. 'My father would not—certainly would not,' she answered unflinchingly. 'It cannot be thought of! My dear friend, please do forget me: I fear I am ruining you and your prospects!'

'Not at all!' said he. 'You are giving this country of yours just sufficient interest to me to make me care to keep alive in it. If my dear land were here also, and my old parent, with you, I could be happy as I am, and would do my best as a soldier. But it is not so. And now listen. This is my plan. That you go with me to my own country, and be my wife there, and live there with my mother and me. I am not a Hanoverian, as you know, though I entered the army as such; my country is by the Saar, and is at peace with France, and if I were once in it I should be free.'

'But how get there?' she asked. Phyllis had been rather amazed than shocked at his proposition. Her position in her father's house was growing irksome and painful in the extreme; his parental affection seemed to be quite dried up. She was not a native of the village, like all the joyous girls around her; and in some way Matthäus Tina had infected her with his own passionate longing for his country, and mother, and home.

'But how?' she repeated, finding that he did not answer. 'Will you buy your discharge?'

'Ah, no,' he said. 'That's impossible in these times. No; I came here against my will; why should I not escape? Now is the time, as we shall soon be striking camp, and I might see you no more. This is my scheme. I will ask you to meet me on the highway two miles off, on some calm night next week that may be appointed. There will be nothing unbecoming in it, or to cause you shame; you will not fly alone with me, for I will bring with me my devoted young friend Christoph, an Alsatian, who has lately joined the regiment, and who has agreed to assist in this enterprise. We shall have come from yonder harbour, where we shall have examined the boats, and found one suited to our purpose. Christoph has already a chart of the Channel, and we will then go to the harbour, and at midnight cut the boat from her moorings, and row away round the point out of sight; and by the next morning we are on the coast of France, near Cherbourg. The rest is easy, for I have saved money for the land journey, and can get a change of clothes. I will write to my mother, who will meet us on the way.'

He added details in reply to her inquiries, which left no doubt in Phyllis's mind of the feasibility of the undertaking. But its magnitude almost appalled her; and it is questionable if she would ever have gone further in the wild adventure if, on entering the house that night, her father had not accosted her in the most significant terms.

'How about the York Hussars?' he said.

'They are still at the camp; but they are soon going away, I believe.'

'It is useless for you to attempt to cloak your actions in that way. You have been meeting one of those fellows; you have been seen walking with him—foreign barbarians, not much better than the French themselves! I have made up my mind—don't speak a word till I have done, please!—I have made up my mind that you shall stay here no longer while they are on the spot. You shall go to your aunt's.'

It was useless for her to protest that she had never taken a walk with any soldier or man under the sun except himself. Her protestations were feeble, too, for though he was not literally correct in his assertion, he was virtually only half in error.

The house of her father's sister was a prison to Phyllis. She had quite recently undergone experience of its gloom; and when her father went on to direct her to pack what would be necessary for her to take, her heart died within her. In after years she never attempted to excuse her conduct during this week of agitation; but the result of her self-communing was that she decided to join in the scheme of her lover and his friend, and fly to the country which he had coloured with such lovely hues in her imagination. She always said that the one feature in his proposal which overcame her hesitation was the obvious purity and straightforwardness of his intentions. He showed himself to be so virtuous and kind; he treated her with a respect to which she had never before been accustomed; and she was braced to the obvious risks of the voyage by her confidence in him.

IV

It was on a soft, dark evening of the following week that they engaged in the adventure. Tina was to meet her at a point in the highway at which the lane to the village branched off. Christoph was to go ahead of them to the harbour where the boat lay, row it round the Nothe—or Look-out as it was called in those days—and pick them up on the other side of the promontory, which they were to reach by crossing the harbour-bridge on foot, and climbing over the Look-out hill.

As soon as her father had ascended to his room she left the house, and, bundle in hand, proceeded at a trot along the lane. At such an hour not a soul was afoot anywhere in the village, and she reached the junction of the lane with the highway unobserved. Here she took up her position in the obscurity formed by the angle of a fence, whence she could discern every one who approached along the turnpike-road, without being herself seen.

She had not remained thus waiting for her lover longer than a minute—though from the tension of her nerves the lapse of even that short time was trying—when, instead of the expected footsteps, the stage-coach could be heard descending the hill. She knew that Tina would not show himself till the road was clear, and waited impatiently for the coach to pass. Nearing the corner where she was it slackened speed, and, instead of going by as usual, drew up within a few yards of her. A passenger alighted, and she heard his voice. It was Humphrey Gould's.

He had brought a friend with him, and luggage. The luggage was deposited on the grass, and the coach went on its route to the royal watering-place.

'I wonder where that young man is with the horse and trap?' said her former admirer to his companion. 'I hope we shan't have to wait here long. I told him half-past nine o'clock precisely.'

'Have you got her present safe?'

'Phyllis's? O, yes. It is in this trunk. I hope it will please her.'

'Of course it will. What woman would not be pleased with such a handsome peace-offering?'

'Well—she deserves it. I've treated her rather badly. But she has been in my mind these last two days much more than I should care to confess to everybody. Ah, well; I'll say no more about that. It cannot be that she is so bad as they make out. I am quite sure that a girl of her good wit would know better than to get entangled with any of those Hanoverian soldiers. I won't believe it of her, and there's an end on't.'

More words in the same strain were casually dropped as the two men waited; words which revealed to her, as by a sudden illumination, the enormity of her conduct. The conversation was at length cut off by the arrival of the man with the vehicle. The luggage was placed in it, and they mounted, and were driven on in the direction from which she had just come.

Phyllis was so conscience-stricken that she was at first inclined to follow them; but a moment's reflection led her to feel that it would only be bare justice to Matthäus to wait till he arrived, and explain candidly that she had changed her mind—difficult as the struggle would be when she stood face to face with him. She bitterly reproached herself for having believed reports which represented Humphrey Gould as false to his engagement, when, from what she now heard from his own lips, she gathered that he had been living full of trust in her. But she knew well enough who had won her love. Without him her life seemed a dreary prospect, yet the more she looked at his proposal the more she feared to accept it—so wild as it was, so vague, so venturesome. She had promised Humphrey Gould, and it was only his assumed faithlessness which had led her to treat that promise as nought. His solicitude in bringing her these gifts touched her; her promise must be kept, and esteem must take the place of love. She would preserve her self-respect. She would stay at home, and marry him, and suffer.

Phyllis had thus braced herself to an exceptional fortitude when, a few minutes later, the outline of Matthäus Tina appeared behind a field-gate, over which he lightly leapt as she stepped forward. There was no evading it, he pressed her to his breast.

'It is the first and last time!' she wildly thought as she stood encircled by his arms.

How Phyllis got through the terrible ordeal of that night she could never clearly recollect. She always attributed her success in carrying out her resolve to her lover's honour, for as soon as she declared to him in feeble words that she had changed her mind, and felt that she could not, dared not, fly with him, he forbore to urge her, grieved as he was at her decision. Unscrupulous pressure on his part, seeing how romantically she had become attached to him, would no doubt have turned the balance in his favour. But he did nothing to tempt her unduly or unfairly.

On her side, fearing for his safety, she begged him to remain. This, he declared, could not be. 'I cannot break faith with my friend,' said he. Had he stood alone he would have abandoned his plan. But Christoph, with the boat and compass and chart, was waiting on the shore; the tide would soon turn; his mother had been warned of his coming; go he must.

Many precious minutes were lost while he tarried, unable to tear himself away. Phyllis held to her resolve, though it cost her many a bitter pang. At last they parted, and he went down the hill. Before his footsteps had quite died away she felt a desire to behold at least his outline once more, and running noiselessly after him regained view of his diminishing figure. For one moment she was sufficiently excited to be on the point of rushing forward and linking her fate with his. But she could not. The courage which at the critical instant failed Cleopatra of Egypt could scarcely be expected of Phyllis Grove.

A dark shape, similar to his own, joined him in the highway. It was Christoph, his friend. She could see no more; they had hastened on in the direction of the town and harbour, four miles ahead. With a feeling akin to despair she turned and slowly pursued her way homeward.

Tattoo sounded in the camp; but there was no camp for her now. It was as dead as the camp of the Assyrians after the passage of the Destroying Angel.

She noiselessly entered the house, seeing nobody, and went to bed. Grief, which kept her awake at first, ultimately wrapped her in a heavy sleep. The next morning her father met her at the foot of the stairs.

'Mr. Gould is come,' he said triumphantly.

Humphrey was staying at the inn, and had already called to inquire for her. He had brought her a present of a very handsome looking-glass in a frame of *repoussé* silverwork, which her father held in his hand. He had promised to call again in the course of an hour, to ask Phyllis to walk with him.

Pretty mirrors were rarer in country-houses at that day than they are now, and the one before her won Phyllis's admiration.

She looked into it, saw how heavy her eyes were, and endeavoured to brighten them. She was in that wretched state of mind which leads a woman to move mechanically onward in what she conceives to be her allotted path. Mr. Humphrey had, in his undemonstrative way, been adhering all along to the old understanding; it was for her to do the same, and to say not a word of her own lapse. She put on her bonnet and tippet, and when he arrived at the hour named she was at the door awaiting him.

V

Phyllis thanked him for his beautiful gift; but the talking was soon entirely on Humphrey's side as they walked along. He told her of the latest movements of the world of fashion—a subject which she willingly discussed to the exclusion of anything more personal—and his measured language helped to still her disquieted heart and brain. Had not her own sadness been what it was she must have observed his embarrassment. At last he abruptly changed the subject.

'I am glad you are pleased with my little present,' he said. 'The truth is that I brought it to propitiate 'ee, and to get you to help me out of a mighty difficulty.'

It was inconceivable to Phyllis that this independent bachelor —whom she admired in some respects—could have a difficulty.

'Phyllis—I'll tell you my secret at once; for I have a monstrous secret to confide before I can ask your counsel. The case is, then, that I am married: yes, I have privately married a dear young belle; and if you knew her, and I hope you will, you would say everything in her praise. But she is not quite the one that my father would have chose for me—you know the paternal idea as well as I—and I have kept it secret. There will be a terrible noise, no doubt; but I think that with your help I may get over it. If you would only do me this good turn—when I have told my father, I mean—say that you never could have married me, you know, or something of that sort—'pon my life it will help to smooth the way vastly. I am so anxious to win him round to my point of view, and not to cause any estrangement.'

What Phyllis replied she scarcely knew, or how she counselled him as to his unexpected situation. Yet the relief that his announcement brought her was perceptible. To have confided her trouble in return was what her aching heart longed to do; and had Humphrey been a woman she would instantly have poured out her tale. But to him she feared to confess; and there was a real reason for silence, till a sufficient time had elapsed to allow her lover and his comrade to get out of harm's way.

As soon as she reached home again she sought a solitary place, and spent the time in half regretting that she had not gone away, and in dreaming over the meetings with Matthäus Tina from their beginning to their end. In his own country, amongst his own countrywomen, he would possibly soon forget her, even to her very name.

Her listlessness was such that she did not go out of the house for several days. There came a morning which broke in fog and mist, behind which the dawn could be discerned in greenish grey; and the outlines of the tents, and the rows of horses at the ropes. The smoke from the canteen fires drooped heavily.

The spot at the bottom of the garden where she had been accustomed to climb the wall to meet Matthäus, was the only inch of English ground in which she took any interest; and in spite of the disagreeable haze prevailing she walked out there till she reached the well-known corner. Every blade of grass was weighted with little liquid globes, and slugs and snails had crept out upon the plots. She could hear the usual faint noises from the camp, and in the other direction the trot of farmers on the road to the town, for it was market-day. She observed that her frequent visits to this corner had quite trodden down the grass in the angle of the wall, and left marks of garden soil on the stepping-stones by which she had mounted to look over the top. Seldom having gone there till dusk, she had not considered that her traces might be visible by day. Perhaps it was these which had revealed her trysts to her father.

While she paused in melancholy regard, she fancied that the customary sounds from the tents were changing their character. Indifferent as Phyllis was to camp doings now, she mounted by the steps to the old place. What she beheld at first awed and perplexed her; then she stood rigid, her fingers hooked to the wall, her eyes staring out of her head, and her face as if hardened to stone.

On the open green stretching before her all the regiments in the camp were drawn up in line, in the mid-front of which two empty coffins lay on the ground. The unwonted sounds which she had noticed came from an advancing procession. It consisted of the band of the York Hussars playing a dead march; next two soldiers of that regiment in a mourning coach, guarded on each side, and accompanied by two priests. Behind came a crowd of rustics who had been attracted by the event. The melancholy procession marched along the front of the line, returned to the centre, and halted beside the coffins, where the two condemned men were blindfolded, and each placed kneeling on his coffin; a few minutes' pause was now given, while they prayed.

A firing-party of twenty-four men stood ready with levelled carbines. The commanding officer, who had his sword drawn, waved it through some cuts of the sword-exercise till he reached the downward stroke, whereat the firing-party discharged their volley. The two victims fell, one upon his face across his coffin, the other backwards.

As the volley resounded there arose a shriek from the wall of Dr. Grove's garden, and someone fell down inside; but nobody among the spectators without noticed it at the time. The two executed Hussars were Matthäus Tina and his friend Christoph. The soldiers on guard placed the bodies in the coffins almost instantly; but the colonel of the regiment, an Englishman, rode up and exclaimed in a stern voice: 'Turn them out—as an example to the men!'

The coffins were lifted endwise, and the dead Germans flung out upon their faces on the grass. Then all the regiments wheeled in sections, and marched past the spot in slow time. When the survey was over the corpses were again coffined, and borne away.

Meanwhile Dr. Grove, attracted by the noise of the volley, had rushed out into his garden, where he saw his wretched daughter lying motionless against the wall. She was taken indoors, but it was long before she recovered consciousness; and for weeks they despaired of her reason.

It transpired that the luckless deserters from the York Hussars had cut the boat from her moorings in the adjacent harbour, according to their plan, and, with two other comrades who were smarting under ill-treatment from their colonel, had sailed in safety across the Channel. But mistaking their bearings they steered into Jersey, thinking that island the French coast. Here they were perceived to be deserters, and delivered up to the authorities. Matthäus and Christoph interceded for the other two at the court-martial, saying that it was entirely by the former's representations that these were induced to go. Their sentence was accordingly commuted to flogging, the death punishment being reserved for their leaders.

The visitor to the well-known old Georgian watering-place, who may care to ramble to the neighbouring village under the hills, and examine the register of burials, will there find two entries in these words:—

'*Matth: Tina (Corpl.) in His Majesty's Regmt. of York Hussars, and Shot for Desertion, was Buried June 30th, 1801, aged 22 years. Born in the town of Sarrbruk, Germany.*

'*Christoph Bless, belonging to His Majesty's Regmt. of York*

Hussars, who was Shot for Desertion, was Buried June 30th, 1801, aged 22 years. Born at Lothaargen, Alsatia.'

Their graves were dug at the back of the little church, near the wall. There is no memorial to mark the spot, but Phyllis pointed it out to me. While she lived she used to keep their mounds neat; but now they are overgrown with nettles, and sunk nearly flat. The older villagers, however, who know of the episode from their parents, still recollect the place where the soldiers lie. Phyllis lies near.

[*Delivered to the publisher*] *October* 1889.

Absentmindedness in a Parish Choir

'It happened on Sunday after Christmas—the last Sunday ever they played in Longpuddle church gallery, as it turned out, though they didn't know it then. As you may know, sir, the players formed a very good band—almost as good as the Mellstock parish players that were led by the Dewys; and that's saying a great deal. There was Nicholas Puddingcome, the leader, with the first fiddle; there was Timothy Thomas, the bass-viol man; John Biles, the tenor fiddler; Dan'l Hornhead, with the serpent; Robert Dowdle, with the clarionet; and Mr. Nicks, with the oboe—all sound and powerful musicians, and strong-winded men—they that blowed. For that reason they were very much in demand Christmas week for little reels and dancing parties; for they could turn a jig or a hornpipe out of hand as well as ever they could turn out a psalm, and perhaps better, not to speak irreverent. In short, one half-hour they could be playing a Christmas carol in the squire's hall to the ladies and gentlemen, and drinking tay and coffee with 'em as modest as saints; and the next, at The Tinker's Arms, blazing away like wild horses with the "Dashing White Sergeant" to nine couple of dancers and more, and swallowing rum-and-cider hot as flame.

'Well, this Christmas they'd been out to one rattling randy after another every night, and had got next to no sleep at all. Then came the Sunday after Christmas, their fatal day. 'Twas so mortal cold that year that they could hardly sit in the gallery; for though the congregation down in the body of the church had a stove to keep off the frost, the players in the gallery had nothing at all. So Nicholas said at morning service, when 'twas freezing an inch an hour, "Please the Lord I won't stand this numbing weather no longer: this afternoon we'll have something in our insides to make us warm, if it cost a king's ransom."

'So he brought a gallon of hot brandy and beer, ready mixed, to church with him in the afternoon, and by keeping the jar well wrapped up in Timothy Thomas's bass-viol bag it kept drinkably warm till they wanted it, which was just a thimbleful in the Absolution, and another after the Creed, and the remainder at the beginning o' the sermon. When they'd had the last pull they felt quite comfortable and warm, and as the sermon went on—most unfortunately for 'em it was a long one that afternoon—they fell asleep, every man jack of 'em; and there they slept on as sound as rocks.

"'Twas a very dark afternoon, and by the end of the sermon all you could see of the inside of the church were the pa'son's two candles alongside of him in the pulpit, and his spaking face behind 'em. The sermon being ended at last, the pa'son gie'd out the Evening Hymn. But no choir set about sounding up the tune, and the people began to turn their heads to learn the reason why, and then Levi Limpet, a boy who sat in the gallery, nudged Timothy and Nicholas, and said, "Begin! begin!"

"'Hey? what?" says Nicholas, starting up; and the church being so dark and his head so muddled he thought he was at the party they had played at all the night before, and away he went, bow and fiddle, at "The Devil among the Tailors", the favourite jig of our neighbourhood at that time. The rest of the band, being in the same state of mind and nothing doubting, followed their leader with all their strength, according to custom. They poured out that there tune till the lower bass notes of "The Devil among the Tailors" made the cobwebs in the roof shiver like ghosts; then Nicholas, seeing nobody moved, shouted out as he scraped (in his usual commanding way at dances when the folk didn't know the figures), "Top couples cross hands! And when I make the fiddle squeak at the end, every man kiss his pardner under the mistletoe!"

'The boy Levi was so frightened that he bolted down the gallery stairs and out homeward like lightning. The pa'son's hair fairly stood on end when he heard the evil tune raging through the church, and thinking the choir had gone crazy he held up his hand and said: "Stop, stop, stop! Stop, stop! What's this?" But they didn't hear'n for the noise of their own playing, and the more he called the louder they played.

'Then the folks came out of their pews, wondering down to the ground, and saying: "What do they mean by such wickedness! We shall be consumed like Sodom and Gomorrah!"

'Then the squire came out of his pew lined wi' green baize, where lots of lords and ladies visiting at the house were worshipping along with him, and went and stood in front of the gallery, and shook his fist in the musicians' faces, saying, "What! In this reverent edifice! What!"

'And at last they heard'n through their playing, and stopped.

"'Never such an insulting, disgraceful thing—never!" says the squire, who couldn't rule his passion.

"'Never!" says the pa'son, who had come down and stood beside him.

"'Not if the Angels of Heaven," says the squire (he was a

62

wickedish man, the squire was, though now for once he happened
to be on the Lord's side)—"not if the Angels of Heaven come
down," he says, "shall one of you villainous players ever sound a
note in this church again; for the insult to me, and my family,
and my visitors, and the parson and God Almighty, that you've
a-perpetrated this afternoon!"

'Then the unfortunate church band came to their senses, and
remembered where they were; and 'twas a sight to see Nicholas
Puddingcome and Timothy Thomas and John Biles creep down
the gallery stairs with their fiddles under their arms, and poor
Dan'l Hornhead with his serpent, and Robert Dowdle with his
clarionet, all looking as little as ninepins; and out they went.
The pa'son might have forgi'ed 'em when he learned the truth
o't, but the squire would not. That very week he sent for a
barrel-organ that would play two-and-twenty new psalm-tunes,
so exact and particular that, however sinful inclined you was,
you could play nothing but psalm-tunes whatsomever. He had a
really respectable man to turn the winch, as I said, and the old
players played no more.'

1891

> *The last eighteen lines, which link this anec-*
> *dote to the next in the story, are here omitted.*

Tony Kytes, The Arch-Deceiver

'I SHALL never forget Tony's face. 'Twas a little, round, firm,
tight face, with a seam here and there left by the smallpox, but
not enough to hurt his looks in a woman's eye, though he'd had
it badish when he was a boy. So very serious looking and un-
smiling 'a was, that young man, that it really seemed as if he
couldn't laugh at all without great pain to his conscience. He
looked very hard at a small speck in your eye when talking to
'ee. And there was no more sign of a whisker or beard on Tony
Kytes's face than on the palm of my hand. He used to sing
"The Tailor's Breeches" with a religious manner, as if it were a
hymn:

"*" O the petticoats went off, and the breeches they went on!*"

and all the rest of the scandalous stuff. He was quite the women's favourite, and in return for their likings he loved 'em in shoals.

'But in course of time Tony got fixed down to one in particular, Milly Richards, a nice, light, small, tender little thing; and it was soon said that they were engaged to be married. One Saturday he had been to market to do business for his father, and was driving home the waggon in the afternoon. When he reached the foot of the very hill we shall be going over in ten minutes who should he see waiting for him at the top but Unity Sallet, a handsome girl, one of the young women he'd been very tender toward before he'd got engaged to Milly.

'As soon as Tony came up to her she said, "My dear Tony, will you give me a lift home?"

'"That I will, darling," said Tony. "You don't suppose I could refuse 'ee?"

'She smiled a smile, and up she hopped, and on drove Tony.

'"Tony," she says, in a sort of tender chide, "why did ye desert me for that other one? In what is she better than I? I should have made 'ee a finer wife, and a more loving one too. 'Tisn't girls that are so easily won at first that are the best. Think how long we've known each other—ever since we were children almost—now haven't we, Tony?"

'"Yes, that we have," says Tony, a-struck with the truth o't.

'"And you've never seen anything in me to complain of, have ye, Tony? Now tell the truth to me?"

'"I never have, upon my life," says Tony.

'"And—can you say I'm not pretty, Tony? Now look at me!"

'He let his eyes light upon her for a long while. "I really can't," says he. "In fact, I never knowed you was so pretty before!"

'"Prettier than she?"

'What Tony would have said to that nobody knows, for before he could speak, what should he see ahead, over the hedge past the turning, but a feather he knew well—the feather in Milly's hat—she to whom he had been thinking of putting the question as to giving out the banns that very week.

'"Unity," says he, as mild as he could, "here's Milly coming. Now I shall catch it mightily if she sees 'ee riding here with me; and if you get down she'll be turning the corner in a moment, and, seeing 'ee in the road, she'll know we've been coming on together. Now, dearest Unity, will ye, to avoid all unpleasantness, which I know ye can't bear any more than I, will ye lie down in the back part of the waggon, and let me cover you over with the tarpaulin till Milly has passed? It will all be done in a minute. Do!—and I'll think over what we've said; and perhaps I shall put a loving question to you after all, instead of to Milly. 'Tisn't true that it is all settled between her and me."

'Well, Unity Sallet agreed, and lay down at the back end of the waggon, and Tony covered her over, so that the waggon seemed to be empty but for the loose tarpaulin; and then he drove on to meet Milly.

'"My dear Tony!" cries Milly, looking up with a little pout at him as he came near. "How long you've been coming home! Just as if I didn't live at Upper Longpuddle at all! And I've come to meet you as you asked me to do, and to ride back with you, and talk over our future home—since you asked me, and I promised. But I shouldn't have come else, Mr. Tony!"

'"Ay, my dear, I did ask 'ee—to be sure I did, now I think of it—but I had quite forgot it. To ride back with me, did you say, dear Milly?"

'"Well, of course! What can I do else? Surely you don't want me to walk, now I've come all this way?"

'"O no, no! I was thinking you might be going on to town to meet your mother. I saw her there—and she looked as if she might be expecting 'ee."

'"O no; she's just home. She came across the fields, and so got back before you."

'"Ah! I didn't know that," says Tony. And there was no help for it but to take her up beside him.

'They talked on very pleasantly, and looked at the trees, and beasts, and birds, and insects, and at the ploughmen at work in the fields, till presently who should they see looking out of the upper window of a house that stood beside the road they were following, but Hannah Jolliver, another young beauty of the place at that time, and the very first woman that Tony had fallen in love with—before Milly and before Unity, in fact—the one that he had almost arranged to marry instead of Milly. She was a much more dashing girl than Milly Richards, though he'd not thought much of her of late. The house Hannah was looking from was her aunt's.

'"My dear Milly—my coming wife, as I may call 'ee," says Tony in his modest way, and not so loud that Unity could overhear, "I see a young woman a-looking out of window, who I think may accost me. The fact is, Milly, she had a notion that I was wishing to marry her, and since she's discovered I've promised another, and a prettier than she, I'm rather afeard of her temper if she sees us together. Now, Milly, would you do me a favour—my coming wife, as I may say?"

'"Certainly, dearest Tony," says she.

'"Then would ye creep under the empty sacks just here in the front of the waggon, and hide there out of sight till we've passed the house? She hasn't seen us yet. You see, we ought to live in peace and good-will since 'tis almost Christmas, and 'twill prevent angry passions rising, which we always should do."

"'I don't mind, to oblige you, Tony," Milly said; and though she didn't care much about doing it, she crept under, and crouched down just behind the seat, Unity being snug at the other end. So they drove on till they got near the road-side cottage. Hannah had soon seen him coming, and waited at the window, looking down upon him. She tossed her head a little disdainful and smiled off-hand.

"'Well, aren't you going to be civil enough to ask me to ride home with you?" she says, seeing that he was for driving past with a nod and a smile.

"'Ah, to be sure! What was I thinking of?" said Tony, in a flutter. "But you seem as if you was staying at your aunt's?"

"'No, I am not," she said. "Don't you see I have my bonnet and jacket on? I have only called to see her on my way home. How can you be so stupid, Tony?"

"'In that case—ah—of course you must come along wi' me," says Tony, feeling a dim sort of sweat rising up inside his clothes. And he reined in the horse, and waited till she'd come downstairs, and then helped her up beside him. He drove on again, his face as long as a face that was a round one by nature well could be.

'Hannah looked round sideways into his eyes. "This is nice, isn't it, Tony?" she says. "I like riding with you."

'Tony looked back into her eyes. "And I with you," he said after a while. In short, having considered her, he warmed up, and the more he looked at her the more he liked her, till he couldn't for the life of him think why he had ever said a word about marriage to Milly or Unity while Hannah Jolliver was in question. So they sat a little closer and closer, their feet upon the footboard and their shoulders touching, and Tony thought over and over again how handsome Hannah was. He spoke tenderer and tenderer, and called her "dear Hannah" in a whisper at last.

"'You've settled it with Milly by this time, I suppose," said she.

"'N—no, not exactly."

"'What? How low you talk, Tony."

"'Yes—I've a kind of hoarseness. I said, not exactly."

"'I suppose you mean to?"

"'Well, as to that——" His eyes rested on her face, and hers on his. He wondered how he could have been such a fool as not to follow up Hannah. "My sweet Hannah!" he bursts out, taking her hand, not being really able to help it, and forgetting Milly and Unity, and all the world besides. "Settled it? I don't think I have!"

66

"'Hark!" says Hannah.

"'What?" says Tony, letting go her hand.

"'Surely I heard a sort of little screaming squeak under those sacks? Why, you've been carrying corn, and there's mice in this waggon, I declare!" She began to haul up the tails of her gown.

"'Oh no; 'tis the axle," said Tony in an assuring way. "It do go like that sometimes in dry weather."

"'Perhaps it was.... Well, now, to be quite honest, dear Tony, do you like her better than me? Because—because, although I've held off so independent, I'll own at last that I do like 'ee, Tony, to tell the truth; and I wouldn't say no if you asked me—you know what."

'Tony was so won over by this pretty offering mood of a girl who had been quite the reverse (Hannah had a backward way with her at times, if you can mind) that he just glanced behind, and then whispered very soft, "I haven't quite promised her, and I think I can get out of it, and ask you that question you speak of."

"'Throw over Milly?—all to marry me! How delightful!" broke out Hannah, quite loud, clapping her hands.

'At this there was a real squeak—an angry, spiteful squeak, and afterward a long moan, as if something had broke its heart, and a movement of the empty sacks.

"'Something's there!" said Hannah, starting up.

"'It's nothing, really," says Tony in a soothing voice, and praying inwardly for a way out of this. "I wouldn't tell 'ee at first, because I wouldn't frighten 'ee. But, Hannah, I've really a couple of ferrets in a bag under there, for rabbiting, and they quarrel sometimes. I don't wish it knowed, as 'twould be called poaching. Oh, they can't get out, bless 'ee—you are quite safe! And—and—what a fine day it is, isn't it, Hannah, for this time of year? Be you going to market next Saturday? How is your aunt now?" And so on, says Tony, to keep her from talking any more about love in Milly's hearing.

'But he found his work cut out for him, and wondering again how he should get out of this ticklish business, he looked about for a chance. Nearing home he saw his father in a field not far off, holding up his hand as if he wished to speak to Tony.

"'Would you mind taking the reins a moment, Hannah," he said, much relieved, "while I go and find out what father wants?"

'She consented, and away he hastened into the field, only too glad to get breathing time. He found that his father was looking at him with rather a stern eye.

"'Come, come, Tony," says old Mr. Kytes, as soon as his son was alongside him, "this won't do, you know."

"'What?' says Tony.

"'Why, if you mean to marry Milly Richards, do it, and there's an end o't. But don't go driving about the country with Jolliver's daughter and making a scandal. I won't have such things done.'

"'I only asked her—that is, she asked me, to ride home.'

"'She? Why, now, if it had been Milly, 'twould have been quite proper; but you and Hannah Jolliver going about by your-selves——'

"'Milly's there too, father.'

"'Milly? Where?'

"'Under the corn-sacks! Yes, the truth is, father, I've got rather into a nunny-watch, I'm afeard! Unity Sallet is there too —yes, at the other end, under the tarpaulin. All three are in that waggon, and what to do with 'em I know no more than the dead! The best plan is, as I'm thinking, to speak out loud and plain to one of 'em before the rest, and that will settle it; not but what 'twill cause 'em to kick up a bit of a miff, for certain. Now which would you marry, father, if you was in my place?'

"'Whichever of 'em did *not* ask to ride with thee.'

"'That was Milly, I'm bound to say, as she only mounted by my invitation. But Milly——'

"'Then stick to Milly, she's the best. . . . But look at that!'

'His father pointed toward the waggon. "She can't hold that horse in. You shouldn't have left the reins in her hands. Run on and take the horse's head, or there'll be some accident to them maids!"

'Tony's horse, in fact, in spite of Hannah's tugging at the reins, had started on his way at a brisk walking pace, being very anxious to get back to the stable, for he had had a long day out. Without another word Tony rushed away from his father to overtake the horse.

'Now of all things that could have happened to wean him from Milly there was nothing so powerful as his father's recom-mending her. No; it could not be Milly, after all. Hannah must be the one, since he could not marry all three as he longed to do. This he thought while running after the waggon. But queer things were happening inside it.

'It was, of course, Milly who had screamed under the sack-bags, being obliged to let off her bitter rage and shame in that way at what Tony was saying, and never daring to show, for very pride and dread o' being laughed at, that she was in hiding. She became more and more restless, and in twisting herself about, what did she see but another woman's foot and white stocking close to her head. It quite frightened her, not knowing that Unity

Sallet was in the waggon likewise. But after the fright was over she determined to get to the bottom of all this, and she crept and crept along the bed of the waggon, under the tarpaulin, like a snake, when lo and behold she came face to face with Unity.

'"Well, if this isn't disgraceful!" says Milly in a raging whisper to Unity.

'"'Tis," says Unity, "to see you hiding in a young man's waggon like this, and no great character belonging to either of ye!"

'"Mind what you are saying!" replied Milly, getting louder. "I am engaged to be married to him, and haven't I a right to be here? What right have you, I should like to know? What has he been promising you? A pretty lot of nonsense, I expect! But what Tony says to other women is all mere wind, and no concern to me!"

'"Don't you be too sure!" says Unity. "He's going to have Hannah, and not you, nor me either; I could hear that."

'Now at these strange voices sounding from under the cloth Hannah was thunderstruck a'most into a swound; and it was just at this time that the horse moved on. Hannah tugged away wildly, not knowing what she was doing; and as the quarrel rose louder and louder Hannah got so horrified that she let go the reins altogether. The horse went on at his own pace, and coming to the corner where we turn round to drop down the hill to Lower Longpuddle he turned too quick, the off wheels went up the bank, the waggon rose sideways till it was quite on edge upon the near axles, and out rolled the three maidens into the road in a heap. The horse looked round and stood still.

'When Tony came up, frightened and breathless, he was relieved enough to see that neither of his darlings was hurt, beyond a few scratches from the brambles of the hedge. But he was rather alarmed when he heard how they were going on at one another.

'"Don't ye quarrel, my dears—don't ye!" says he, taking off his hat out of respect to 'em. And then he would have kissed them all round, as fair and square as a man could, but they were in too much of a taking to let him, and screeched and sobbed till they was quite spent.

'"Now I'll speak out honest, because I ought to," says Tony, as soon as he could get heard. "And this is the truth," says he. "I've asked Hannah to be mine, and she is willing, and we are going to put up the banns next——"

'Tony had not noticed that Hannah's father was coming up behind, nor had he noticed that Hannah's face was beginning to bleed from the scratch of a bramble. Hannah had seen her father, and had run to him, crying worse than ever.

'"My daughter is *not* willing, sir!" says Mr. Jolliver hot and strong. "Be you willing, Hannah? I ask ye to have spirit enough to refuse him, if yer virtue is left to 'ee and you run no risk?"

'"She's as sound as a bell for me, that I'll swear!" says Tony, flaring up. "And so's the others, come to that, though you may think it an onusual thing in me!"

'"I have spirit, and I do refuse him!" says Hannah, partly because her father was there, and partly, too, in a tantrum because of the discovery, and the scratch that might be left on her face. "Little did I think when I was so soft with him just now that I was talking to such a false deceiver!"

'"What, you won't have me, Hannah?" says Tony, his jaw hanging down like a dead man's.

'"Never—I would sooner marry no—nobody at all!" she gasped out, though with her heart in her throat, for she would not have refused Tony if he had asked her quietly, and her father had not been there, and her face had not been scratched by the bramble. And having said that, away she walked upon her father's arm, thinking and hoping he would ask her again.

'Tony didn't know what to say next. Milly was sobbing her heart out; but as his father had strongly recommended her he couldn't feel inclined that way. So he turned to Unity.

'"Well, will you, Unity dear, be mine?" he says.

'"Take her leavings? Not I!" says Unity. "I'd scorn it!" And away walks Unity Sallet likewise, though she looked back when she's gone some way, to see if he was following her.

'So there at last were left Milly and Tony by themselves, she crying in watery streams, and Tony looking like a tree struck by lightning.

'"Well, Milly," he says at last, going up to her, "it do seem as if fate had ordained that it should be you and I, or nobody. And what must be must be, I suppose. Hey, Milly?"

'"If you like, Tony. You didn't really mean what you said to them?"

'"Not a word of it!" declares Tony, bringing down his fist upon his palm.

'And then he kissed her, and put the waggon to rights, and they mounted together; and their banns were put up the very next Sunday. I was not able to go to their wedding, but it was a rare party they had, by all account.'

The last ten lines, which link this anecdote to the next in the story, are here omitted.

A Tryst at an Ancient Earthwork

At one's every step forward it rises higher against the south sky, with an obtrusive personality that compels the senses to regard it and consider. The eyes may bend in another direction, but never without the consciousness of its heavy, high-shouldered presence at its point of vantage. Across the intervening levels the gale races in a straight line from the fort, as if breathed out of it hitherward. With the shifting of the clouds the faces of the steeps vary in colour and in shade, broad lights appearing where mist and vagueness had prevailed, dissolving in their turn into melancholy grey, which spreads over and eclipses the luminous bluffs. In this so-thought immutable spectacle all is change.

Out of the invisible marine region on the other side birds soar suddenly into the air, and hang over the summits of the heights with the indifference of long familiarity. Their forms are white against the tawny concave of cloud, and the curves they exhibit in their floating signify that they are sea-gulls which have journeyed inland from expected stress of weather. As the birds rise behind the fort, so do the clouds rise behind the birds, almost as it seems, stroking with their bagging bosoms the uppermost flyers.

The profile of the whole stupendous ruin, as seen at a distance of a mile eastward, is cleanly cut as that of a marble inlay. It is varied with protuberances, which from hereabouts have the animal aspect of warts, wens, knuckles, and hips. It may indeed be likened to an enormous many-limbed organism of an antediluvian time—partaking of the cephalopod in shape—lying lifeless, and covered with a thin green cloth, which hides its substance, while revealing its contour. This dull green mantle of herbage stretches down towards the levels, where the ploughs have essayed for centuries to creep up near and yet nearer to the base of the castle, but have always stopped short before reaching it. The furrows of these environing attempts show themselves distinctly, bending to the incline as they trench upon it; mounting in steeper curves, till the steepness baffles them, and their parallel threads show like the striae of waves pausing on the curl. The peculiar place of which these are some of the features is 'Mai-Dun,' 'The Castle of the Great Hill,' said to be the Dunium of Ptolemy, the capital of the Durotriges, which eventually came into Roman occupation, and was finally deserted on their withdrawal from the island.

The evening is followed by a night on which an invisible moon bestows a subdued yet pervasive light—without radiance, as without blackness. From the spot whereon I am ensconced in a cottage, a mile away, the fort has now ceased to be visible; yet, as by day, to anybody whose thoughts have been engaged with it and its barbarous grandeurs of past time the form asserts its existence behind the night gauzes as persistently as if it had a voice. Moreover, the south-west wind continues to feed the intervening arable flats with vapours brought directly from its sides.

The midnight hour for which there has been occasion to wait at length arrives, and I journey towards the stronghold in obedience to a request urged earlier in the day. It concerns an appointment, which I rather regret my decision to keep now that night is come. The route thither is hedgeless and treeless—I need not add deserted. The moonlight is sufficient to disclose the pale riband-like surface of the way as it trails along between the expanses of darker fallow. Though the road passes near the fortress it does not conduct directly to its fronts. As the place is without an inhabitant, so it is without a trackway. So presently leaving the macadamized road to pursue its course elsewhither, I step off upon the fallow, and plod stumblingly across it. The castle looms out of the shade by degrees, like a thing waking up and asking what I want there. It is now so enlarged by nearness that its whole shape cannot be taken in at one view. The ploughed ground ends as the rise sharpens, the sloping basement of grass begins, and I climb upward to invade Mai-Dun.

Impressive by day as this largest Ancient-British work in the kingdom undoubtedly is, its impressiveness is increased now. After standing still and spending a few minutes in adding its age to its size, and its size to its solitude, it becomes appallingly mournful in its growing closeness. A squally wind blows in the face with an impact which proclaims that the vapours of the air sail low to-night. The slope that I so laboriously clamber up the wind skips sportively down. Its track can be discerned even in this light by the undulations of the withered grass-bents—the only produce of this upland summit except moss. Four minutes of ascent, and a vantage-ground of some sort is gained. It is only the crest of the outer rampart. Immediately within this a chasm gapes; its bottom is imperceptible, but the counterscarp slopes not too steeply to admit of a sliding descent if cautiously performed. The shady bottom, dank and chilly, is thus gained, and reveals itself as a kind of winding lane, wide enough for a waggon to pass along, floored with rank herbage, and trending away, right and left, into obscurity, between the concentric walls of earth. The towering closeness of these on each hand, their impenetrability, and their ponderousness, are felt as a physical pressure. The way is now up the second of them, which stands steeper and higher than the first. To turn aside, as did Christian's companion, from such a Hill Difficulty, is the more natural tendency; but the way to the interior is upward. There is, of course, an entrance to the fortress; but that lies far off on the other side. It might possibly have been the wiser course to seek for easier ingress there.

However, being here, I ascend the second acclivity. The grass stems—the grey beard of the hill—sway in a mass close to my stooping face. The dead heads of these various grasses—fescues, fox-tails, and ryes—bob and twitch as if pulled by a string underground. From a few thistles a whistling proceeds; and even the moss speaks, in its humble way, under the stress of the blast.

That the summit of the second line of defence has been gained is suddenly made known by a contrasting wind from a new quarter, coming over with the curve of a cascade. These novel gusts raise a sound from the whole camp or castle, playing upon it bodily as upon a harp. It is with some difficulty that a foothold can be preserved under their sweep. Looking aloft for a moment I perceive that the sky is much more overcast than it has been hitherto, and in a few instants a dead lull in what is now a gale ensues with almost preternatural abruptness. I take advantage of this to sidle down the second counterscarp, but by the time the ditch is reached the lull reveals itself to be but the precursor of a storm. It begins with a heave of the whole atmosphere, like the sigh of a weary strong man on turning to re-commence unusual exertion, just as I stand here in the second fosse. That which now radiates from the sky upon the scene is not so much light as vaporous phosphorescence.

The wind, quickening, abandons the natural direction it has pursued on the open upland, and takes the course of the gorge's length, rushing along therein helter-skelter, and carrying thick rain upon its back. The rain is followed by hailstones which fly through the defile in battalions—rolling, hopping, ricochetting, snapping, clattering down the shelving banks in an undefinable haze of confusion. The earthen sides of the fosse seem to quiver under the drenching onset, though it is practically no more to them than the blows of Thor upon the giant of Jotun-land. It is impossible to proceed further till the storm somewhat abates, and

I draw up behind a spur of the inner scarp, where possibly a barricade stood two thousand years ago; and thus await events.

The roar of the storm can be heard travelling the complete circuit of the castle—a measured mile—coming round at intervals like a circumambulating column of infantry. Doubtless such a column has passed this way in its time, but the only columns which enter in these latter days are the columns of sheep and oxen that are sometimes seen here now; while the only semblance of heroic voices heard are the utterances of such, and of the many winds which make their passage through the ravines.

The expected lightning radiates round, and a rumbling as from its subterranean vaults—if there are any—fills the castle. The lightning repeats itself, and, coming after the aforesaid thoughts of martial men, it bears a fanciful resemblance to swords moving in combat. It has the very brassy hue of the ancient weapons that here were used. The so sudden entry upon the scene of this metallic flame is as the entry of a presiding exhibitor who unrolls the maps, uncurtains the pictures, unlocks the cabinets, and effects a transformation by merely exposing the materials of his science, unintelligibly cloaked till then. The abrupt configuration of the bluffs and mounds is now for the first time clearly revealed—mounds whereon, doubtless, spears and shields have frequently lain while their owners loosened their sandals and yawned and stretched their arms in the sun. For the first time, too, a glimpse is obtainable of the true entrance used by its occupants of old, some way ahead.

There, where all passage has seemed to be inviolably barred by an almost vertical façade, the ramparts are found to overlap each other like loosely clasped fingers, between which a zigzag path may be followed—a cunning construction that puzzles the uninformed eye. But its cunning, even where not obscured by dilapidation, is now wasted on the solitary forms of a few wild badgers, rabbits, and hares. Men must have often gone out by those gates in the morning to battle with the Roman legions under Vespasian; some to return no more, others to come back at evening, bringing with them the noise of their heroic deeds. But not a page, not a stone, has preserved their fame.

Acoustic perceptions multiply to-night. We can almost hear the stream of years that have borne those deeds away from us. Strange articulations seem to float on the air from that point, the gateway, where the animation in past times must frequently have concentrated itself at hours of coming and going, and general excitement. There arises an ineradicable fancy that they

74

are human voices; if so, they must be the lingering air-borne vibrations of conversations uttered at least fifteen hundred years ago. The attention is attracted from mere nebulous imaginings about yonder spot by a real moving of something close at hand.

I recognize by the now moderate flashes of lightning, which are sheet-like and nearly continuous, that it is the gradual elevation of a small mound of earth. At first no larger than a man's fist, it reaches the dimensions of a hat, then sinks a little and is still. It is but the heaving of a mole who chooses such weather as this to work in from some instinct that there will be nobody abroad to molest him. As the fine earth lifts and lifts and falls loosely aside fragments of burnt clay roll out of it—clay that once formed part of cups or other vessels used by the inhabitants of the fortress.

The violence of the storm has been counterbalanced by its transitoriness. From being immersed in well-nigh solid media of cloud and hail shot with lightning, I find myself uncovered of the humid investiture and left bare to the mild gaze of the moon, which sparkles now on every wet grass-blade and frond of moss.

But I am not yet inside the fort, and the delayed ascent of the third and last escarpment is now made. It is steeper than either. The first was a surface to walk up, the second to stagger up, the third can only be ascended on the hands and toes. On the summit obtrudes the first evidence which has been met with in these precincts that the time is really the nineteenth century; it is in the form of a white notice-board on a post, and the wording can just be discerned by the rays of the setting moon:

CAUTION.—Any Person found removing Relics, Skeletons, Stones, Pottery, Tiles, or other Material from this Earthwork, or cutting up the Ground, will be Prosecuted as the Law directs.

Here one observes a difference underfoot from what has gone before: scraps of Roman tile and stone chippings protrude through the grass in meagre quantity, but sufficient to suggest that masonry stood on the spot. Before the eye stretches under the moonlight the interior of the fort. So open and so large is it as to be practically an upland plateau, and yet its area lies wholly within the walls of what may be designated as one building. It is a long-violated retreat; all its corner-stones, plinths, and architraves were carried away to build neighbouring villages even before mediaeval or modern history began. Many a block which once may have helped to form a bastion here rests now in broken and diminished shape as part of the chimney-corner of some shepherd's cottage within the distant horizon, and the corner-stones of this heathen altar may form the base-course of some adjoining village church.

Yet the very bareness of these inner courts and wards, their condition of mere pasturage, protects what remains of them as no defences could do. Nothing is left visible that the hands can seize on or the weather overturn, and a permanence of general outline at least results, which no other condition could ensure.

The position of the castle on this isolated hill bespeaks deliberate and strategic choice exercised by some remote mind capable of prospective reasoning to a far extent. The natural configuration of the surrounding country and its bearing upon such a stronghold were obviously long considered and viewed mentally before its extensive design was carried into execution. Who was the man that said, 'Let it be built here!'—not on that hill yonder, or on that ridge behind, but on this best spot of all? Whether he were some great one of the Belgae, or of the Durotriges, or the travelling engineer of Britain's united tribes, must for ever remain time's secret; his form cannot be realized, nor his countenance, nor the tongue that he spoke, when he set down his foot with a thud and said, 'Let it be here!'

Within the innermost enclosure, though it is so wide that at a superficial glance the beholder has only a sense of standing on a breezy down, the solitude is rendered yet more solitary by the knowledge that between the benighted sojourner herein and all kindred humanity are those three concentric walls of earth which no being would think of scaling on such a night as this, even were he to hear the most pathetic cries issuing hence that could be uttered by a spectre-chased soul. I reach a central mound or platform—the crown and axis of the whole structure. The view from here by day must be of almost limitless extent. On this raised floor, daïs, or rostrum, harps have probably twanged more or less tuneful notes in celebration of daring, strength, or cruelty; of worship, superstition, love, birth, and death; of simple loving-kindness perhaps never. Many a time must the king or leader have directed his keen eyes hence across the open lands towards the ancient road, the Icening Way, still visible in the distance, on the watch for armed companies approaching either to succour or to attack.

I am startled by a voice pronouncing my name. Past and present have become so confusedly mingled under the associations of the spot that for a time it has escaped my memory that this mound was the place agreed on for the aforesaid appointment. I turn and behold my friend. He stands with a dark lantern in his hand and a spade and light pickaxe over his shoulder. He expresses both delight and surprise that I have come. I tell him I had set out before the bad weather began.

He, to whom neither weather, darkness, nor difficulty seems to have any relation or significance, so entirely is his soul wrapped up in his own deep intentions, asks me to take the lantern and accompany him. I take it and walk by his side. He is a man about sixty, small in figure, with grey old-fashioned whiskers cut to the shape of a pair of crumb-brushes. He is entirely in black broadcloth—or rather, at present, black and brown, for he is bespattered with mud from his heels to the crown of his low hat. He has no consciousness of this—no sense of anything but his purpose, his ardour for which causes his eyes to shine like those of a lynx, and gives his motions all the elasticity of an athlete's.

'Nobody to interrupt us at this time of night!' he chuckles with fierce enjoyment.

We retreat a little way and find a sort of angle, an elevation in the sod, a suggested squareness amid the mass of irregularities around. Here, he tells me, if anywhere, the king's house stood. Three months of measurement and calculation have confirmed him in this conclusion.

He requests me now to open the lantern, which I do, and the light streams out upon the wet sod. At last divining his proceedings I say that I had no idea, in keeping the tryst, that he was going to do more at such an unusual time than meet me for a meditative ramble through the stronghold. I ask him why, having a practicable object, he should have minded interruptions and not have chosen the day? He informs me, quietly pointing to his spade, that it was because his purpose is to dig, then signifying with a grim nod the gaunt notice-post against the sky beyond. I inquire why, as a professed and well-known antiquary with capital letters at the tail of his name, he did not obtain the necessary authority, considering the stringent penalties for this sort of thing; and he chuckles fiercely again with suppressed delight, and says, 'Because they wouldn't have given it!'

He at once begins cutting up the sod, and, as he takes the pickaxe to follow on with, assures me that, penalty or no penalty, honest men or marauders, he is sure of one thing, that we shall not be disturbed at our work till after dawn.

I remember to have heard of men who, in their enthusiasm for some special science, art, or hobby, have quite lost the moral sense which would restrain them from indulging it illegitimately; and I conjecture that here, at last, is an instance of such an one. He probably guesses the way my thoughts travel, for he stands up and solemnly asserts that he has a distinctly justifiable intention in this matter; namely, to uncover, to search, to verify a theory or displace it, and to cover up again. He means to take away nothing—not a grain of sand. In this he says he sees no such monstrous sin. I inquire if this is really a promise to me? He repeats that it is a promise, and resumes digging. My contribution to the labour is that of directing the light constantly upon the hole. When he has reached something more than a foot deep he digs more cautiously, saying that, be it much or little there, it will not lie far below the surface; such things never are deep. A few minutes later the point of the pickaxe clicks upon a stony substance. He draws the implement out as feelingly as if it had entered a man's body. Taking up the spade he shovels with care, and a surface, level as an altar, is presently disclosed. His eyes flash anew; he pulls handfuls of grass and mops the surface clean, finally rubbing it with his handkerchief. Grasping the lantern from my hand he holds it close to the ground, when the rays reveal a complete mosaic—a pavement of minute tesserae of many colours, of intricate pattern, a work of much art, of much time, and of much industry. He exclaims in a shout that he knew it always—that it is not a Celtic stronghold exclusively, but also a Roman; the former people having probably contributed little more than the original framework which the latter took and adapted till it became the present imposing structure.

I ask, What if it is Roman?

A great deal, according to him. That it proves all the world to be wrong in this great argument, and himself alone to be right! Can I wait while he digs further?

I agree—reluctantly; but he does not notice my reluctance. At an adjoining spot he begins flourishing the tools anew with the skill of a navvy, this venerable scholar with letters after his name. Sometimes he falls on his knees, burrowing with his hands in the manner of a hare, and where his old-fashioned broadcloth touches the sides of the hole it gets plastered with the damp earth. He continually murmurs to himself how important, how very important, this discovery is! He draws out an object; we wash it in the same primitive way by rubbing it with the wet grass, and it proves to be a semi-transparent bottle of iridescent beauty, the sight of which draws groans of luxurious sensibility from the digger. Further and further search brings out a piece of a weapon. It is strange indeed that by merely peeling off a wrapper of modern accumulations we have lowered ourselves into an ancient world. Finally a skeleton is uncovered, fairly perfect. He lays it out on the grass, bone to its bone.

My friend says the man must have fallen fighting here, as this is no place of burial. He turns again to the trench, scrapes, feels, till from a corner he draws out a heavy lump—a small image four or five inches high. We clean it as before. It is a statuette, apparently of gold, or, more probably, of bronze-gilt—a figure of Mercury, obviously, its head being surmounted with the petasus or winged hat, the usual accessory of that deity. Further inspection reveals the workmanship to be of good finish and detail, and, preserved by the limy earth, to be as fresh in every line as on the day it left the hands of its artificer.

We seem to be standing in the Roman Forum and not on a hill in Wessex. Intent upon this truly valuable relic of the old empire of which even this remote spot was a component part, we do not notice what is going on in the present world till reminded of it by the sudden renewal of the storm. Looking up I perceive that the wide extinguisher of cloud has again settled down upon the fortress-town, as if resting upon the edge of the inner rampart, and shutting out the moon. I turn my back to the tempest, still directing the light across the hole. My companion digs on unconcernedly; he is living two thousand years ago, and despises things of the moment as dreams. But at last he is fairly beaten, and standing up beside me looks round on what he has done. The rays of the lantern pass over the trench to the tall skeleton stretched upon the grass on the other side. The beating rain has washed the bones clean and smooth, and the forehead, cheek-bones, and two-and-thirty teeth of the skull glisten in the candle shine as they lie.

This storm, like the first, is of the nature of a squall, and it ends as abruptly as the other. We dig no further. My friend says that it is enough—he has proved his point. He turns to replace the bones in the trench and covers them. But they fall to pieces under his touch: the air has disintegrated them, and he can only sweep in the fragments. The next act of his plan is more than difficult, but is carried out. The treasures are inhumed again in their respective holes: they are not ours. Each deposition seems to cost him a twinge; and at one moment I fancied I saw him slip his hand into his coat pocket.

'We must re-bury them *all*,' say I.

'O yes,' he answers with integrity. 'I was wiping my hand.'

The beauties of the tesselated floor of the governor's house are once again consigned to darkness; the trench is filled up; the sod laid smoothly down; he wipes the perspiration from his forehead with the same handkerchief he had used to mop the skeleton and tesserae clean; and we make for the eastern gate of the fortress.

Dawn bursts upon us suddenly as we reach the opening. It comes by the lifting and thinning of the clouds that way till we are bathed in a pink light. The direction of his homeward journey is not the same as mine, and we part under the outer slope.

Walking along quickly to restore warmth I muse upon my eccentric friend, and cannot help asking myself this question: Did he really replace the gilded image of the god Mercurius with the rest of the treasures? He seemed to do so; and yet I could not testify to the fact. Probably, however, he was as good as his word.

It was thus I spoke to myself, and so the adventure ended. But one thing remains to be told, and that is concerned with seven years after. Among the effects of my friend, at that time just deceased, was found, carefully preserved, a gilt statuette representing Mercury, labelled 'Debased Roman.' No record was attached to explain how it came into his possession. The figure was bequeathed to the Casterbridge Museum.

1885.

William and the Pious Bull: An Incident

'ONCE there was a old aged man over at Mellstock—William Dewy by name—one of the family that used to do a good deal of business as tranters over there, Jonathan, do ye mind?—I knowed the man by sight as well as I know my own brother, in a manner of speaking. Well, this man was a coming home-along from a wedding where he had been playing his fiddle, one fine moonlight night, and for shortness' sake he took a cut across Forty-acres, a field lying that way, where a bull was out to grass. The bull seed William, and took after him, horns aground, begad; and though William runned his best, and hadn't *much* drink in him (considering 'twas a wedding, and the folks well off), he found he'd never reach the fence and get over in time to save himself. Well, as a last thought, he pulled out his fiddle as he runned, and struck up a jig, turning to the bull, and backing towards the corner. The bull softened down, and stood still, looking hard at William Dewy, who fiddled on and on; till a sort of a smile stole over the bull's face. But no sooner did William stop his playing and turn to get over hedge than the bull would stop his smiling and lower his horns towards the seat of William's breeches. Well, William had to turn about and play

on, willy-nilly; and 'twas only three o'clock in the world, and a'
knowed that nobody would come that way for hours, and he so
leery and tired that 'a didn't know what to do. When he had
scraped till about four o'clock he felt that he verily would have
to give over soon, and he said to himself, "There's only this last
tune between me and eternal welfare! Heaven save me, or I'm a
done man." Well, then he called to mind how he'd seen the cattle
kneel o' Christmas Eves in the dead o' night. It was not Christmas
Eve then, but it came into his head to play a trick upon the bull.
So he broke into the 'Tivity Hymn, just as at Christmas carol-
singing; when, lo and behold, down went the bull on his bended
knees, in his ignorance, just as if 'twere the true 'Tivity night and
and hour. As soon as his horned friend were down, William
turned, clinked off like a long-dog, and jumped safe over hedge,
before the praying bull had got on his feet again to take after
him. William used to say that he's seen a man look a fool a
good many times, but never such a fool as that bull looked when
he found his pious feelings had been played upon, and 'twas not
Christmas Eve. ... Yes, William Dewy, that was the man's
name; and I can tell you to a foot where's he a-lying in Mellstock
Churchyard at this very moment—just between the second yew-
tree and the north aisle.'

'It's a curious story; it carries us back to mediæval times, when
faith was a living thing!'

Tess of the d'Urbervilles, 1891.

The Deserters: A Scene

SCENE I OF ACT THREE OF *THE DYNASTS*, PART SECOND

SPAIN. A ROAD NEAR ASTORGA

The eye of the spectator rakes the road from the interior of a cellar which opens upon it, and forms the basement of a deserted house, the roof, doors, and shutters of which have been pulled down and burnt for bivouac fires. The season is the beginning of January, and the country is covered with a sticky snow. The road itself is intermittently encumbered with heavy traffic, the surface being churned to a yellow mud that lies half knee-deep, and at the numerous holes in the track forming still deeper quagmires.

In the gloom of the cellar are heaps of damp straw, in which ragged figures are lying half-buried, many of the men in the uniform of English line-regiments, and the women and children in clouts of all descriptions, some being nearly naked. At the back of the cellar is revealed, through a burst door, an inner vault, where are discernible some wooden-hooped wine-casks; in one sticks a gimlet, and the broaching-cork of another has been driven in. The wine runs into pitchers, washing-basins, shards, chamber-vessels, and other extemporized receptacles. Most of the inmates are drunk; some to insensibility.

So far as the characters are doing anything they are contemplating the almost incessant traffic outside, passing in one direction. It includes a medley of stragglers from the Marquis of ROMANA's *Spanish forces and the retreating English army under* SIR JOHN MOORE—*to which the concealed deserters belong.*

FIRST DESERTER

Now he's one of the Eighty-first, and I'd gladly let that poor blade know that we've all that man can wish for here—good wine and buxom women. But if I do, we shan't have room for ourselves—hey?

[He signifies a man limping past with neither fire-lock nor knapsack. Where the discarded knapsack has rubbed for weeks against his shoulderblades the jacket and shirt are fretted away, leaving his skin exposed.]

SECOND DESERTER (*drowsily*)

He may be the Eighty-firsht, or th' Eighty-second; but what I say is, without fear of contradiction, I wish to the Lord I was back in old Bristol again. I'd sooner have a nipperkin of our own real 'Bristol milk' than a mash-tub full of this barbarian wine!

THIRD DESERTER

'Tis like thee to be ungrateful, after putting away such a skinful on't. I am as much Bristol as thee, but would as soon be here as there. There ain't near such willing women, that are strict respectable too, there as hereabout, and no open cellars.—As there's many a slip in this country I'll have the rest of my allowance now.

[*He crawls on his elbows to one of the barrels, and turning on his back lets the wine run down his throat.*]

FOURTH DESERTER (*to a fifth, who is snoring*)

Don't treat us to such a snoaching there, mate. Here's some more coming, and they'll sight us if we don't mind!

[*Enter without a straggling flock of military objects, some with fragments of shoes on, others bare-footed, many of the latter's feet bleeding. The arms and waists of some are clutched by women as tattered and bare-footed as themselves. They pass on.*]

[*The Retreat continues. More of* ROMANA'S *Spanish limp along in disorder; then enters a miscellaneous group of English cavalry soldiers, some on foot, some mounted, the rearmost of the latter bestriding a shoeless foundered creature whose neck is vertebræ and mane only. While passing it falls from exhaustion; the trooper extricates himself and pistols the animal through the head. He and the rest pass on.*]

FIRST DESERTER (*a new plashing of feet being heard*)

Here's something more in order, or I am much mistaken. (*He cranes out.*) Yes, a sergeant of the Forty-third, and what's left of their second battalion. And, by God, not far behind I see shining helmets. 'Tis a whole squadron of French dragoons!

[*Enter the sergeant. He has a racking cough, but endeavours, by stiffening himself up, to hide how it is wasting away his life. He halts, and looks back, till the remains of the Forty-third are abreast, to the number of some three hundred, about half of whom are crippled invalids, the other half being presentable and armed soldiery.*]

SERGEANT

Now show yer nerve, and be men. If you die to-day you won't have to die to-morrow. Fall in! (*The miscellany falls in.*) All

invalids and men without arms march ahead as well as they can.
Quick—maw-w-w-ch! (*Exeunt invalids, etc.*) Now! Tention!
Shoulder-r-r-r—fawlocks! (*Order obeyed.*)

[*The sergeant hastily forms these into platoons, who prime and
load, and seem preternaturally changed from what they were into
alert soldiers.*

[*Enter French dragoons at the left-back of the scene. The rear
platoon of the Forty-third turns, fires, and proceeds. The next
platoon covering them does the same. This is repeated several times,
staggering the pursuers. Exeunt French dragoons, giving up the
pursuit. The coughing sergeant and the remnant of the Forty-third
march on.*]

FOURTH DESERTER (*to a woman lying beside him*)
What d'ye think o' that, my honey? It fairly makes me a man
again. Come, wake up! We must be getting along somehow. (*He
regards the woman more closely.*) Why—my little chick? Look
here, friends. (*They look, and the woman is found to be dead.*) If I
didn't think that her poor knees felt cold! . . . And only an hour
go I swore I'd marry her!

[*They remain silent. The Retreat continues in the snow without,
now in the form of a file of ox-carts, followed by a mixed rabble of
English and Spanish, and mules, and muleteers hired by English
officers to carry their baggage. The muleteers, looking about and
seeing that the French dragoons have been there, cut the bands
which hold on the heavy packs, and scamper off with their mules.*]

A VOICE (*behind*)
The Commander-in-Chief is determined to maintain discipline,
and they must suffer. No more pillaging here. It is the worst
case of brutality and plunder that we have had in this wretched
time!

[*Enter an English captain of hussars, a lieutenant, a guard of about
a dozen, and three men as prisoners.*]

CAPTAIN
If they choose to draw lots, only one need be made an example
of. But they must be quick about it. The advance-guard of the
enemy is not far behind.

[*The three prisoners appear to draw lots, and the one on whom the
lot falls is blindfolded. Exeunt the hussars behind a wall, with
carbines. A volley is heard and something falls. The wretches in
the cellar shudder.*]

FOURTH DESERTER

'Tis the same for us but for this heap of straw. Ah—my doxy is
the only one of us who is safe and sound!
(*He kisses the dead woman.*)

[*Retreat continues. A train of six-horse baggage-waggons lumbers
past, a mounted sergeant alongside. Among the baggage lie
wounded soldiers and sick women.*]

SERGEANT OF THE WAGGON-TRAIN

If so be they are dead, ye may as well drop 'em over the tail-
board. 'Tis no use straining the horses unnecessary.

[*Waggons halt. Two of the wounded who have just died are taken
out, laid down by the roadside, and some muddy snow scraped over
them. Exeunt waggons and sergeant.*

*An interval. More English troops pass on horses, mostly shoeless
and foundered.*

Enter SIR JOHN MOORE *and officers.* MOORE *appears in the pale
evening light as a handsome man, far on in the forties, the orbits
of his dark eyes showing marks of deep anxiety. He is talking to
some of his staff with vehement emphasis and gesture. They cross
the scene and go on out of sight, and the squashing of their horses'
hoofs in the snowy mud dies away.*]

FIFTH DESERTER (*incoherently in his sleep*)

Poise fawlocks—open pans—right hands to pouch—handle
ca'tridge—bring it—quick motion—bite top well off—prime—
shut pans—cast about—load——

FIRST DESERTER (*throwing a shoe at the sleeper*)

Shut up that! D'ye think you are a 'cruity in the awkward squad
still?

SECOND DESERTER

I don't know what he thinks, but I know what I feel! Would that
I were at home in England again, where there's old-fashioned
tipple, and a proper God A'mighty instead of this eternal
'Ooman and baby;—ay, at home a-leaning against old Bristol
Bridge, and no questions asked, and the winter sun slanting
friendly over Baldwin Street as 'a used to do! 'Tis my very belief,
though I have lost all sure reckoning, that if I wer there, and in
good health, 'twould be New Year's day about now. What it is
over here I don't know. Ay, to-night we should be a-setting in the
tap of the 'Adam and Eve'—lifting up the tune of 'The Light
o' the Moon.' 'Twer a romantical thing enough. 'A used to go
som'at like this (*he sings in a nasal tone*):

85

'*O I thought it had been day,*
And I stole from her away;
But it proved to be the light o' the moon!'

[*Retreat continues, with infantry in good order. Hearing the singing, one of the officers looks around, and detaching a patrol enters the ruined house with the file of men, the body of soldiers marching on. The inmates of the cellar bury themselves in the straw. The officer peers about, and seeing no-one prods the straw with his sword.*]

VOICES (*under the straw*)
Oh! Hell! Stop it! We'll come out! Mercy! Quarter!

[*The lurkers are uncovered.*]

OFFICER
If you are well enough to sing bawdy songs, you are well enough to march. So out of it—or you'll be shot, here and now!

SEVERAL
You may shoot us, captain, or the French may shoot us, or the devil may take us; we don't care which! Only we can't stir. Pity the women, captain, but do what you will with us!

[*The searchers pass over the wounded, and stir out those capable of marching, both men and women, so far as they discover them. They are pricked on by the patrol. Exeunt patrol and deserters in its charge.*
Those who remain look stolidly at the highway. The English Rear-guard of cavalry crosses the scene and passes out. An interval. It grows dusk.]

SPIRIT IRONIC
Quaint poesy, and real romance of war!

SPIRIT OF THE PITIES
Mock on, Shade, if thou wilt! But others find
Poesy ever lurk where pit-pats poor mankind!

[*The scene is cloaked in darkness.*]

The Three Wayfarers

Characters

THE SHEPHERD (*age 28*)
THE PARISH CONSTABLE (*age 50*)
TIMOTHY SOMMERS (*a condemned sheepstealer, age 30*)
JOSEPH SOMMERS (*his brother, age 32*)
THE HANGMAN (*age 55*)
THE SERPENT PLAYER
A BOY FIDDLER
A MAGISTRATE
A TURNKEY
ELIJAH
THE SHEPHERD'S WIFE
A DAMSEL (*betrothed to the* CONSTABLE)

Other PEASANTS, *male and female, guests of the Shepherd*

TIME: *A March evening at the beginning of the last century*

Details of the Dance: The College Hornpipe
The Three Wayfarers

The couples stand in two lines, gentlemen in one, ladies in the other, partners facing each other. The three top couples join hands in a circle, dance half round, and back again to places. (*End of first part of tune*)

The three top gentlemen take their partners and promenade round two and two in a complete circle to places. (*End of repeated first part of tune*)

The three (or two) top couples dance down the middle and up again. (*End of second part of tune*)

The three (or two) top couples swing partners and return to places, except that the original top couple takes now the second couple's place. (*End of repeated second part of tune*)

Tune recommences. The original top couple, now the second couple, does the same with the next two couples, and so work their way to the bottom of the dance.

The Three Wayfarers

SHEPHERD

In a few hours we shall have the folk hurrying past here to get to the sight early.

SERPENT PLAYER

'Twasn't one of your sheep that 'a stole, shepherd?

SHEPHERD

Oh, no. I haven't lost one this winter. 'Twas from some farm up by Shottsford. I don't know the place at all.

SERPENT PLAYER

Who'll do the gallus job now our hangman is dead?

CONSTABLE

They'll have to send for a new hand, I reckon.

SHEPHERD'S WIFE

Well, heaven send that they'll let the poor man drop easy, though some die hard, that's true. . . .

TIMOTHY SOMMERS

(*To* SHEPHERD'S WIFE) I'll take a seat in the chimney-corner if you've nothing to say against it, ma'am, for I am a little moist on the side that was next the rain.

SHEPHERD'S WIFE

Ay, sure. (*He enters chimney-corner and stretches out legs.*) Your boots are the worse for wear.

TIMOTHY SOMMERS

Yes—I am rather thin in the vamp. And I'm not well fitted, either. I have seen some rough times lately, and have been forced to pick up what I could get in the way of wearing; but I must find a suit better fitted for working days when I get home.

SHEPHERD'S WIFE

One of hereabouts?

TIMOTHY SOMMERS

Not quite, ma'am. Further up the country.

SHEPHERD'S WIFE

I thought so. And so be I. And by your tongue you seem to come from my neighbourhood.

TIMOTHY SOMMERS

(*Hastily*) But you would hardly have heard of me. (*Blandly*) My time would be long before yours, ma'am, you see. . . . Really, if I'd not met you here as a married woman, I should have said to 'ee 'my dear young girl'!

SHEPHERD'S WIFE

(*Simpering*) Get along with thee!

TIMOTHY SOMMERS

Really I should! When was you married, ma'am?

SHEPHERD'S WIFE

I've been married five years, and have three children.

TIMOTHY SOMMERS

No! Impossible! Really, married women shouldn't look such maiden deceptions. 'Tisn't moral of 'em! Why, I won't say that I shouldn't have asked to pay my addresses to 'ee, if I'd been a younger fellow, and as well off as I was formerly.

SHEPHERD'S WIFE

Ah—poor man. (*To* SHEPHERD, *who has been helping guests to liquor*) Pour out some for the stranger. I never met a civiller man.

TIMOTHY SOMMERS

(*To* SHEPHERD) There is only one thing more wanted to make me happy. And that's a little baccy, which I'm sorry to say I'm out of.

SHEPHERD

I'll fill your pipe.

TIMOTHY SOMMERS

I must ask you to lend me a pipe, likewise.

SHEPHERD

A smoker, and no pipe about 'ee?

TIMOTHY SOMMERS

(*Confused*) I've dropped it somewhere on the road.

SHEPHERD

(*Handing pipe*) Hand me your baccy box—I'll fill that, too, now I'm about it. (TIMOTHY SOMMERS *searches pockets*). . . . Lost that, too?

TIMOTHY SOMMERS

I'm afraid so. Give it to me in a screw of paper. (*Lights pipe.*)

SHEPHERD

Neighbours, another dance? Shall it be hands across this time?

GUESTS

Ay, ay, maister—hands across.

SHEPHERD

Strike up, fiddler.
(*Country dance. Two top couples hands across and back again. Swing partners. The other couples do the same.*)

SHEPHERD'S WIFE

Get the man some more mead.
(*Knocking.* TIMOTHY SOMMERS *starts up and sits again. Dance ceases.*)

SHEPHERD

What—another?

CONSTABLE, ETC.

Another visitor!

SHEPHERD

Walk in!
(*Enter* HANGMAN R. C., *bag in hand.*)

HANGMAN

I must beg for a few minutes shelter, comrades, or I shall be wetted to my skin before I reach Casterbridge.

SHEPHERD

Make yerself at home, master—make yerself at home, though you be a stranger.
(HANGMAN *removes great-coat, shakes out and hangs up hat. He advances to table by chimney-corner, deposits bag thereon, and sits down outside* TIMOTHY SOMMERS, *who nods and hands mug. Other* GUESTS *play at forfeits or some silent game.*)

HANGMAN

(*Drinks.*) I knew it! When I walked up your garden afore coming in, and saw the hives all of a row, I said to myself, 'Where there's bees there's honey, and where there's honey there's mead,' but mead of such a truly comfortable sort as this I really didn't expect to meet my lips in older days!
(*Drinks again deeply.*)

SHEPHERD

Glad you enjoy it!

SHEPHERD'S WIFE

(*Grudgingly*) It is goodish mead, and trouble enough to make, and we can hardly afford to have it drunk wastefully. . . . I hardly think we shall make any more, for honey sells well, and we can make shift without such strong liquor.

HANGMAN

Oh, but you'll never have the heart! (*Drinks again.*) I love mead, when 'tis old like this, as I love to go to church o' Sundays, or relieve the poor and needy any day of the week.

TIMOTHY SOMMERS

Good—very good! Ha-ha-ha!

HANGMAN

(*Spreading himself in chair*) Well, well, as I say, I am going to Casterbridge, and to Casterbridge I must go. I should have been almost there by this time, if the rain hadn't driven me in here; and I'm not sorry for it.

SHEPHERD

You don't live in Casterbridge, sir, seemingly?

HANGMAN

Not as yet. I shortly mean to move there.

SHEPHERD

Going to set up in trade, perhaps?

SHEPHERD'S WIFE

No, no. It is easy to see that the gentleman is rich and don't need to work at anything.

HANGMAN

(*After a pause*) Rich is not quite the word for me, dame. I do work, and I must work. And even if I only get to Casterbridge by midnight, I must get to work there by eight to-morrow morning. ... Yes, het or wet, blow or snow, famine or sword, my day's work to-morrow must be done.

(TIMOTHY SOMMERS *droops in agitation*.)

SHEPHERD'S WIFE

Indeed! Then in spite o' seeming, you are worse off than we?

HANGMAN

It lies rather in the nature of my trade, men and maidens. It is the peculiarity of my business more than my poverty. ... But, really and truly, I must up and away, or I shan't get a lodging in the town. ... There's time for one more draught of friendship before I go, and I'd perform it at once if the mug were not dry.

SHEPHERD'S WIFE

Here's a mug of small. Small we call it, though 'tis only the first wash of the combs.

HANGMAN

No! I won't spoil your kindness by partaking of your second.

SHEPHERD

Certainly not. We don't increase and multiply every day, and I'll fill the mug wi' strong again!

(*Goes to barrel in corner.*)

SHEPHERD'S WIFE

(*Following him*) Why should you do this? He emptied it at once, though it held enough for ten people; and now he's not content with the small, but must needs call for more of the strong! And a stranger unbeknown to any of us! For my part I don't like the look of this man at all!

SHEPHERD

But he's in the house, my dear and tender. And 'tis a wet night, and our baby's christening! Daze it, what's a cup o' mead more or less?

SHEPHERD'S WIFE

Very well, this time, then. But what's the man's calling, and where does he come from, that he should burst in and join us like this!

SHEPHERD

I don't know. I'll ask him again.
(*They return to* HANGMAN, *she pouring out a very small cupful, keeping the mug at a distance.*)

SHEPHERD

(*To* HANGMAN) And as to this trade of yours, what did you say it might be?

TIMOTHY SOMMERS

(*Affecting frankness*) Anybody may know *my* trade. I'm a wheelwright.

SHEPHERD'S WIFE

A very good trade for these parts—

HANGMAN

And anybody may know mine—if they've the wit to find out. . . .

CONSTABLE

You may mostly tell what a man is by his claws: Though I be a servant o' the Crown as regards my constableship, I be a hedge-carpenter by trade, and my fingers be as full of thorns as a pin-cushion is of pins.
(TIMOTHY SOMMERS *quickly hides his hands.*)

HANGMAN

True. But the oddity of my trade is that instead of setting a mark upon me, it sets a mark upon my customers!

SHEPHERD'S WIFE

That's strange. [*Aside*] I don't like the man at all. . . . (*To the other* GUESTS) Will somebody favour us with a song?

GUESTS

(*Severally*) I've got no voice . . . I've forgot the first verse, etc.

HANGMAN

Well—to start the company I'll sing one myself.
(*Sings*)
> O, my trade it is the rarest one,
> > Simple shepherds all—
> My trade is a sight to see;
> For my customers I tie, and take them up on high,
> > And waft 'em to a far countree—

(TIMOTHY SOMMERS *drops and breaks pipe in his agitation.*)
> > Hee-hee!
> And waft 'em to a far countree!

(*Drinks.*)

94

The Three Wayfarers

TIMOTHY SOMMERS

(*Sings*)
> And waft 'em to a far countree!

SHEPHERD'S WIFE

What do the man mean?
(SHEPHERD *shakes his head.*)

TIMOTHY SOMMERS

Second verse, stranger!

HANGMAN

(*Sings*)
> My tools are but common ones (*tapping bag*),
> > Simple shepherds all—
> My tools are no sight to see;
> A little hempen string and a post whereon to swing
> > Are implements enough for me—
> > > Hee-hee!
> Are implements enough for me!

(*Pulls end of rope from bag.* TIMOTHY SOMMERS *tries to hide his agitation.*)

GUESTS

(*Starting*) Oh!
(DAMSEL *faints*—CONSTABLE *catches her.*

CONSTABLE

Oh—he's the hangman!

SEVERAL

He's come to hang Tim Sommers at Casterbridge gaol to-morrow morning!

OTHERS

The man condemned for sheep-stealing, what we were talking of! —the poor clockmaker who used to live at Shottsford! His family was starving, and so he went out of Shottsford by the high road and took a sheep in open daylight. . . . He (*pointing to* HANGMAN) is come up from the country to do it. Then it's he who is going to have the berth here now our own man is dead!

TIMOTHY SOMMERS

(*Sings*)
> Are implements enough for me!
(*Clinks cups with* HANGMAN.)

HANGMAN

Next verse.
(*Sings*)
> To-morrow is— (*knocking without.*)
(SHEPHERD *rises.* WIFE *tries to prevent his speaking.*)

95

CONSTABLE

Another of 'em!

SEVERAL

What do it mean?

SHEPHERD

Walk in!
(*Enter* JOSEPH SOMMERS R. C. *Begins wiping shoes.*)

JOSEPH SOMMERS

Can you tell me the way to— (*starts.*) [*Aside*] My brother Tim
escaped—sitting with his own hangman!

HANGMAN

(*Sings*)
> To-morrow is my working day,
>   Simple shepherds all—
> To-morrow is a working day for me;
> For the farmer's sheep is slain, and the lad who did it ta'en,
>   And on his soul may God ha' mer-cy—

TIMOTHY SOMMERS

(*Waving cup, joins in.*)
> Hee-hee!
> And on his soul may God ha' mer-cy!

(JOSEPH SOMMERS *aghast, staggers and nearly falls in a fit.*)
[*Exit* JOSEPH SOMMERS, *slamming door.*]

SHEPHERD

What man could he be?
(*Silence. Company stare at* HANGMAN. *Rain without.* TIMOTHY
SOMMERS *smokes unconcerned. Report of a gun.*)

HANGMAN

(*Jumping up*) Be jiggered! (*Rope falls on floor.*) The prison gun!

TIMOTHY SOMMERS

What does that mean?

SHEPHERD'S WIFE

A prisoner escaped from the gaol—that's what it means!

TIMOTHY SOMMERS

(*After a pause*) I've often been told that in this county they fire
a gun at such times, but I never heard it till now.

HANGMAN

I wonder if it is *my* man?

SHEPHERD

Surely it is! And surely we've seen him! The little man who
knocked at the door by now, and quivered like a leaf when he
saw 'ee and heard your song!

SHEPHERD'S WIFE

Yes! His teeth chattered, and the breath went out of his body!

CONSTABLE

And his heart seemed to sink within him like a stone.

OTHERS

And he bolted as if he'd been shot at.

TIMOTHY SOMMERS

(*Elaborately*) True—true. His teeth chattered and his heart seemed to sink, and he bolted as if he'd been shot at.

HANGMAN

I didn't notice it.

DAMSEL

We were all wondering what made him run off in such a fright, and now 'tis explained!
(*Gun at slow intervals*)

HANGMAN

Is there a parish constable here? If so, let him step forward.
(CONSTABLE *advances*, DAMSEL *abandoning him reluctantly and sobbing over back of chair*.)

HANGMAN

You are a sworn constable?

CONSTABLE

I be, sir!

HANGMAN

Then pursue the criminal at once with assistance and bring him back. He can't have gone far.

CONSTABLE

I will, sir—I will—when I've got my staff of office. I'll go home and get it, and come sharp here and start in a body!

HANGMAN

Staff—never mind your staff! The man'll be gone!

CONSTABLE

But I can't do nothing without my staff—can I, Shepherd, and Elijah, and John? No, for there's the King's royal crown a-painted on en in yaller and gold, and the lion and the unicorn, so as when I raise en up and hit my prisoner 'tis made a lawful blow thereby. I wouldn't attempt to take up a man without my staff—no, not I. If I hadn't the law to give me courage, why, instead o' my taking him up, he might take up me!

DAMSEL

(*Clinging to him*) Don't 'ee risk your life, dear. Don't 'ee!

HANGMAN

Now, I'm a king's man myself, and can give you authority enough for this. Now then, all of ye, be ready. Have ye any lanterns?

CONSTABLE

Yes. Have ye any lanterns? I demand it.

HANGMAN

And the rest of you able-bodied men—

CONSTABLE

Able-bodied men, yes—the rest of ye!

HANGMAN

Have you some good stout staves and pitchforks—

CONSTABLE

Staves and pitchforks in the name of the law. And take 'em in your hands and go in quest, and do as we in authority tell ye!
[*Exeunt all* R.C. *except the women, with lanterns, staves, etc. Rope discovered. Start affrighted.* DAMSEL *faints. Baby cries from another room.*]

SHEPHERD'S WIFE

Oh, my poor baby! 'Tis of ill omen for her—all this gallows work at her christening! I wouldn't have had her if I'd known!
(*Exeunt* WOMEN U.R.]

(*Enter stealthily* TIMOTHY SOMMERS. *Helps himself to food and drink.*)

TIMOTHY SOMMERS

Hunger will tame a lion, and a convict! To think they should fancy my brother the man, and not me!
(*Enter* HANGMAN R.C.)

HANGMAN

Ah—you here, friend? I thought you had gone to help in the capture. (*Staggers to mug.*)

TIMOTHY SOMMERS

And I thought you had.

HANGMAN

Well, on second thoughts I felt there were enough to do it without me, and such a night as it is, too. Besides, 'tis the business of the Government to take care of its criminals till they reach my hands.

TIMOTHY SOMMERS

True—so it is. And I felt, as you did, that there were enough without me.

HANGMAN

I don't want to break my limbs running over the humps and hollows of this wild country!

The Three Wayfarers

TIMOTHY SOMMERS

Nor I either, between you and me.

HANGMAN

These shepherd-folk are used to it—simple-minded souls, you know—stirred up to anything in a moment. They'll have him before the morning, ready for me to pinion and turn off. (*Suiting action to word.*) And no trouble to me at all. Besides me fee, his clothes will fetch me a guinea or two, I hope, when I've stripped his corpse afore burial.

TIMOTHY SOMMERS

True, true. A guinea or two for certain—when you've stripped his corpse!

HANGMAN

By the way, I've dropped my rope somewhere. I always carry my own halter with me—the new ones they make for ye won't draw tight under the ear like an old one.

TIMOTHY SOMMERS

Exactly. Not like an old one, tight under the ear! Ha-ha! Here 'tis, sir. (*Picking up rope.*)

HANGMAN

Thank 'ee friend. Oh, I wouldn't make a *long* strangling of it for the world. I'm too kind-hearted for that.

TIMOTHY SOMMERS

Ve-ry kind-hearted! Ha-ha! (*Edging off*) Good-bye—my way is—

HANGMAN

And my way is to Casterbridge, and it is as much as my legs will do to carry me that far. Going the same way?

TIMOTHY SOMMERS

No, I'm sorry to say. I've to get home over north'ard there, and I feel as you do that I must be stepping on. Good-night t' ye!

HANGMAN

Good-night! Till we meet again.
(*They shake hands.*)

TIMOTHY SOMMERS

Till we meet again!   [*Exeunt severally.*]
(*Enter* TURNKEY *and* MAGISTRATE.)

MAGISTRATE

Nobody here?
(*Enter* SHEPHERD'S WIFE, DAMSEL, *and other* WOMEN.)

SHEPHERD'S WIFE

They are gone in pursuit, sir.

MAGISTRATE

Ah—I think I hear them returning. Then they've caught him.
(*Enter* CONSTABLE, SHEPHERD, MUSICIANS, *other* PEASANTS, *and*
JOSEPH SOMMERS.)

CONSTABLE

Gentlemen, I have brought back your man, not without risk and
danger, but everyone must do his duty. I pursued him, and when
I was a safe distance I said, 'Prisoner at the bar, surrender in
the name of the Saints of —'

SHEPHERD

The Crown, the Crown.

CONSTABLE

If you had all the weight of this undertaking on your mind,
you'd say the wrong word, perhaps! So I said, 'Surrender in the
name of the Crown! We arrest 'ee on the charge of not staying
in Casterbridge gaol in a decent, proper manner to be hung
to-morrow morning!' That's the words I said.

MAGISTRATE

Well, well—where is the man?

CONSTABLE

He's inside this circle of able-bodied persons, sir. Men, bring
forward your prisoner!
(*They advance with* JOSEPH SOMMERS.)

TURNKEY

Who is this man?

CONSTABLE

The culprit!

TURNKEY

Certainly not!
(*Re-enter* HANGMAN.)

CONSTABLE

But how can he be otherwise? Why was he so terrified at the
sight of that singing instrument of the law? (*Pointing to* HANG-
MAN.)

TURNKEY

Can't explain it. All I know is that this is not the condemned
man. He's quite a different character—gaunt—dark-haired—
and a voice you'd never mistake as long as you lived.

CONSTABLE

Why, souls—'twas the man in the chimney-corner!

SEVERAL

Ay—'twas the man in the chimney-corner.

MAGISTRATE

Hey? What—haven't you got the man after all?

CONSTABLE

Well, sir, he's the man we were in search of, that's true, and yet he's not the man we were in search of. For the man we were in search of was not the man we wanted—if you understand my everyday way, sir—for 'twas the man in the chimley-corner!

MAGISTRATE

A pretty kettle of fish altogether! You had better start for the other man at once.

JOSEPH SOMMERS

Sir, the time has come when I may as well speak. I have done nothing. My crime is that the condemned man is my brother.

SEVERAL

His brother!

JOSEPH SOMMERS

Yes. Early this afternoon I left home to tramp to Casterbridge gaol to bid him farewell. I was benighted and called here to rest and ask the way.

HANGMAN

Like myself.

JOSEPH SOMMERS

When I opened the door, I saw before me the very man, my brother Tim, that I thought to see in the condemned cell at Casterbridge. He was in this chimney-corner, and jammed close to him was the executioner who had come to take his life—

HANGMAN

According to law, according to law!

JOSEPH SOMMERS

—and singing a song about it, and my brother joining in to save appearances.

HANGMAN

A deceitful rascal. How I do despise a man who won't die legal.

JOSEPH SOMMERS

Tim threw a look of agony upon me, and I knew it meant, 'Don't reveal what you see—my life depends on it!' I was so terrified that I turned and hurried away.

MAGISTRATE

And do you know where your brother is at present?

JOSEPH SOMMERS

I do not. I have not seen him since I closed the door.

CONSTABLE

I can testify to that. We kept well between 'em with our weapons, at a safe distance.

MAGISTRATE

Where does he think to fly to? What's his occupation?

JOSEPH SOMMERS

A watch- and clock-maker, sir.

CONSTABLE

'A said 'a was a wheelwright—a wicked rogue!

SHEPHERD

He meant the wheels o' clocks and watches, perhaps. I thought his hands were whitish for his trade.

MAGISTRATE

Well—it appears to me that nothing can be gained by retaining this poor man in custody. Your business lies with the other, unquestionably.

(*Enter a* PEASANT, *a* BOY *etc.*)

BOY

And he's gone far enough!

PEASANT

Yes—he's gone! Nobody can find he to-night, now the moon is down, and by to-morrow morning he'll be half across the Channel.

HANGMAN

'Twas an unprincipled thing! To cheat an honest man of his perquisites, and take away his trade. How am I to live?

SHEPHERD'S WIFE

I'm unlawfully glad of it. He were a nice civil man, and his punishment would ha' been too heavy for his sin. So brave and daring and cool as he was to sit here as he did! I pray they'll never catch him. And I hope that you, sir, will never do your morning's work at Casterbridge, or meet our friend anywhere for *business* purposes.

SHEPHERD

Well, neighbours, I now do hope this little dy-ver-sion is ended, and I don't see why our christening party should be cut short by such a' onseemly interruption. Another jig, friends. We don't have a baby every day!

WOMEN

God forbid!

SHEPHERD

Come, then; choose your partners; form a line; and to it again till daylight.

HANGMAN

Wi' all my heart! My day's work being lost, faith, I may as well make a night of it, too, and hope for better luck at the next assizes!

SHEPHERD

Now start the tune, fiddler!

(*They form again for the six-hands round. College Hornpipe.* HANGMAN *tries to get each woman severally as partner: all refuse. At last* HANGMAN *dances in the figure by himself, with an imaginary partner, and pulls out rope.* JOSEPH SOMMERS *looks on pensively.*)

CURTAIN

AESTHETICS AND POETRY

POEMS

Dates printed at the foot of certain poems are dates of composition added by the author; those in square brackets have been ascertained from other sources.

Hardy on his Aesthetics and his Poetry

These remarks, of greater and lesser seriousness, are representative of Hardy's thinking about his art over fifty years: while they afford some interesting comments by a poet on poetry, it is not to be expected that notebook jotting or ponderously studied Apology will lay down final truths about that poetry.
Unless otherwise stated the extracts are from Florence Emily Hardy's The Life of Thomas Hardy (*1962*)

At this time the real state of his mind was, in his own words, that 'A sense of the truth of poetry, of its supreme place in literature, had awakened itself in me. At the risk of ruining all my wordly prospects I dabbled in it . . .' in verse was concentrated the essence of all imaginative and emotional literature . . . [The Sixties]

The business of the poet and novelist is to show the sorriness underlying the grandest things, and the grandeur underlying the sorriest things. [1885]

My art is to intensify the expression of things, as is done by Crivelli, Bellini, etc., so that the heart and inner meaning is made vividly visible. [1886]

To find beauty in ugliness is the province of the poet. [1888]

Art consists in so depicting the common events of life as to bring out the features which illustrate the author's idiosyncratic mode of regard; making old incidents and things seem as new. [1890]

Art is a disproportioning—(i.e. distorting, throwing out of proportion)—of realities, to show more clearly the features that matter in those realities, which, if merely copied or reported inventorially, might possibly be observed, but would more probably be overlooked. Hence 'realism' is not Art. [1890]

Poetry. Perhaps I can express more fully in verse ideas and emotions which run counter to the inert crystallized opinion—

hard as a rock—which the vast body of men have vested interests in supporting. To cry out in a passionate poem that (for instance) the Supreme Mover or Movers, the Prime Force or Forces, must be either limited in power, unknowing, or cruel—which is obvious enough, and has been for centuries—will cause them merely a shake of the head; but to put it in argumentative prose will make them sneer, or foam, and set all the literary contortionists jumping upon me, a harmless agnostic, as if I were a clamorous atheist, which in their crass illiteracy they seem to think is the same thing. . . . If Galileo had said in verse that the world moved, the Inquisition might have let him alone. [1896]

The change, after all [from prose to verse], was not so great as it seemed. It was not as if he had been a writer of novels proper, and as more specifically understood, that is, stories of modern artificial life and manners showing a certain smartness of treatment. He had mostly aimed at keeping his narratives close to natural life and as near to poetry in their subject as the conditions would allow, and had often regretted that those conditions would not let him keep them nearer still. [1897–8]

Whenever an ancient and legitimate word of the district, for which there was no equivalent in received English, suggested itself as the most natural, nearest, and often only expression of a thought, it has been made use of, on what seemed good grounds. [1898] From the Preface to *Wessex Poems*

He wrote somewhere: 'There is no new poetry; but the new poet —if he carry the flame on further (and if not he is no new poet) —comes with a new note. And that new note it is that troubles the critical waters.

'Poetry is emotion put into measure. The emotion must come by nature, but the measure can be acquired by art.'

[The value of irregularity.] That the author loved the art of concealing art was undiscerned [by commentators]. For instance, as to rhythm. Years earlier he had decided that too regular a beat was bad art. He had fortified himself in his opinion by thinking of the analogy of architecture, between which art and that of poetry he had discovered, to use his own words, that there existed a close and curious parallel, both arts, unlike some others, having to carry a rational content inside their artistic form. He knew that in architecture cunning irregularity is of enormous worth, and it is obvious that he carried on into his verse, perhaps in part unconsciously, the Gothic art-principle in which he had been trained—the principle of spontaneity, found in mouldings, tracery, and such like—resulting in the 'unforeseen' (as it has been called) character of his metres and stanzas, that of stress rather than of syllable, poetic texture rather than poetic veneer.... [1899–1900]

... It will probably be found, therefore, to possess little cohesion of thought or harmony of colouring. I do not greatly regret this. Unadjusted impressions have their value, and the road to a true philosophy of life seems to lie in humbly recording diverse readings of its phenomena as they are forced upon us by chance and change. [1901] From the Preface to *Poems of the Past and the Present*

... how much more concise and quintessential expression becomes when given in rhythmic form than when shaped in the language of prose ...

Differing natures find their tongue in the presence of differing spectacles. Some natures become vocal at tragedy, some are made vocal by comedy, and it seems to me that to whichever of these aspects of life a writer's instinct for expression the more readily responds, to that he should allow it to respond. [1911] From the General Preface to the Novels and Poems, written for the Wessex Edition and printed in *Tess of the d'Urbervilles*

[On *Moments of Vision*] I do not expect much notice will be taken of these poems: they mortify the human sense of self-importance by showing, or suggesting, that human beings are of no matter or appreciable value in this nonchalant universe. [1917]

My opinion is that a poet should express the emotion of all the ages and the thought of his own. [1919]

[Florence Emily Hardy] Speaking generally there is more auto-biography in a hundred lines of Mr. Hardy's poetry than in all the novels. [1919]

Apology

The Apology, which prefaces *Late Lyrics and Earlier* (1922), is given here in its entirety.

ABOUT half the verses that follow were written quite lately. The rest are older, having been held over in MS. when past volumes were published, on considering that these would contain a sufficient number of pages to offer readers at one time, more especially during the distractions of the war. The unusually far back poems to be found here are, however, but some that were overlooked in gathering previous collections. A freshness in them, now unattainable, seemed to make up for their inexperience and to justify their inclusion. A few are dated; the dates of others are not discoverable.

The launching of a volume of this kind in neo-Georgian days by one who began writing in mid-Victorian, and has published nothing to speak of for some years, may seem to call for a few words of excuse or explanation. Whether or no, readers may feel assured that a new book is submitted to them with great hesitation at so belated a date. Insistent practical reasons, however, among which were requests from some illustrious men of letters who are in sympathy with my productions, the accident that several of the poems have already seen the light, and that dozens of them have been lying about for years, compelled the course adopted, in spite of the natural disinclination of a writer whose works have been so frequently regarded askance by a pragmatic section here and there, to draw attention to them once more.

I do not know that it is necessary to say much on the contents of the book, even in deference to suggestions that will be mentioned presently. I believe that those readers who care for my poems at all—readers to whom no passport is required—will care for this new instalment of them, perhaps the last, as much as for any that have preceded them. Moreover, in the eyes of a less friendly class the pieces, though a very mixed collection indeed, contain, so far as I am able to see, little or nothing in technic or teaching that can be considered a Star-Chamber matter, or so much as agitating to a ladies' school; even though, to use Wordsworth's observation in his Preface to *Lyrical Ballads*, such readers may suppose 'that by the act of writing in verse an author makes a formal engagement that he will gratify certain known habits of association: that he not only thus apprises the reader that certain classes of ideas and expressions will be found in his book, but that others will be carefully excluded'.

It is true, nevertheless, that some grave, positive, stark, delineations are interspersed among those of the passive, lighter, and traditional sort presumably nearer to stereotyped tastes. For—while I am quite aware that a thinker is not expected, and, indeed, is scarcely allowed, now more than heretofore, to state all that crosses his mind concerning existence in this universe, in his attempts to explain or excuse the presence of evil and the incongruity of penalizing the irresponsible—it must be obvious to open intelligences that, without denying the beauty and faithful service of certain venerable cults, such disallowance of 'obstinate questionings' and 'blank misgivings' tends to a paralysed intellectual stalemate. Heine observed nearly a hundred years ago that the soul has her eternal rights; that she will not be darkened by statutes, nor lullabied by the music of bells. And what is to-day, in allusions to the present author's pages, alleged to be 'pessimism' is, in truth, only such 'questionings' in the exploration of reality, and is the first step towards the soul's betterment, and the body's also.

If I may be forgiven for quoting my own old words, let me repeat what I printed in this relation more than twenty years ago, and wrote much earlier, in a poem entitled 'In Tenebris':

If way to the Better there be, it exacts a full look at the Worst:

that is to say, by the exploration of reality, and its frank recognition stage by stage along the survey, with an eye to the best consummation possible: briefly, evolutionary meliorism. But it is called pessimism nevertheless; under which word, expressed with condemnatory emphasis, it is regarded by many as some pernicious new thing (though so old as to underlie the Gospel scheme, and even to permeate the Greek drama); and the subject is charitably left to decent silence, as if further comment were needless.

Happily there are some who feel such Levitical passing-by to be, alas, by no means a permanent dismissal of the matter; that comment on where the world stands is very much the reverse of needless in these disordered years of our prematurely afflicted century: that amendment and not madness lies that way. And looking down the future these few hold fast to the same: that whether the human and kindred animal races survive till the exhaustion or destruction of the globe, or whether these races perish and are succeeded by others before that conclusion comes, pain to all upon it, tongued or dumb, shall be kept down to a minimum by loving-kindness, operating through scientific knowledge, and actuated by the modicum of free will conjecturally possessed by organic life when the mighty necessitating forces—unconscious or other—that have 'the balancings of the clouds', happen to be in equilibrium, which may or may not be often.

To conclude this question I may add that the argument of the so-called optimists is neatly summarized in a stern pronouncement against me by my friend Mr. Frederic Harrison in a late essay of his, in the words: 'This view of life is not mine.' The solemn declaration does not seem to me to be so annihilating to the said 'view' (really a series of fugitive impressions which I have never tried to co-ordinate) as is complacently assumed. Surely it embodies a too human fallacy quite familiar in logic. Next, a knowing reviewer, apparently a Roman Catholic young man, speaks, with some rather gross instances of the *suggestio falsi* in his whole article, of 'Mr. Hardy refusing consolation', the 'dark gravity of his ideas', and so on. When a Positivist and a Romanist agree there must be something wonderful in it, which should make a poet sit up. But . . . O that 'twere possible!

I would not have alluded in this place or anywhere else to such casual personal criticisms—for casual and unreflecting they must be—but for the satisfaction of two or three friends in whose opinion a short answer was deemed desirable, on account of the continual repetition of these criticisms, or more precisely, quizzings. After all, the serious and truly literary inquiry in this connection is: Should a shaper of such stuff as dreams are made on disregard considerations of what is customary and expected, and apply himself to the real function of poetry, the application of ideas to life (in Matthew Arnold's familiar phrase)? This bears more particularly on what has been called the 'philosophy' of these poems—usually reproved as 'queer'. Whoever the author may be that undertakes such application of ideas in this 'philosophic' direction—where it is specially required—glacial judgments must inevitably fall upon him amid opinion whose arbiters largely decry individuality, to whom *ideas* are oddities to smile at, who are moved by a yearning the reverse of that of the Athenian inquirers on Mars Hill; and stiffen their features not only at sound of a new thing, but at a restatement of old things in new terms. Hence should anything of this sort in the following adumbrations seem 'queer'—should any of them seem to good

Panglossians to embody strange and disrespectful conceptions of this best of all possible worlds, I apologize; but cannot help it.

Such divergences, which, though piquant for the nonce, it would be affectation to say are not saddening and discouraging likewise, may, to be sure, arise sometimes from superficial aspect only, writer and reader seeing the same thing at different angles. But in palpable cases of divergence they arise, as already said, whenever a serious effort is made towards that which the authority I have cited—who would now be called old-fashioned, possibly even parochial—affirmed to be what no good critic could deny as the poet's province, the application of ideas to life. One might shrewdly guess, by the by, that in such recommendation the famous writer may have overlooked the cold-shouldering results upon an enthusiastic disciple that would be pretty certain to follow his putting the high aim in practice, and have forgotten the disconcerting experience of Gil Blas with the Archbishop.

To add a few more words to what has already taken up too many, there is a contingency liable to miscellanies of verse that I have never seen mentioned, so far as I can remember; I mean the chance little shocks that may be caused over a book of various character like the present and its predecessors by the juxtaposition of unrelated, even discordant, effusions; poems perhaps years apart in the making, yet facing each other. An odd result of this has been that dramatic anecdotes of a satirical and humorous intention following verse in graver voice, have been read as misfires because they raise the smile that they were intended to raise, the journalist, deaf to the sudden change of key, being unconscious that he is laughing with the author and not at him. I admit that I did not foresee such contingencies as I ought to have done, and that people might not perceive when the tone altered. But the difficulties of arranging the themes in a graduated kinship of moods would have been so great that irrelation was almost unavoidable with efforts so diverse. I must trust for right note-catching to those finely-touched spirits who can divine without half a whisper, whose intuitiveness is proof against all the accidents of inconsequence. In respect of the less alert, however, should any one's train of thought be thrown out of gear by a consecuting piping of vocal reeds in jarring tonics, without a semiquaver's rest between, and be led thereby to miss the writer's aim and meaning in one out of two contiguous compositions, I shall deeply regret it.

Having at last, I think, finished with the personal points that I was recommended to notice, I will forsake the immediate object of this Preface; and, leaving *Late Lyrics* to whatever fate it deserves, digress for a few moments to more general considerations. The thoughts of any man of letters concerned to keep poetry alive cannot but run uncomfortably on the precarious prospects of English verse at the present day. Verily the hazards and casualties surrounding the birth and setting forth of almost every modern creation in numbers are ominously like those of one of Shelley's paper-boats on a windy lake. And a forward conjecture scarcely permits the hope of a better time, unless men's tendencies should change. So indeed of all art, literature, and 'high thinking' nowadays. Whether owing to the barbarizing of taste in the younger minds by the dark madness of the late war, the unabashed cultivation of selfishness in all classes, the plethoric growth of knowledge simultaneously with the stunting of wisdom, 'a degrading thirst after outrageous stimulation' (to quote Wordsworth again), or from any other cause, we seem threatened with a new Dark Age.

I formerly thought, like other much exercised writers, that so far as literature was concerned a partial cause might be impotent or mischievous criticism; the satirizing of individuality, the lack of whole-seeing in contemporary estimates of poetry and kindred work, the knowingness affected by junior reviewers, the overgrowth of meticulousness in their peerings for an opinion, as if it were a cultivated habit in them to scrutinize the toll-marks and be blind to the building, to harken for the key-creaks and be deaf to the diapason, to judge the landscape by a nocturnal exploration with a flash-lantern. In other words, to carry on the old game of sampling the poem or drama by quoting the worst line or worst passage only, in ignorance or not of Coleridge's proof that a versification of any length neither can be nor ought to be all poetry; of reading meanings into a book that its author never dreamt of writing there. I might go on interminably.

But I do not now think any such temporary obstructions to be the cause of the hazard, for these negligences and ignorances, though they may have stifled a few true poets in the run of generations, disperse like stricken leaves before the wind of next week, and are no more heard of again in the region of letters than their writers themselves. No: we may be convinced that something of the deeper sort mentioned must be the cause.

In any event poetry, pure literature in general, religion—I include religion, in its essential and undogmatic sense, because poetry and religion touch each other, or rather modulate into each other; are, indeed, often but different names for the same thing—these, I say, the visible signs of mental and emotional life, must like all other things keep moving, becoming; even though at present, when belief in witches of Endor is displacing the Darwinian theory and 'the truth that shall make you free', men's minds appear, as above noted, to be moving backwards rather than on. I speak somewhat sweepingly, and should except many thoughtful writers in verse and prose; also men in certain worthy but small bodies of various denominations, and perhaps in the homely quarter where advance might have been the very least expected a few years back—the English Church—if one reads it rightly as showing evidence of 'removing those things that are shaken', in accordance with the wise Epistolary recommendation to the Hebrews. For since the historic and once august hierarchy of Rome some generation ago lost its chance of being the religion of the future by doing otherwise, and throwing over the little band of New Catholics who were making a struggle for continuity by applying the principle of evolution to their own faith, joining hands with modern science, and outflanking the hesitating English instinct towards liturgical restatement (a flank march which I at the time quite expected to witness, with the gathering of many millions of waiting agnostics into its fold); since then, one may ask, what other purely English establishment than the Church, of sufficient dignity and footing, with such strength of old association, such scope for transmutability, such architectural spell, is left in this country to keep the shreds of morality together? *

It may indeed be a forlorn hope, a mere dream, that of an alliance between religion, which must be retained unless the world is to perish, and complete rationality, which must come, unless also the world is to perish, by means of the interfusing effect of poetry—'the breath and finer spirit of all knowledge; the impassioned expression of science', as it was defined by an English poet who was quite orthodox in his ideas. But if it be

---

* However, one must not be too sanguine in reading signs, and since the above was written evidence that the Church will go far in the removal of 'things that are shaken' has not been encouraging.

true, as Comte argued, that advance is never in a straight line, but in a looped orbit, we may, in the aforesaid ominous moving backward, be doing it *pour mieux sauter*, drawing back for a spring. I repeat that I forlornly hope so, notwithstanding the supercilious regard of hope by Schopenhauer, von Hartmann, and other philosophers down to Einstein who have my respect. But one dares not prophesy. Physical, chronological, and other contingencies keep me in these days from critical studies and literary circles

> Where once we held debate, a band
> Of youthful friends, on mind and art

(if one may quote Tennyson in this century). Hence I cannot know how things are going so well as I used to know them, and the aforesaid limitations must quite prevent my knowing henceforward.

February 1922.

Let Me Enjoy

I

LET me enjoy the earth no less
Because the all-enacting Might
That fashioned forth its loveliness
Had other aims than my delight.

II

About my path there flits a Fair,
Who throws me not a word or sign;
I'll charm me with her ignoring air,
And laud the lips not meant for mine.

III

From manuscripts of moving song
Inspired by scenes and dreams unknown
I'll pour out raptures that belong
To others, as they were my own.

IV

And some day hence, towards Paradise
And all its blest—if such should be—
I will lift glad, afar-off eyes,
Though it contain no place for me.

[April 1909]

He Never Expected Much

[A REFLECTION] ON MY EIGHTY-SIXTH BIRTHDAY

WELL, World, you have kept faith with me,
    Kept faith with me;
Upon the whole you have proved to be
    Much as you said you were.
Since as a child I used to lie
Upon the leaze and watch the sky,
Never, I own, expected I
    That life would all be fair.

'Twas then you said, and since have said,
    Times since have said,
In that mysterious voice you shed
    From clouds and hills around:
'Many have loved me desperately,
Many with smooth serenity,
While some have shown contempt of me
    Till they dropped underground.

'I do not promise overmuch,
    Child; overmuch;
Just neutral-tinted haps and such,'
    You said to minds like mine.
Wise warning for your credit's sake!
Which I for one failed not to take,
And hence could stem such strain and ache
    As each year might assign.

[*c.* 2 June 1926]

During Wind and Rain

THEY sing their dearest songs—
He, she, all of them—yea,
Treble and tenor and bass,
    And one to play;
With the candles mooning each face. . . .
    Ah, no; the years O!
How the sick leaves reel down in throngs!

During Wind and Rain

They clear the creeping moss—
Elders and juniors—aye,
Making the pathways neat
    And the garden gay;
And they build a shady seat. . . .
    Ah, no; the years, the years;
See, the white storm-birds wing across.

They are blithely breakfasting all—
Men and maidens—yea,
Under the summer tree,
    With a glimpse of the bay,
While pet fowl come to the knee. . . .
    Ah, no; the years O!
And the rotten rose is ript from the wall.

They change to a high new house,
He, she, all of them—aye,
Clocks and carpets and chairs
    On the lawn all day,
And brightest things that are theirs. . . .
    Ah, no; the years, the years;
Down their carved names the rain-drop ploughs.

Proud Songsters

THE thrushes sing as the sun is going,
    And the finches whistle in ones and pairs,
And as it gets dark loud nightingales
        In bushes
Pipe, as they can when April wears,
    As if all Time were theirs.

These are brand-new birds of twelve-months' growing,
Which a year ago, or less than twain,
No finches were, nor nightingales,
        Nor thrushes,
But only particles of grain,
    And earth, and air, and rain.

119

Julie-Jane

SING; how 'a would sing!
How 'a would raise the tune
When we rode in the waggon from harvesting
　　By the light o' the moon!

Dance; how 'a would dance!
If a fiddlestring did but sound
She would hold out her coats, give a slanting glance,
　　And go round and round.

Laugh; how 'a would laugh!
Her peony lips would part
As if none such a place for a lover to quaff
　　At the deeps of a heart.

Julie, O girl of joy,
Soon, soon that lover he came.
Ah, yes; and gave thee a baby-boy,
　　But never his name. . . .

—Tolling for her, as you guess;
And the baby too. . . . 'Tis well.
You knew her in maidhood likewise?—Yes,
　　That's her burial bell.

'I suppose,' with a laugh, she said,
'I should blush that I'm not a wife;
But how can it matter, so soon to be dead,
　　What one does in life!'

When we sat making the mourning
By her death-bed side, said she,
'Dears, how can you keep from your lovers, adorning
　　In honour of me!'

Bubbling and brightsome eyed!
But now—O never again.
She chose her bearers before she died
　　From her fancy-men.

NOTE.—It is, or was, a common custom in Wessex, and probably other country places, to prepare the mourning beside the death-bed, the dying person sometimes assisting, who also selects his or her bearers on such occasions.
'Coats' (line 7), old name for petticoats.

The Convergence of the Twain

(*Lines on the loss of the 'Titanic'*)

I

In a solitude of the sea
Deep from human vanity,
And the Pride of Life that planned her, stilly couches she.

II

Steel chambers, late the pyres
Of her salamandrine fires,
Cold currents thrid, and turn to rhythmic tidal lyres.

III

Over the mirrors meant
To glass the opulent
The sea-worm crawls—grotesque, slimed, dumb, indifferent.

IV

Jewels in joy designed
To ravish the sensuous mind
Lie lightless, all their sparkles bleared and black and blind.

V

Dim moon-eyed fishes near
Gaze at the gilded gear   .
And query: 'What does this vaingloriousness down here?' ...

VI

Well: while was fashioning
This creature of cleaving wing,
The Immanent Will that stirs and urges everything

VII

Prepared a sinister mate
For her—so gaily great—
A Shape of Ice, for the time far and dissociate.

VIII

And as the smart ship grew
In stature, grace, and hue,
In shadowy silent distance grew the Iceberg too.

The Convergence of the Twain

IX

Alien they seemed to be:
No mortal eye could see
The intimate welding of their later history,

X

Or sign that they were bent
By paths coincident
On being anon twin halves of one august event,

XI

Till the Spinner of the Years
Said 'Now!' And each one hears,
And consummation comes, and jars two hemispheres.

[24 April 1912]

Logs on the Hearth

A MEMORY OF A SISTER

THE fire advances along the log
Of the tree we felled,
Which bloomed and bore striped apples by the peck
Till its last hour of bearing knelled.

The fork that first my hand would reach
And then my foot
In climbings upward inch by inch, lies now
Sawn, sapless, darkening with soot.

Where the bark chars is where, one year,
It was pruned, and bled—
Then overgrew the wound. But now, at last,
Its growings all have stagnated.

My fellow-climber rises dim
From her chilly grave—
Just as she was, her foot near mine on the bending limb,
Laughing, her young brown hand awave.

December 1915

Going And Staying

I

THE moving sun-shapes on the spray,
The sparkles where the brook was flowing,
Pink faces, plightings, moonlit May,
These were the things we wished would stay;
    But they were going.

II

Seasons of blankness as of snow,
The silent bleed of a world decaying,
The moan of multitudes in woe,
These were the things we wished would go;
    But they were staying.

III

Then we looked closelier at Time,
And saw his ghostly arms revolving
To sweep off woeful things with prime,
Things sinister with things sublime
    Alike dissolving.

Afternoon Service at Mellstock

(*Circa* 1850)

ON afternoons of drowsy calm
    We stood in the panelled pew,
Singing one-voiced a Tate-and-Brady psalm
    To the tune of 'Cambridge New'.

We watched the elms, we watched the rooks,
    The clouds upon the breeze,
Between the whiles of glancing at our books,
    And swaying like the trees.

Afternoon Service at Mellstock

So mindless were those outpourings!—
    Though I am not aware
That I have gained by subtle thought on things
    Since we stood psalming there.

The Impercipient

(AT A CATHEDRAL SERVICE)

THAT with this bright believing band
    I have no claim to be,
That faiths by which my comrades stand
    Seem fantasies to me,
And mirage-mists their Shining Land,
    Is a strange destiny.

Why thus my soul should be consigned
    To infelicity,
Why always I must feel as blind
    To sights my brethren see,
Why joys they've found I cannot find,
    Abides a mystery.

Since heart of mine knows not that ease
    Which they know; since it be
That He who breathes All's Well to these
    Breathes no All's Well to me,
My lack might move their sympathies
    And Christian charity!

I am like a gazer who should mark
    An inland company
Standing upfingered, with, 'Hark! hark!
    The glorious distant sea!'
And feel, 'Alas, 'tis but yon dark
    And wind-swept pine to me!'

The Impercipient

Yet I would bear my shortcomings
    With meet tranquillity,
But for the charge that blessed things
    I'd liefer not have be.
O, doth a bird deprived of wings
    Go earth-bound wilfully!

Enough. As yet disquiet clings
    About us. Rest shall we.

The Oxen

CHRISTMAS EVE, and twelve of the clock.
    'Now they are all on their knees,'
An elder said as we sat in a flock
    By the embers in hearthside ease.

We pictured the meek mild creatures where
    They dwelt in their strawy pen,
Nor did it occur to one of us there
    To doubt they were kneeling then.

So fair a fancy few would weave
    In these years! Yet, I feel,
If someone said on Christmas Eve,
    'Come; see the oxen kneel

'In the lonely barton by yonder coomb
    Our childhood used to know,'
I should go with him in the gloom,
    Hoping it might be so.

1915

Christmas: 1924

'PEACE upon earth!' was said. We sing it,
And pay a million priests to bring it.
After two thousand years of mass
We've got as far as poison-gas.

1924

A Cathedral Façade at Midnight

ALONG the sculptures of the western wall
    I watched the moonlight creeping:
It moved as if it hardly moved at all,
    Inch by inch thinly peeping
Round on the pious figures of freestone, brought
And poised there when the Universe was wrought
To serve its centre, Earth, in mankind's thought.

The lunar look skimmed scantly toe, breast, arm,
    Then edged on slowly, slightly,
To shoulder, hand, face; till each austere form
    Was blanched its whole length brightly
Of prophet, king, queen, cardinal in state,
That dead men's tools had striven to simulate;
And the stiff images stood irradiate.

A frail moan from the martyred saints there set
    Mid others of the erection
Against the breeze, seemed sighings of regret
    At the ancient faith's rejection
Under the sure, unhasting, steady stress
Of Reason's movement, making meaningless
The coded creeds of old-time godliness.

[1897]

By the Earth's Corpse

I

'O LORD, why grievest Thou?—
    Since Life has ceased to be
Upon this globe, now cold
    As lunar land and sea,
And humankind, and fowl, and fur
    Are gone eternally,
All is the same to Thee as ere
    They knew mortality.'

II

'O Time,' replied the Lord,
    'Thou readest me ill, I ween;
Were all *the same*, I should not grieve
    At that late earthly scene,
Now blestly past—though planned by me
    With interest close and keen!—
Nay, nay: things now are *not* the same
    As they have earlier been.

III

    'Written indelibly
    On my eternal mind
    Are all the wrongs endured
    By Earth's poor patient kind,
Which my too oft unconscious hand
    Let enter undesigned.
No god can cancel deeds foredone,
    Or thy old coils unwind!

IV

    'As when, in Noë's days,
    I whelmed the plains with sea,
    So at this last, when flesh
    And herb but fossils be,
And, all extinct, their piteous dust
    Revolves obliviously,
That I made Earth, and life, and man,
    It still repenteth me!'

At a Lunar Eclipse

THY shadow, Earth, from Pole to Central Sea,
Now steals along upon the Moon's meek shine
In even monochrome and curving line
Of imperturbable serenity.

How shall I link such sun-cast symmetry
With the torn troubled form I know as thine,
That profile, placid as a brow divine,
With continents of moil and misery?

And can immense Mortality but throw
So small a shade, and Heaven's high human scheme
Be hemmed within the coasts yon arc implies?

Is such the stellar gauge of earthly show,
Nation at war with nation, brains that teem,
Heroes, and women fairer than the skies?

[186–]

Hap

IF but some vengeful god would call to me
From up the sky, and laugh: 'Thou suffering thing,
Know that thy sorrow is my ecstasy,
That thy love's loss is my hate's profiting!'

Then would I bear it, clench myself, and die,
Steeled by the sense of ire unmerited;
Half-eased in that a Powerfuller than I
Had willed and meted me the tears I shed.

But not so. How arrives it joy lies slain,
And why unblooms the best hope ever sown?
—Crass Casualty obstructs the sun and rain,
And dicing Time for gladness casts a moan. . . .
These purblind Doomsters had as readily strown
Blisses about my pilgrimage as pain.

[16 *Westbourne Park Villas*,] 1866

The Aërolite

I THOUGHT a germ of Consciousness
Escaped on an aërolite
    Aions ago
From some far globe, where no distress
Had means to mar supreme delight;

But only things abode that made
The power to feel a gift uncloyed
    Of gladsome glow,
And life unendingly displayed
Emotions loved, desired, enjoyed.

And that this stray, exotic germ
Fell wanderingly upon our sphere,
    After its wingings,
Quickened, and showed to us the worm
That gnaws vitalities native here,

And operated to unblind
Earth's old-established ignorance
    Of stains and stingings,
Which grin no griefs while not opined,
But cruelly tax intelligence.

'How shall we,' then the seers said,
'Oust this awareness, this disease
    Called sense, here sown,
Though good, no doubt, where it was bred,
And wherein all things work to please?'

Others cried: 'Nay, we rather would,
Since this untoward gift is sent
    For ends unknown,
Limit its registerings to good,
And hide from it all anguishment.'

I left them pondering. This was how
(Or so I dreamed) was waked on earth
    The mortal moan
Begot of sentience. Maybe now
Normal unawareness waits rebirth.

The Unborn

I ROSE at night, and visited
    The Cave of the Unborn:
And crowding shapes surrounded me
For tidings of the life to be,
Who long had prayed the silent Head
    To haste its advent morn.

Their eyes were lit with artless trust,
    Hope thrilled their every tone;
'A scene the loveliest, is it not?
A pure delight, a beauty-spot
Where all is gentle, true and just,
    And darkness is unknown?'

My heart was anguished for their sake,
    I could not frame a word;
And they descried my sunken face,
And seemed to read therein, and trace
The news that pity would not break,
    Nor truth leave unaverred.

And as I silently retired
    I turned and watched them still,
And they came helter-skelter out,
Driven forward like a rabble rout
Into the world they had so desired,
    By the all-immanent Will.

1905

The Reminder

WHILE I watch the Christmas blaze
Paint the room with ruddy rays,
Something makes my vision glide
To the frosty scene outside.

There, to reach a rotting berry,
Toils a thrush,—constrained to very
Dregs of food by sharp distress,
Taking such with thankfulness.

The Reminder

Why, O starving bird, when I
One day's joy would justify,
And put misery out of view,
Do you make me notice you!

The New Dawn's Business

WHAT are you doing outside my walls,
    O Dawn of another day?
I have not called you over the edge
    Of the heathy ledge,
    So why do you come this way,
With your furtive footstep without sound here,
    And your face so deedily grey?

'I show a light for killing the man
    Who lives not far from you,
And for bringing to birth the lady's child,
    Nigh domiciled,
    And for earthing a corpse or two,
And for several other such odd jobs round here
    That Time to-day must do.

'But you he leaves alone (although,
    As you have often said,
You are always ready to pay the debt
    You don't forget
    You owe for board and bed):
The truth is, when men willing are found here
    He takes those loth instead.'

Timing Her

(*Written to an old folk-tune*)

LALAGE's coming:
Where is she now, O?
Turning to bow, O,
And smile, is she,
Just at parting,
Parting, parting,
As she is starting
To come to me?

Where is she now, O,
Now, and now, O,
Shadowing a bough, O,
Of hedge or tree
As she is rushing,
Rushing, rushing,
Gossamers brushing
To come to me?

Lalage's coming;
Where is she now, O;
Climbing the brow, O,
Of hills I see?
Yes, she is nearing,
Nearing, nearing,
Weather unfearing
To come to me.

Near is she now, O,
Now, and now, O;
Milk the rich cow, O,
Forward the tea;
Shake the down bed for her,
Linen sheets spread for her,
Drape round the head for her
Coming to me.

132

Timing Her

Lalage's coming,
She's nearer now, O,
End anyhow, O,
To-day's husbandry!
Would a gilt chair were mine.
Slippers of vair were mine,
Brushes for hair were mine
Of ivory!

What will she think, O,
She who's so comely,
Viewing how homely
A sort are we!
Nothing resplendent,
No prompt attendant,
Not one dependent
Pertaining to me!

Lalage's coming;
Where is she now, O?
Fain I'd avow, O,
Full honestly
Nought here's enough for her,
All is too rough for her,
Even my love for her
Poor in degree.

She's nearer now, O,
Still nearer now, O,
She 'tis, I vow, O,
Passing the lea.
Rushing down to meet her there,
Call out and greet her there,
Never a sweeter there
Crossed to me!

Lalage's come; aye,
Come is she now, O!...
Does Heaven allow, O,
A meeting to be?
Yes, she is here now,
Here now, here now,
Nothing to fear now,
Here's Lalage!

Lines to A Movement in Mozart's E-Flat Symphony

SHOW me again the time
When in the Junetide's prime
We flew by meads and mountains northerly!—
Yea, to such freshness, fairness, fulness, fineness, freeness,
    Love lures life on.

Show me again the day
When from the sandy bay
We looked together upon the pestered sea!—
Yea, to such surging, swaying, sighing, swelling, shrinking,
    Love lures life on.

Show me again the hour
When by the pinnacled tower
We eyed each other and feared futurity!—
Yea, to such bodings, broodings, beatings, blanchings, blessings,
    Love lures life on.

Show me again just this:
The moment of that kiss
Away from the prancing folk, by the strawberry-tree!—
Yea, to such rashness, ratheness, rareness, ripeness, richness,
    Love lures life on.

Begun November 1898

Coming Up Oxford Street: Evening

THE sun from the west glares back,
And the sun from the watered track,
And the sun from the sheets of glass,
And the sun from each window-brass;
Sun-mirrorings, too, brighten
From show-cases beneath
The laughing eyes and teeth
Of ladies who rouge and whiten.
And the same warm god explores
Panels and chinks of doors;
Problems with chymists' bottles
Profound as Aristotle's
He solves, and with good cause,
Having been ere man was.

Also he dazzles the pupils of one who walks west,
A city-clerk, with eyesight not of the best,
Who sees no escape to the very verge of his days
From the rut of Oxford Street into open ways;
And he goes along with head and eyes flagging forlorn,
Empty of interest in things, and wondering why he was born.

As seen July 4, 1872

Epeisodia

I

PAST the hills that peep
Where the leaze is smiling,
On and on beguiling
Crisply-cropping sheep;
Under boughs of brushwood
Linking tree and tree
In a shade of lushwood,
        There caressed we!

135

II

Hemmed by city walls
That outshut the sunlight,
In a foggy dun light,
Where the footstep falls
With a pit-pat wearisome
In its cadency
On the flagstones drearisome
    There pressed we!

III

Where in wild-winged crowds
Blown birds show their whiteness
Up against the lightness
Of the clammy clouds;
By the random river
Pushing to the sea,
Under bents that quiver
    There shall rest we.

Great Things

SWEET cyder is a great thing,
    A great thing to me,
Spinning down to Weymouth town
    By Ridgway thirstily,
And maid and mistress summoning
    Who tend the hostelry:
O cyder is a great thing,
    A great thing to me!

The dance it is a great thing,
    A great thing to me,
With candles lit and partners fit
    For night-long revelry;
And going home when day-dawning
    Peeps pale upon the lea:
O dancing is a great thing,
    A great thing to me!

Great Things

Love is, yea, a great thing,
    A great thing to me,
When, having drawn across the lawn
    In darkness silently,
A figure flits like one a-wing
    Out from the nearest tree:
O love is, yes, a great thing,
    A great thing to me!

Will these be always great things,
    Great things to me? . . .
Let it befall that One will call,
    'Soul, I have need of thee:'
What then? Joy-jaunts, impassioned flings,
    Love, and its ecstasy,
Will always have been great things,
    Great things to me!

Weathers

I

This is the weather the cuckoo likes,
        And so do I;
When showers betumble the chestnut spikes,
        And nestlings fly:
And the little brown nightingale bills his best,
And they sit outside at 'The Travellers' Rest,'
And maids come forth sprig-muslin drest,
And citizens dream of the south and west,
        And so do I.

II

This is the weather the shepherd shuns,
        And so do I;
When beeches drip in browns and duns,
        And thresh, and ply;
And hill-hid tides throb, throe on throe,
And meadow rivulets overflow,
And drops on gate-bars hang in a row,
And rooks in families homeward go,
        And so do I.

Mad Judy

WHEN the hamlet hailed a birth
  Judy used to cry:
When she heard our christening mirth
  She would kneel and sigh.
She was crazed, we knew, and we
Humoured her infirmity.

When the daughters and the sons
  Gathered them to wed,
And we like-intending ones
  Danced till dawn was red,
She would rock and mutter, 'More
Comers to this stony shore!'

When old Headsman Death laid hands
  On a babe or twain,
She would feast, and by her brands
  Sing her songs again.
What she liked we let her do,
Judy was insane, we knew.

The Young Glass-Stainer

'THESE Gothic windows, how they wear me out
With cusp and foil, and nothing straight or square,
Crude colours, leaden borders roundabout,
And fitting in Peter here, and Matthew there!

'What a vocation! Here do I draw now
The abnormal, loving the Hellenic norm;
Martha I paint, and dream of Hera's brow,
Mary, and think of Aphrodite's form.'

[23] November 1893

Tess's Lament

I

I WOULD that folk forgot me quite,
   Forgot me quite!
I would that I could shrink from sight,
  And no more see the sun.
Would it were time to say farewell,
To claim my nook, to need my knell,
Time for them all to stand and tell
  Of my day's work as done.

II

Ah! dairy where I lived so long,
   I lived so long;
Where I would rise up staunch and strong,
  And lie down hopefully.
'Twas there within the chimney-seat
He watched me to the clock's slow beat—
Loved me, and learnt to call me Sweet,
  And whispered words to me.

III

And now he's gone; and now he's he's gone; . . .
   And now he's gone!
The flowers we potted perhaps are thrown
  To rot upon the farm.
And where we had our supper-fire
May now grow nettle, dock, and briar,
And all the place be mould and mire
  So cozy once and warm.

IV

And it was I who did it all,
   Who did it all;
'Twas I who made the blow to fall
  On him who thought no guile.
Well, it is finished—past, and he
Has left me to my misery,
And I must take my Cross on me
  For wronging him awhile.

V

How gay we looked that day we wed,
        That day we wed!
'May joy be with ye!' they all said
        A-standing by the durn.
I wonder what they say o'us now,
And if they know my lot; and how
She feels who milks my favourite cow,
        And takes my place at churn!

VI

It wears me out to think of it,
        To think of it;
I cannot bear my fate as writ,
        I'd have my life unbe;
Would turn my memory to a blot,
Make every relic of me rot,
My doings be as they were not,
        And gone all trace of me!

Lonely Days

LONELY her fate was,
Environed from sight
In the house where the gate was
Past finding at night.
None there to share it,
No one to tell:
Long she'd to bear it,
And bore it well.

Elsewhere just so she
Spent many a day;
Wishing to go she
Continued to stay.
And people without
Basked warm in the air,
But none sought her out,
Or knew she was there.

140

Lonely Days

Even birthdays were passed so,
Sunny and shady:
Years did it last so
For this sad lady.
Never declaring it,
No one to tell,
Still she kept bearing it—
Bore it well.

The days grew chillier,
And then she went
To a city, familiar
In years forespent,
When she walked gaily
Far to and fro,
But now, moving frailly,
Could nowhere go.
The cheerful colour
Of houses she's known
Had died to a duller
And dingier tone.
Streets were now noisy
Where once had rolled
A few quiet coaches,
Or citizens strolled.
Through the party-wall
Of the memoried spot
They danced at a ball
Who recalled her not.
Tramlines lay crossing
Once gravelled slopes,
Metal rods clanked,
And electric ropes.
So she endured it all,
Thin, thinner wrought,
Until time cured it all,
And she knew nought.

Versified from a Diary

141

In a Museum

I

HERE'S the mould of a musical bird long passed from light.
Which over the earth before man came was winging;
There's a contralto voice I heard last night,
That lodges in me still with its sweet singing.

II

Such a dream is Time that the coo of this ancient bird
Has perished not, but is blent, or will be blending
Mid visionless wilds of space with the voice that I heard,
In the full-fugued song of the universe unending.

Exeter [? June 1915]

The Self-Unseeing

HERE is the ancient floor,
Footworn and hollowed and thin,
Here was the former door
Where the dead feet walked in.

She sat here in her chair,
Smiling into the fire;
He who played stood there,
Bowing it higher and higher.

Childlike, I danced in a dream;
Blessings emblazoned that day;
Everything glowed with a gleam;
Yet we were looking away!

The Clasped Skeletons

SURMISED DATE 1800 B.C.

(In an Ancient British barrow near the writer's house)

O WHY did we uncover to view
　　So closely clasped a pair?
Your chalky bedclothes over you,
　　This long time here!

Ere Paris lay with Helena—
　　The poets' dearest dear—
Ere David bedded Bathsheba
　　You two were bedded here.

Aye, even before the beauteous Jael
　　Bade Sisera doff his gear
And lie in her tent; then drove the nail,
　　You two lay here.

Wicked Aholah, in her youth,
　　Colled loves from far and near
Until they slew her without ruth;
　　But you had long colled here.

Aspasia lay with Pericles,
　　And Philip's son found cheer
At eves in lying on Thais' knees
　　While you lay here.

Cleopatra with Antony,
　　Resigned to dalliance sheer,
Lay, fatuous he, insatiate she,
　　Long after you'd lain here.

Pilate by Procula his wife
　　Lay tossing at her tear
Of pleading for an innocent life;
　　You tossed not here.

Ages before Monk Abélard
　　Gained tender Héloïse' ear,
And loved and lay with her till scarred,
　　Had you lain loving here.

143

The Clasped Skeletons

So long, beyond chronology,
    Lovers in death as 'twere,
So long in placid dignity
    Have you lain here!

Yet what is length of time? But dream!
    Once breathed this atmosphere
Those fossils near you, met the gleam
    Of day as you did here;

But so far earlier theirs beside
    Your life-span and career,
That they might style of yestertide
    Your coming here!

Best Times

We went a day's excursion to the stream,
Basked by the bank, and bent to the ripple-gleam,
    And I did not know
    That life would show,
However it might flower, no finer glow.

I walked in the Sunday sunshine by the road
That wound towards the wicket of your abode,
    And I did not think
    That life would shrink
To nothing ere it shed a rosier pink.

Unlooked for I arrived on a rainy night,
And you hailed me at the door by the swaying light,
    And I full forgot
    That life might not
Again be touching that ecstatic height.

And that calm eve when you walked up the stair,
After a gaiety prolonged and rare,
    No thought soever
    That you might never
Walk down again, struck me as I stood there.

Rewritten from an old draft

Shut out that Moon

CLOSE up the casement, draw the blind,
    Shut out that stealing moon,
She wears too much the guise she wore
    Before our lutes were strewn
With years-deep dust, and names we read
    On a white stone were hewn.

Step not forth on the dew-dashed lawn
    To view the Lady's Chair,
Immense Orion's glittering form,
    The Less and Greater Bear:
Stay in; to such sights we were drawn
    When faded ones were fair.

Brush not the bough for midnight scents
    That come forth lingeringly,
And wake the same sweet sentiments
    They breathed to you and me
When living seemed a laugh, and love
    All it was said to be.

Within the common lamp-lit room
    Prison my eyes and thought;
Let dingy details crudely loom,
    Mechanic speech be wrought:
Too fragrant was Life's early bloom,
    Too tart the fruit it brought!

1904

At Day-Close in November

THE ten hours' light is abating,
    And a late bird wings across,
Where the pines, like waltzers waiting,
    Give their black heads a toss.

At Day-Close in November

Beech leaves, that yellow the noon-time,
    Float past like specks in the eye;
I set every tree in my June time,
    And now they obscure the sky.

And the children who ramble through here
    Conceive that there never has been
A time when no tall trees grew here,
    That none will in time be seen.

Amabel

I MARKED her ruined hues,
Her custom-straitened views,
And asked, 'Can there indwell
    My Amabel?'

I looked upon her gown,
Once rose, now earthen brown;
The change was like the knell
    Of Amabel.

Her step's mechanic ways
Had lost the life of May's;
Her laugh, once sweet in swell,
    Spoilt Amabel.

I mused: 'Who sings the strain
I sang ere warmth did wane?
Who thinks its numbers spell
    His Amabel?'—

Knowing that, though Love cease,
Love's race shows no decrease;
All find in dorp or dell
    An Amabel.

—I felt that I could creep
To some housetop, and weep
That Time the tyrant fell
    Ruled Amabel!

146

Amabel

I said (the while I sighed
That love like ours had died),
'Fond things I'll no more tell
    To Amabel,

'But leave her to her fate,
And fling across the gate,
"Till the Last Trump, farewell,
    O Amabel!"'

[16 *Westbourne Park Villas*,] 1865

A Merrymaking in Question

'I WILL get a new string for my fiddle,
    And call to the neighbours to come,
And partners shall dance down the middle
    Until the old pewter-wares hum:
    And we'll sip the mead, cyder, and rum!'

From the night came the oddest of answers:
    A hollow wind, like a bassoon,
And headstones all ranged up as dancers,
    And cypresses droning a croon,
    And gurgoyles that mouthed to the tune.

The Five Students

THE sparrow dips in his wheel-rut bath,
    The sun grows passionate-eyed,
And boils the dew to smoke by the paddock-path;
    As strenuously we stride,—
Five of us; dark He, fair He, dark She, fair She, I,
    All beating by.

The air is shaken, the high-road hot,
    Shadowless swoons the day,
The greens are sobered and cattle at rest; but not
    We on our urgent way,—
Four of us; fair She, dark She, fair He, I, are there,
    But one—elsewhere.

The Five Students

Autumn moulds the hard fruit mellow,
    And forward still we press
Through moors, briar-meshed plantations, clay-pits yellow,
    As in the spring hours—yes,
Three of us; fair He, fair She, I, as heretofore,
    But—fallen one more.

The leaf drops: earthworms draw it in
    At night-time noiselessly,
The fingers of birch and beech are skeleton-thin,
    And yet on the beat are we,—
Two of us; fair She, I. But no more left to go
    The track we know.

Icicles tag the church-aisle leads,
    The flag-rope gibbers hoarse,
The home-bound foot-folk wrap their snow-flaked heads,
    Yet I still stalk the course—
One of us. . . . Dark and fair He, dark and fair She, gone:
    The rest—anon.

The Place on the Map

I

I LOOK upon the map that hangs by me—
Its shires and towns and rivers lined in varnished artistry—
    And I mark a jutting height
Coloured purple, with a margin of blue sea.

II

—'Twas a day of latter summer, hot and dry;
Ay, even the waves seemed drying as we walked on, she and I
    By this spot where, calmly quite,
She unfolded what would happen by and by.

III

This hanging map depicts the coast and place,
And re-creates therewith our unforeboded troublous case
    All distinctly to my sight,
And her tension, and the aspect of her face.

IV

Weeks and weeks we had loved beneath that blazing blue,
Which had lost the art of raining, as her eyes to-day had too,
 While she told what, as by sleight,
Shot our firmament with rays of ruddy hue.

V

For the wonder and the wormwood of the whole
Was that what in realms of reason would have joyed our double
  soul
 Wore a torrid tragic light
Under order-keeping's rigorous control.

VI

So, the map revives her words, the spot, the time,
And the thing we found we had to face before the next year's
  prime;
 The charted coast stares bright,
And its episode comes back in pantomime.

Wessex Heights

THERE are some heights in Wessex, shaped as if by a kindly hand
For thinking, dreaming, dying on, and at crises when I stand,
Say, on Ingpen Beacon eastward, or on Wylls-Neck westwardly,
I seem where I was before my birth, and after death may be.

In the lowlands I have no comrade, not even the lone man's
  friend—
Her who suffereth long and is kind; accepts what he is too weak
  to mend:
Down there they are dubious and askance; there nobody thinks
  as I,
But mind-chains do not clank where one's next neighbour is the
  sky.

149

Wessex Heights

In the towns I am tracked by phantoms having weird detective
    ways—
Shadows of beings who fellowed with myself of earlier days:
They hang about at places, and they say harsh heavy things—
Men with a wintry sneer, and women with tart disparagings.

Down there I seem to be false to myself, my simple self that was,
And is not now, and I see him watching, wondering what crass
    cause
Can have merged him into such a strange continuator as this,
Who yet has something in common with himself, my chrysalis.

I cannot go to the great grey Plain; there's a figure against the
    moon,
Nobody sees it but I, and it makes my breast beat out of tune;
I cannot go to the tall-spired town, being barred by the forms
    now passed
For everybody but me, in whose long vision they stand there fast.

There's a ghost at Yell'ham Bottom chiding loud at the fall of
    the night,
There's a ghost in Froom-side Vale, thin-lipped and vague, in a
    shroud of white,
There is one in the railway train whenever I do not want it near,
I see its profile against the pane, saying what I would not hear.

As for one rare fair woman, I am now but a thought of hers,
I enter her mind and another thought succeeds me that she
    prefers;
Yet my love for her in its fulness she herself even did not know;
Well, time cures hearts of tenderness, and now I can let her go.

So I am found on Ingpen Beacon, or on Wylls-Neck to the west,
Or else on homely Bulbarrow, or little Pilsdon Crest,
Where men have never cared to haunt, nor women have walked
    with me,
And ghosts then keep their distance; and I know some liberty.

14 December 1896

A Thought in Two Moods

I SAW it—pink and white—revealed
    Upon the white and green;
The white and green was a daisied field,
    The pink and white Ethleen.

And as I looked it seemed in kind
    That difference they had none;
The two fair bodiments combined
    As varied miens of one.

A sense that, in some mouldering year,
    As one they both would lie,
Made me move quickly on to her
    To pass the pale thought by.

She laughed and said: 'Out there, to me,
    You looked so weather-browned,
And brown in clothes, you seemed to be
    Made of the dusty ground!'

Seen by the Waits

THROUGH snowy woods and shady
    We went to play a tune
To the lonely manor-lady
    By the light of the Christmas moon.

We violed till, upward glancing
    To where a mirror leaned,
It showed her airily dancing,
    Deeming her movements screened;

151

Dancing alone in the room there,
　　Thin-draped in her robe of night;
Her postures, glassed in the gloom there,
　　Were a strange phantasmal sight.

She had learnt (we heard when homing)
　　That her roving spouse was dead:
Why she had danced in the gloaming
　　We thought, but never said.

Near Lanivet, 1872

THERE was a stunted handpost just on the crest,
　　Only a few feet high:
She was tired, and we stopped in the twilight-time for her rest,
　　At the crossways close thereby.

She leant back, being so weary, against its stem,
　　And laid her arms on its own,
Each open palm stretched out to each end of them,
　　Her sad face sideways thrown.

Her white-clothed form at this dim-lit cease of day
　　Made her look as one crucified
In my gaze at her from the midst of the dusty way,
　　And hurriedly 'Don't,' I cried.

I do not think she heard. Loosing thence she said,
　　As she stepped forth ready to go,
'I am rested now.—Something strange came into my head;
　　I wish I had not leant so!'

And wordless we moved onward down from the hill
　　In the west cloud's murked obscure,
And looking back we could see the handpost still
　　In the solitude of the moor.

'It struck her too,' I thought, for as if afraid
 She heavily breathed as we trailed;
Till she said, 'I did not think how 'twould look in the shade,
 When I leant there like one nailed.'

I, lightly: 'There's nothing in it. For *you*, anyhow!
 —'O I know there is not,' said she . . .
'Yet I wonder . . . If no one is bodily crucified now,
 In spirit one may be!'

And we dragged on and on, while we seemed to see
 In the running of Time's far glass
Her crucified, as she had wondered if she might be
 Some day.—Alas, alas!

Her Dilemma

(IN ⸺ CHURCH)

THE two were silent in a sunless church,
 Whose mildewed walls, uneven paving stones,
And wasted carvings passed antique research;
 And nothing broke the clock's dull monotones.

Leaning against a wormy poppy-head,
 So wan and worn that he could scarcely stand,
—For he was soon to die,—he softly said,
 'Tell me you love me!'—holding long her hand.

She would have given a world to breathe 'yes' truly,
 So much his life seemed hanging on her mind,
And hence she lied, her heart persuaded throughly
 'Twas worth her soul to be a moment kind.

But the sad need thereof, his nearing death,
 So mocked humanity that she shamed to prize
A world conditioned thus, or care for breath
 Where Nature such dilemmas could devise.

1866

'Ah, are you Digging on my Grave?'

'AH, are you digging on my grave,
      My loved one?—planting rue?'
—'No: yesterday he went to wed
One of the brightest wealth has bred.
"It cannot hurt her now," he said,
      "That I should not be true."'

'Then who is digging on my grave?
      My nearest dearest kin?'
—'Ah, no: they sit and think, "What use!
What good will planting flowers produce?
No tendance of her mound can loose
      Her spirit from Death's gin."'

'But some one digs upon my grave?
      My enemy?—prodding sly?'
—'Nay: when she heard you had passed the Gate
That shuts on all flesh soon or late,
She thought you no more worth her hate,
      And cares not where you lie.'

'Then, who is digging on my grave?
      Say—since I have not guessed!'
—'O it is I, my mistress dear,
Your little dog, who still lives near,
And much I hope my movements here
      Have not disturbed your rest?'

'Ah, yes! *You* dig upon my grave . . .
      Why flashed it not on me
That one true heart was left behind!
What feeling do we ever find
To equal among human kind
      A dog's fidelity!'

'Mistress, I dug upon your grave
      To bury a bone, in case
I should be hungry near this spot
When passing on my daily trot.
I am sorry, but I quite forgot
      It was your resting-place.'

A Wife Comes Back

THIS is the story a man told me
Of his life's one day of dreamery.

A woman came into his room
Between the dawn and the creeping day:
She was the years-wed wife from whom
He had parted, and who lived far away,
    As if strangers they.

He wondered, and as she stood
She put on youth in her look and air,
And more was he wonderstruck as he viewed
Her form and flesh bloom yet more fair
    While he watched her there;

Till she freshed to the pink and brown
That were hers on the night when first they met,
When she was the charm of the idle town,
And he the pick of the club-fire set. . . .
    His eyes grew wet,

And he stretched his arms: 'Stay—rest!—'
He cried. 'Abide with me so, my own!'
But his arms closed in on his hard bare breast;
She had vanished with all he had looked upon
    Of her beauty: gone.

He clothed, and drew downstairs,
But she was not in the house, he found;
And he passed out under the leafy pairs
Of the avenue elms, and searched around
    To the park-pale bound.

He mounted, and rode till night
To the city to which she had long withdrawn,
The vision he bore all day in his sight
Being her young self as pondered on
    In the dim of dawn.

'—The lady here long ago—
Is she now here?—young—or such age as she is?'
'—She is still here.'—'Thank God. Let her know;
She'll pardon a comer so late as this
    Whom she'd fain not miss.'

A Wife Comes Back

She received him—an ancient dame,
Who hemmed, with features frozen and numb,
'How strange!—I'd almost forgotten your name!—
A call just now—is troublesome;
    Why did you come?'

Satires of Circumstance

IN FIFTEEN GLIMPSES

I. AT TEA

THE kettle descants in a cosy drone,
And the young wife looks in her husband's face,
And then at her guest's, and shows in her own
Her sense that she fills an envied place;
And the visiting lady is all abloom,
And says there was never so sweet a room.

And the happy young housewife does not know
That the woman beside her was first his choice,
Till the fates ordained it could not be so. . . .
Betraying nothing in look or voice
The guest sits smiling and sips her tea,
And he throws her a stray glance yearningly.

II. IN CHURCH

'AND now to God the Father,' he ends,
And his voice thrills up to the topmost tiles:
Each listener chokes as he bows and bends,
And emotion pervades the crowded aisles.
Then the preacher glides to the vestry-door,
And shuts it, and thinks he is seen no more.

The door swings softly ajar meanwhile,
And a pupil of his in the Bible class,
Who adores him as one without gloss or guile,
Sees her idol stand with a satisfied smile
And re-enact at the vestry-glass
Each pulpit gesture in deft dumb-show
That had moved the congregation so.

Satires of Circumstance

VI. IN THE CEMETERY

'You see those mothers squabbling there?'
Remarks the man of the cemetery.
'One says in tears, "'*Tis mine lies here!*"
Another, "*Nay, mine, you Pharisee!*"
Another, "*How dare you move my flowers
And put your own on this grave of ours!*"
But all their children were laid therein
At different times, like sprats in a tin.

'And then the main drain had to cross,
And we moved the lot some nights ago,
And packed them away in the general foss
With hundreds more. But their folks don't know,
And as well cry over a new-laid drain
As anything else, to ease your pain!'

VIII. IN THE STUDY

He enters, and mute on the edge of a chair
Sits a thin-faced lady, a stranger there,
A type of decayed gentility;
And by some small signs he well can guess
That she comes to him almost breakfastless.

'I have called—I hope I do not err—
I am looking for a purchaser
Of some score volumes of the works
Of eminent divines I own,—
Left by my father—though it irks
My patience to offer them.' And she smiles
As if necessity were unknown;
'But the truth of it is that oftenwhiles
I have wished, as I am fond of art,
To make my rooms a little smart,
And these old books are so in the way.'
And lightly still she laughs to him,
As if to sell were a mere gay whim,
And that, to be frank, Life were indeed
To her not vinegar and gall,
But fresh and honey-like; and Need
No household skeleton at all.

XII. AT THE DRAPER'S

'I STOOD at the back of the shop, my dear,
    But you did not perceive me.
Well, when they deliver what you were shown
    I shall know nothing of it, believe me!'

And he coughed and coughed as she paled and said,
    'O, I didn't see you come in there—
Why couldn't you speak?'—'Well, I didn't. I left
    That you should not notice I'd been there.

'You were viewing some lovely things. "*Soon required
    For a widow, of latest fashion*";
And I knew 'twould upset you to meet the man
    Who had to be cold and ashen

'And screwed in a box before they could dress you
    "*In the last new note in mourning,*"
As they defined it. So, not to distress you,
    I left you to your adorning.'

XV. IN THE MOONLIGHT

'O LONELY workman, standing there
In a dream, why do you stare and stare
At her grave, as no other grave there were?

'If your great gaunt eyes so importune
Her soul by the shine of this corpse-cold moon,
Maybe you'll raise her phantom soon!'

'Why, fool, it is what I would rather see
Than all the living folk there be;
But alas, there is no such joy for me!'

'Ah—she was one you loved, no doubt,
Through good and evil, through rain and drought,
And when she passed, all your sun went out?'

'Nay: she was the woman I did not love,
Whom all the others were ranked above,
Whom during her life I thought nothing of.'

1910

Neutral Tones

WE stood by a pond that winter day,
And the sun was white, as though chidden of God,
And a few leaves lay on the starving sod;
    —They had fallen from an ash, and were grey.

Your eyes on me were as eyes that rove
Over tedious riddles of years ago;
And some words played between us to and fro
    On which lost the more by our love.

The smile on your mouth was the deadest thing
Alive enough to have strength to die;
And a grin of bitterness swept thereby
    Like an ominous bird a-wing. . . .

Since then, keen lessons that love deceives,
And wrings with wrong, have shaped to me
Your face, and the God-curst sun, and a tree,
    And a pond edged with greyish leaves.

[*16 Westbourne Park Villas,*] 1867

Faintheart in a Railway Train

AT nine in the morning there passed a church,
At ten there passed me by the sea,
At twelve a town of smoke and smirch,
At two a forest of oak and birch,
    And then, on a platform, she:

A radiant stranger, who saw not me.
I said, 'Get out to her do I dare?'
But I kept my seat in my search for a plea,
And the wheels moved on. O could it but be
    That I had alighted there!

'We Sat at the Window'

(*Bournemouth*, 1875)

WE sat at the window looking out,
And the rain came down like silken strings
That Swithin's day. Each gutter and spout
Babbled unchecked in the busy way
    Of witless things:
Nothing to read, nothing to see
Seemed in that room for her and me
      On Swithin's day.

We were irked by the scene, by our own selves; yes,
For I did not know, nor did she infer
How much there was to read and guess
By her in me, and to see and crown
    By me in her.
Wasted were two souls in their prime,
And great was the waste, that July time
      When the rain came down.

The Division

RAIN on the windows, creaking doors,
    With blasts that besom the green,
And I am here, and you are there,
    And a hundred miles between!

O were it but the weather, Dear,
    O were it but the miles
That summed up all our severance,
    There might be room for smiles.

But that thwart thing betwixt us twain,
    Which nothing cleaves or clears,
Is more than distance, Dear, or rain,
    And longer than the years!

1893

Thoughts of Phena at News of her Death

NOT a line of her writing have I,
       Not a thread of her hair,
No mark of her late time as dame in her dwelling, whereby
       I may picture her there;
   And in vain do I urge my unsight
       To conceive my lost prize
At her close, whom I knew when her dreams were upbrimming
       with light,
       And with laughter her eyes.

What scenes spread around her last days,
       Sad, shining, or dim?
Did her gifts and compassions enray and enarch her sweet ways
       With an aureate nimb?
   Or did life-light decline from her years,
       And mischances control
Her full day-star; unease, or regret, or forebodings, or fears
       Disennoble her soul?

Thus I do but the phantom retain
       Of the maiden of yore
As my relic; yet haply the best of her—fined in my brain
       It may be the more
   That no line of her writing have I,
       Nor a thread of her hair,
No mark of her late time as dame in her dwelling, whereby
       I may picture her there.

March 1890

The Harbour Bridge

FROM here, the quay, one looks above to mark
The bridge across the harbour, hanging dark
Against the day's-end sky, fair-green in glow
Over and under the middle archway's bow:
It draws its skeleton where the sun has set,
Yea, clear from cutwater to parapet;
On which mild glow, too, lines of rope and spar
       Trace themselves black as char.

161

The Harbour Bridge

Down here in shade we hear the painters shift
Against the bollards with a drowsy lift,
As moved by the incoming stealthy tide.
High up across the bridge the burghers glide
As cut black-paper portraits hastening on
In conversation none knows what upon:
Their sharp-edged lips move quickly word by word
       To speech that is not heard.

There trails the dreamful girl, who leans and stops,
There presses the practical woman to the shops,
There is a sailor, meeting his wife with a start,
And we, drawn nearer, judge they are keeping apart.
Both pause. She says: 'I've looked for you. I thought
We'd make it up.' Then no words can be caught.
At last: 'Won't you come home?' She moves still nigher:
       ''Tis comfortable, with a fire.'

'No,' he says gloomily. 'And, anyhow,
I can't give up the other woman now:
You should have talked like that in former days,
When I was last home.' They go different ways.
And the west dims, and yellow lamplights shine:
And soon above, like lamps more opaline,
White stars ghost forth, that care not for men's wives,
       Or any other lives.

Weymouth

At Rushy-Pond

ON the frigid face of the heath-hemmed pond
       There shaped the half-grown moon:
Winged whiffs from the north with a husky croon
       Blew over and beyond.

And the wind flapped the moon in its float on the pool,
       And stretched it to oval form;
Then corkscrewed it like a wriggling worm;
       Then wanned it weariful.

And I cared not for conning the sky above
    Where hung the substant thing,
For my thought was earthward sojourning
    On the scene I had vision of.

Since there it was once, in a secret year,
    I had called a woman to me
From across this water, ardently—
    And practised to keep her near;

Till the last weak love-words had been said,
    And ended was her time,
And blurred the bloomage of her prime,
    And white the earlier red.

And the troubled orb in the pond's sad shine
    Was her very wraith, as scanned
When she withdrew thence, mirrored, and
    Her days dropped out of mine.

Lost Love

I PLAY my sweet old airs—
    The airs he knew
    When our love was true—
    But he does not balk
    His determined walk,
And passes up the stairs.

I sing my songs once more,
    And presently hear
    His footstep near
    As if it would stay;
    But he goes his way,
And shuts a distant door.

So I wait for another morn,
    And another night
    In this soul-sick blight;
    And I wonder much
    As I sit, why such
A woman as I was born!

The Protean Maiden

(SONG)

THIS single girl is two girls:
  How strange such things should be!
One noon eclipsed by few girls,
  The next no beauty she.

And daily cries the lover,
  In voice and feature vext:
'My last impression of her
  Is never to be the next!

'She's plain: I will forget her!
  She's turned to fair. Ah no,
Forget?—not I! I'll pet her
  With kisses swift and slow.'

The Ruined Maid

'O 'MELIA, my dear, this does everything crown!
Who could have supposed I should meet you in Town?
And whence such fair garments, such prosperi-ty?'—
'O didn't you know I'd been ruined?' said she.

—'You left us in tatters, without shoes or socks,
Tired of digging potatoes, and spudding up docks;
And now you've gay bracelets and bright feathers three!'—
'Yes: that's how we dress when we're ruined,' said she.

—'At home in the barton you said "thee" and "thou,"
And "thik oon," and "theäs oon," and "t'other"; but now
Your talking quite fits 'ee for high compa-ny!'—
'Some polish is gained with one's ruin,' said she.

—'Your hands were like paws then, your face blue and bleak
But now I'm bewitched by your delicate cheek,
And your little gloves fit as on any la-dy!'—
'We never do work when we're ruined,' said she.

—'You used to call home-life a hag-ridden dream,
And you'd sigh, and you'd sock; but at present you seem
To know not of megrims or melancho-ly!'—
'True. One's pretty lively when ruined,' said she.

The Ruined Maid

—'I wish I had feathers, a fine sweeping gown,
And a delicate face, and could strut about Town!'—
'My dear—a raw country girl, such as you be,
Cannot quite expect that. You ain't ruined,' said she.

[16 Westbourne Park Villas] 1866

At the Word 'Farewell'

SHE looked like a bird from a cloud
    On the clammy lawn,
Moving alone, bare-browed
    In the dim of dawn.
The candles alight in the room
    For my parting meal
Made all things withoutdoors loom
    Strange, ghostly, unreal.

The hour itself was a ghost,
    And it seemed to me then
As of chances the chance furthermost
    I should see her again.
I beheld not where all was so fleet
    That a Plan of the past
Which had ruled us from birthtime to meet
    Was in working at last:

No prelude did I there perceive
    To a drama at all,
Or foreshadow what fortune might weave
    From beginnings so small;
But I rose as if quicked by a spur
    I was bound to obey,
And stepped through the casement to her
    Still alone in the grey.

'I am leaving you. . . . Farewell!' I said,
    As I followed her on
By an alley bare boughs overspread;
    'I soon must be gone!'
Even then the scale might have been turned
    Against love by a feather,
—But crimson one cheek of hers burned
    When we came in together.

A Countenance

HER laugh was not in the middle of her face quite,
   As a gay laugh springs,
It was plain she was anxious about some things
   I could not trace quite.
Her curls were like fir-cones—piled up, brown—
   Or rather like tight-tied sheaves:
It seemed they could never be taken down. ...

And her lips were too full, some might say:
I did not think so. Anyway,
The shadow her lower one would cast
Was green in hue whenever she passed
   Bright sun on midsummer leaves.
Alas, I knew not much of her,
And lost all sight and touch of her!

If otherwise, should I have minded
The shy laugh not in the middle of her mouth quite,
And would my kisses have died of drouth quite
   As love became unblinded?

1884

The Bride-Night Fire

'O Tim, my *own* Tim I must call 'ee—I will!
　　All the world has turned round on me so!
Can you help her who loved 'ee, though acting so ill?
Can you pity her misery—feel for her still?
When worse than her body so quivering and chill
　　Is her heart in its winter o' woe!

'I think I mid[1] almost ha' borne it,' she said,
　　'Had my griefs one by one come to hand;
But O, to be slave to thik husbird,[2] for bread,
And then, upon top o' that, driven to wed,
And then, upon top o' that, burnt out o' bed,
　　Is more than my nater can stand!'

Like a lion 'ithin en Tim's spirit outsprung—
(Tim had a great soul when his feelings were wrung)—
　　'Feel for 'ee, dear Barbree?' he cried;
And his warm working-jacket then straightway he flung
Round about her, and horsed her by jerks, till she clung
Like a chiel on a gipsy, her figure uphung
　　By the sleeves that he tightly had tied.

Over piggeries, and mixens,[3] and apples, and hay,
　　They lumpered[4] straight into the night;
And finding ere long where a halter-path[5] lay,
Sighted Tim's house by dawn, on'y seen on their way
By a naibour or two who were up wi' the day,
　　But who gathered no clue to the sight.

Then tender Tim Tankens he searched here and there
　　For some garment to clothe her fair skin;
But though he had breeches and waistcoats to spare,
He had nothing quite seemly for Barbree to wear,
Who, half shrammed[6] to death, stood and cried on a chair
　　At the caddle[7] she found herself in.

There was one thing to do, and that one thing he did,
　　He lent her some clothes of his own,
And she took 'em perforce; and while swiftly she slid
Them upon her Tim turned to the winder, as bid,
Thinking, 'O that the picter my duty keeps hid
　　To the sight o' my eyes mid[8] be shown!'

---

[1] *mid*, might.　　　　　　　　[2] *thik husbird*, that rascal.
[3] *mixens*, manure-heaps.　　　[4] *lumpered*, stumbled.
[5] *halter-path*, bridle-path.　　[6] *shrammed*, numbed.
[7] *caddle*, quandary.　　　　　[8] *mid*, might.

171

The Bride-Night Fire

In the tallet[1] he stowed her; there huddied[2] she lay,
   Shortening sleeves, legs, and tails to her limbs;
But most o' the time in a mortal bad way,
Well knowing that there'd be the divel to pay
If 'twere found that, instead o' the element's prey,
   She was living in lodgings at Tim's.

'Where's the tranter?' said men and boys; 'where can he be?'
   'Where's the tranter?' said Barbree alone.
'Where on e'th is the tranter?' said everybod-y:
They sifted the dust of his perished roof-tree,
   And all they could find was a bone.

Then the uncle cried, 'Lord, pray have mercy on me!'
   And in terror began to repent.
But before 'twas complete, and till sure she was free,
Barbree drew up her loft-ladder, tight turned her key—
Tim bringing up breakfast and dinner and tea—
   Till the news of her hiding got vent.

Then followed the custom-kept rout, shout, and flare
Of a skimmity-ride[3] through the naibourhood, ere
   Folk had proof o' wold[4] Sweatley's decay.
Whereupon decent people all stood in a stare,
Saying Tim and his lodger should risk it, and pair:
So he took her to church. An' some laughing lads there
Cried to Tim, 'After Sweatley!' She said, 'I declare
   I stand as a maiden to-day!'

Written 1866; *printed* 1875

---

[1] *tallet*, loft.
[2] *huddied*, hidden.
[3] *skimmity-ride*, satirical procession with effigies.
[4] *wold*, old.

The Chapel-Organist

(A.D. 185–)

I'VE been thinking it through, as I play here to-night, to play
    never again,
By the light of that lowering sun peering in at the window-pane,
And over the back-street roofs, throwing shades from the boys
    of the chore
In the gallery, right upon me, sitting up to these keys once
    more. . . .

How I used to hear tongues ask, as I sat here when I was new:
'Who is she playing the organ? She touches it mightily true!'
'She travels from Havenpool Town,' the deacon would softly
    speak,
'The stipend can hardly cover her fare hither twice in the week.'
(It fell far short of doing, indeed; but I never told,
For I have craved minstrelsy more than lovers, or beauty, or gold.)

'Twas so he answered at first, but the story grew different later:
'It cannot go on much longer, from what we hear of her now!'
At the meaning wheeze in the words the inquirer would shift his
    place
Till he could see round the curtain that screened me from people
    below.
'A handsome girl,' he would murmur, upstaring (and so I am).
'But—too much sex in her build; fine eyes, but eyelids too heavy;
A bosom too full for her age; in her lips too voluptuous a dye.'
(It may be. But who put it there? Assuredly it was not I.)

I went on playing and singing when this I had heard, and more,
Though tears half-blinded me; yes, I remained going on and on,
Just as I used me to chord and to sing at the selfsame time! . . .
For it's a contralto—my voice is; they'll hear it again here to-night
In the psalmody notes that I love far beyond every lower delight.

Well, the deacon, in fact, that day had learnt new tidings about
    me;
They troubled his mind not a little, for he was a worthy man.
(He trades as a chemist in High Street, and during the week he
    had sought
His fellow-deacon, who throve as a bookbinder over the way.)

173

'These are strange rumours,' he said. 'We must guard the good
  name of the chapel.
If, sooth, she's of evil report, what else can we do but dismiss
  her?'
'—But get such another to play here we cannot for double the
  price!'
It settled the point for the time, and I triumphed awhile in their
  strait,
And my much-beloved grand semibreves went living on, pending
  my fate.

At length in the congregation more headshakes and murmurs
  were rife,
And my dismissal was ruled, though I was not warned of it then.
But a day came when they declared it. The news entered me as a
  sword;
I was broken; so pallid of face that they thought I should faint,
  they said.
I rallied. 'O, rather than go, I will play you for nothing!' said I.
'Twas in much desperation I spoke it, for bring me to forfeit I
  could not
Those melodies chorded so richly for which I had laboured and
  lived.
They paused. And for nothing I played at the chapel through
  Sundays again,
Upheld by that art which I loved more than blandishments
  lavished of men.

But it fell that murmurs anew from the flock broke the pastor's
  peace.
Some member had seen me at Havenpool, comrading close a
  sea-captain.
(O yes; I was thereto constrained, lacking means for the fare to
  and fro.)
Yet God knows, if aught He knows ever, I loved the Old-
  Hundredth, Saint Stephen's,
Mount Zion, New Sabbath, Miles-Lane, Holy Rest, and Arabia,
  and Eaton,
Above all embraces of body by wooers who sought me and
  won! . . .
Next week 'twas declared I was seen coming home with a swain
  ere the sun.
The deacons insisted then, strong; and forgiveness I did not
  implore.

I saw all was lost for me, quite, but I made a last bid in my
     throbs.
My bent, finding victual in lust, men's senses had libelled my soul,
But the soul should die game, if I knew it! I turned to my masters
     and said:
'I yield, Gentlemen, without parlance. But—let me just hymn
     you *once* more!

It's a little thing, Sirs, that I ask; and a passion is music with me!'
They saw that consent would cost nothing, and show as good
     grace, as knew I,
Though tremble I did, and feel sick, as I paused thereat, dumb
     for their words.
They gloomily nodded assent, saying, 'Yes, if you care to. Once
     more,
And only once more, understand.' To that with a bend I agreed.
—'You've a fixed and a-far-reaching look,' spoke one who had
     eyed me awhile.
'I've a fixed and a far-reaching plan, and my look only showed
     it,' I smile.

This evening of Sunday is come—the last of my functioning here.
'She plays as if she were possessed!' they exclaim, glancing
     upward and round.
'Such harmonies I never dreamt the old instrument capable of!'
Meantime the sun lowers and goes; shades deepen; the lights are
     turned up,
And the people voice out the last singing: tune Tallis: the Evening
     Hymn.
(I wonder Dissenters sing Ken: it shows them more liberal in
     spirit
At this little chapel down here than at certain new others I know.)
I sing as I play. Murmurs some one: 'No woman's throat richer
     than hers!'
'True: in these parts,' think I. 'But, my man, never more will its
     richness outspread.'
And I sing with them onward: 'The grave dread as little do I as
     my bed.'

I lift up my feet from the pedals; and then, while my eyes are still
     wet
From the symphonies born of my fingers, I do that whereon I
     am set,
And draw from my 'full round bosom' (their words; how can *I*
     help its heave?)
A bottle blue-coloured and fluted—a vinaigrette, they may
     conceive—

175

And before the choir measures my meaning, reads aught in my
    moves to and fro,
I drink from the phial at a draught, and they think it a pick-me-up;
    so.
Then I gather my books as to leave, bend over the keys as to
    pray.
When they come to me motionless, stooping, quick death will
    have whisked me away.

'Sure, nobody meant her to poison herself in her haste, after all!'
The deacons will say as they carry me down and the night
    shadows fall,
'Though the charges were true,' they will add. 'It's a case red
    as scarlet withal!'
I have never once minced it. Lived chaste I have not. Heaven
    knows it above! . . .
But past all the heavings of passion—it's music has been my
    life-love! . . .
That tune did go well—this last playing! . . . I reckon they'll
    bury me here. . . .
Not a soul from the seaport my birthplace—will come, or bestow
    me . . . a tear.

In the Servants' Quarters

'MAN, you too, aren't you, one of these rough followers of the
    criminal?
All hanging hereabout to gather how he's going to bear
Examination in the hall.' She flung disdainful glances on
The shabby figure standing at the fire with others there,
    Who warmed them by its flare.

'No indeed, my skipping maiden: I know nothing of the trial
    here,
Or criminal, if so he be.—I chanced to come this way,
And the fire shone out into the dawn, and morning airs are cold
    now;
I, too, was drawn in part by charms I see before me play,
    That I see not every day.'

'Ha, ha!' then laughed the constables who also stood to warm
      themselves,
The while another maiden scrutinized his features hard,
As the blaze threw into contrast every line and knot that wrinkled
      them,
Exclaiming, 'Why, last night when he was brought in by the
      guard,
      You were with him in the yard!'

'Nay, nay, you teasing wench, I say! You know you speak
      mistakenly.
Cannot a tired pedestrian who has legged it long and far
Here on his way from northern parts, engrossed in humble
      marketings,
Come in and rest awhile, although judicial doings are
      Afoot by morning star?'

'O, come, come!' laughed the constables. 'Why, man, you speak
      the dialect
He uses in his answers; you can hear him up the stairs.
So own it. We sha'n't hurt ye. There he's speaking now! His
      syllables
Are those you sound yourself when you are talking unawares,
      As this pretty girl declares.'

'And you shudder when his chain clinks!' she rejoined. 'O yes,
      I noticed it.
And you winced, too, when those cuffs they gave him echoed to
      us here.
They'll soon be coming down, and you may then have to defend
      yourself
Unless you hold your tongue, or go away and keep you clear
      When he's led to judgment near!'

'No! I'll be damned in hell if I know about the man!
No single thing about him more than everybody knows!
Must not I even warm my hands but I am charged with
      blasphemies?' . . .
—His face convulses as the morning cock that moment crows,
      And he droops, and turns, and goes.

A Trampwoman's Tragedy

(182—)

I

FROM Wynyard's Gap the livelong day
    The livelong day,
We beat afoot the northward way
    We had travelled times before.
The sun-blaze burning on our backs,
Our shoulders sticking to our packs,
By fosseway, fields, and turnpike tracks
    We skirted sad Sedge-Moor.

II

Full twenty miles we jaunted on,
    We jaunted on,—
My fancy-man, and jeering John,
    And Mother Lee, and I.
And, as the sun drew down to west,
We climbed the toilsome Poldon crest,
And saw, of landskip sights the best,
    The inn that beamed thereby.

III

For months we had padded side by side,
    Ay, side by side
Through the Great Forest, Blackmoor wide,
    And where the Parret ran.
We'd faced the gusts on Mendip ridge,
Had crossed the Yeo unhelped by bridge,
Been stung by every Marshwood midge,
    I and my fancy-man.

A Trampwoman's Tragedy

IV

Lone inns we loved, my man and I,
    My man and I;
'King's Stag,' 'Windwhistle' high and dry,
    'The Horse' on Hintock Green,
The cosy house at Wynyard's Gap,
'The Hut' renowned on Bredy Knap,
And many another wayside tap
    Where folk might sit unseen.

V

Now as we trudged—O deadly day,
    O deadly day!—
I teased my fancy-man in play
    And wanton idleness.
I walked alongside jeering John,
I laid his hand my waist upon;
I would not bend my glances on
    My lover's dark distress.

VI

Thus Poldon top at last we won,
    At last we won,
And gained the inn at sink of sun
    Far-famed as 'Marshal's Elm.'
Beneath us figured tor and lea,
From Mendip to the western sea—
I doubt if finer sight there be
    Within this royal realm.

'Windwhistle' (Stanza IV). The highness and dryness of Windwhistle Inn was impressed upon the writer two or three years ago, when, after climbing on a hot afternoon to the beautiful spot near which it stands and entering the inn for tea, he was informed by the landlady that none could be had, unless he would fetch water from a valley half a mile off, the house containing not a drop, owing to its situation. However, a tantalizing row of full barrels behind her back testified to a wetness of a certain sort, which was not at that time desired.

'Marshal's Elm' (Stanza VI), so picturesquely situated, is no longer an inn, though the house, or part of it, still remains. It used to exhibit a fine old swinging sign.

VII

Inside the settle all a-row—
    All four a-row
We sat, I next to John, to show
    That he had wooed and won.
And then he took me on his knee,
And swore it was his turn to be
My favoured mate, and Mother Lee
    Passed to my former one.

VIII

Then in a voice I had never heard,
    I had never heard,
My only Love to me: 'One word,
    My lady, if you please!
Whose is the child you are like to bear?—
His? After all my months o' care?'
God knows 'twas not! But, O despair!
    I nodded—still to tease.

IX

Then up he sprung, and with his knife—
    And with his knife
He let out jeering Johnny's life,
    Yes; there, at set of sun.
The slant ray through the window nigh
Gilded John's blood and glazing eye,
Ere scarcely Mother Lee and I
    Knew that the deed was done.

X

The taverns tell the gloomy tale,
    The gloomy tale,
How that at Ivel-chester jail
    My Love, my sweetheart swung;
Though stained till now by no misdeed
Save one horse ta'en in time o' need;
(Blue Jimmy stole right many a steed
    Ere his last fling he flung.)

A Trampwoman's Tragedy

XI

Thereaft I walked the world alone,
    Alone, alone!
On his death-day I gave my groan
    And dropt his dead-born child.
'Twas nigh the jail, beneath a tree,
None tending me; for Mother Lee
Had died at Glaston, leaving me
    Unfriended on the wild.

XII

And in the night as I lay weak,
    As I lay weak,
The leaves a-falling on my cheek,
    The red moon low declined—
The ghost of him I'd die to kiss
Rose up and said: 'Ah, tell me this!
Was the child mine, or was it his?
    Speak, that I rest may find!'

XIII

O doubt not but I told him then,
    I told him then,
That I had kept me from all men
    Since we joined lips and swore.
Whereat he smiled, and thinned away
As the wind stirred to call up day . . .
—'Tis past! And here alone I stray
    Haunting the Western Moor.

April 1902.

'Blue Jimmy' (Stanza x) was a notorious horse-stealer of Wessex in those days, who appropriated more than a hundred horses before he was caught, among others one belonging to a neighbour of the writer's grandfather. He was hanged at the now demolished Ivel-chester or Ilchester jail above mentioned—that building formerly of so many sinister associations in the minds of the local peasantry, and the continual haunt of fever, which at last led to its condemnation. Its site is now an innocent-looking green meadow.

'When I Set Out for Lyonnesse'

(1870)

WHEN I set out for Lyonnesse,
　　A hundred miles away,
　　The rime was on the spray,
And starlight lit my lonesomeness
When I set out for Lyonnesse
　　A hundred miles away.

What would bechance at Lyonnesse
　　While I should sojourn there
　　No prophet durst declare,
Nor did the wisest wizard guess
What would bechance at Lyonnesse
　　While I should sojourn there.

When I came back from Lyonnesse
　　With magic in my eyes,
　　All marked with mute surmise
My radiance rare and fathomless,
When I came back from Lyonnesse
　　With magic in my eyes!

'A Man was Drawing Near to Me'

ON that grey night of mournful drone,
Apart from aught to hear, to see,
I dreamt not that from shires unknown
　　In gloom, alone,
　　By Halworthy,
A man was drawing near to me.

I'd no concern at anything,
No sense of coming pull-heart play;
Yet, under the silent outspreading
　　Of even's wing
　　Where Otterham lay,
A man was riding up my way.

'A Man was Drawing Near to Me'

I thought of nobody—not of one,
But only of trifles—legends, ghosts—
Though, on the moorland dim and dun
    That travellers shun
    About these coasts,
The man had passed Tresparret Posts.

There was no light at all inland,
Only the seaward pharos-fire,
Nothing to let me understand
    That hard at hand
    By Hennett Byre
The man was getting nigh and nigher.

There was a rumble at the door,
A draught disturbed the drapery,
And but a minute passed before,
    With gaze that bore
    My destiny,
The man revealed himself to me.

The Going

WHY did you give no hint that night
That quickly after the morrow's dawn,
And calmly, as if indifferent quite,
You would close your term here, up and be gone
    Where I could not follow
    With wing of swallow
To gain one glimpse of you ever anon!

    Never to bid good-bye,
    Or lip me the softest call,
Or utter a wish for a word, while I
Saw morning harden upon the wall,
    Unmoved, unknowing
    That your great going
Had place that moment, and altered all.

Why do you make me leave the house
And think for a breath it is you I see
At the end of the alley of bending boughs
Where so often at dusk you used to be;
    Till in darkening dankness
    The yawning blankness
Of the perspective sickens me!

You were she who abode
By those red-veined rocks far West,
You were the swan-necked one who rode
Along the beetling Beeny Crest,
And, reining nigh me,
Would muse and eye me,
While Life unrolled us its very best.

Why, then, latterly did we not speak,
Did we not think of those days long dead,
And ere your vanishing strive to seek
That time's renewal? We might have said,
'In this bright spring weather
We'll visit together
Those places that once we visited.'

Well, well! All's past amend,
Unchangeable. It must go.
I seem but a dead man held on end
To sink down soon. . . . O you could not know
That such swift fleeing
No soul foreseeing—
Not even I—would undo me so!

December 1912

'I Found Her out There'

I FOUND her out there
On a slope few see,
That falls westwardly
To the salt-edged air,
Where the ocean breaks
On the purple strand,
And the hurricane shakes
The solid land.

I brought her here,
And have laid her to rest
In a noiseless nest
No sea beats near.
She will never be stirred
In her loamy cell
By the waves long heard
And loved so well.

184

'I Found Her out There'

So she does not sleep
By those haunted heights
The Atlantic smites
And the blind gales sweep,
Whence she often would gaze
At Dundagel's famed head,
While the dipping blaze
Dyed her face fire-red;

And would sigh at the tale
Of sunk Lyonnesse,
As a wind-tugged tress
Flapped her cheek like a flail;
Or listen at whiles
With a thought-bound brow
To the murmuring miles
She is far from now.

Yet her shade, maybe,
Will creep underground
Till it catch the sound
Of that western sea
As it swells and sobs
Where she once domiciled,
And joy in its throbs
With the heart of a child.

[December 1912]

The Haunter

HE does not think that I haunt here nightly:
    How shall I let him know
That whither his fancy sets him wandering
    I, too, alertly go?—
Hover and hover a few feet from him
    Just as I used to do,
But cannot answer the words he lifts me—
    Only listen thereto!

The Haunter

When I could answer he did not say them:
    When I could let him know
How I would like to join in his journeys
    Seldom he wished to go.
Now that he goes and wants me with him
    More than he used to do,
Never he sees my faithful phantom
    Though he speaks thereto.

Yes, I companion him to places
    Only dreamers know,
Where the shy hares print long paces,
    Where the night rooks go;
Into old aisles where the past is all to him,
    Close as his shade can do,
Always lacking the power to call to him,
    Near as I reach thereto!

What a good haunter I am, O tell him!
    Quickly make him know
If he but sigh since my loss befell him
    Straight to his side I go.
Tell him a faithful one is doing
    All that love can do
Still that his path may be worth pursuing,
    And to bring peace thereto.

The Voice

Woman much missed, how you call to me, call to me,
Saying that now you are not as you were
When you had changed from the one who was all to me,
But as at first, when our day was fair.

Can it be you that I hear? Let me view you, then,
Standing as when I drew near to the town
Where you would wait for me: yes, as I knew you then,
Even to the original air-blue gown!

The Voice

Or is it only the breeze, in its listlessness
Travelling across the wet mead to me here,
You being ever dissolved to wan wistlessness
Heard no more again far or near?

Thus I; faltering forward,
Leaves around me falling,
Wind oozing thin through the thorn from norward,
And the woman calling.

December 1912

After a Journey

HERETO I come to view a voiceless ghost;
    Whither, O whither will its whim now draw me?
Up the cliff, down, till I'm lonely, lost,
    And the unseen waters' ejaculations awe me.
Where you will next be there's no knowing,
    Facing round about me everywhere,
        With your nut-coloured hair,
And grey eyes, and rose-flush coming and going.

Yes: I have re-entered your olden haunts at last;
    Through the years, through the dead scenes I have tracked you;
What have you now found to say of our past—
    Scanned across the dark space wherein I have lacked you?
Summer gave us sweets, but autumn wrought division?
    Things were not lastly as firstly well
        With us twain, you tell?
But all's closed now, despite Time's derision.

I see what you are doing: you are leading me on
    To the spots we knew when we haunted here together,
The waterfall, above which the mist-bow shone
    At the then fair hour in the then fair weather,
And the cave just under, with a voice still so hollow
    That it seems to call out to me from forty years ago,
        When you were all aglow,
And not the thin ghost that I now fraily follow!

After a Journey

Ignorant of what there is flitting here to see,
   The waked birds preen and the seals flop lazily;
Soon you will have, Dear, to vanish from me,
   For the stars close their shutters and the dawn whitens hazily.
Trust me, I mind not, though Life lours,
   The bringing me here; nay, bring me here again!
     I am just the same as when
Our days were a joy, and our paths through flowers.

Pentargan Bay, March 1913

Beeny Cliff

March 1870—*March* 1913

I

O THE opal and the sapphire of that wandering western sea,
And the woman riding high above with bright hair flapping
   free—
The woman whom I loved so, and who loyally loved me.

II

The pale mews plained below us, and the waves seemed far away
In a nether sky, engrossed in saying their ceaseless babbling say,
As we laughed light-heartedly aloft on that clear-sunned March
   day.

III

A little cloud then cloaked us, and there flew an irised rain,
And the Atlantic dyed its levels with a dull misfeatured stain,
And then the sun burst out again, and purples prinked the main.

IV

—Still in all its chasmal beauty bulks old Beeny to the sky,
And shall she and I not go there once again now March is nigh,
And the sweet things said in that March say anew there by and
   by?

V

What if still in chasmal beauty looms that wild weird western
   shore,
The woman now is—elsewhere—whom the ambling pony bore,
And nor knows nor cares for Beeny, and will laugh there never-
   more.

At Castle Boterel

As I drive to the junction of lane and highway,
    And the drizzle bedrenches the waggonette,
I look behind at the fading byway,
        And see on its slope, now glistening wet,
            Distinctly yet

Myself and a girlish form benighted
    In dry March weather. We climb the road
Beside a chaise. We had just alighted
        To ease the sturdy pony's load
            When he sighed and slowed.

What we did as we climbed, and what we talked of
    Matters not much, nor to what it led,—
Something that life will not be balked of
        Without rude reason till hope is dead,
            And feeling fled.

It filled but a minute. But was there ever
    A time of such quality, since or before,
In that hill's story? To one mind never,
        Though it has been climbed, foot-swift, foot-sore,
            By thousands more.

Primaeval rocks form the roads' steep border,
    And much have they faced there, first and last,
Of the transitory in Earth's long order;
        But what they record in colour and cast
            Is—that we two passed.

And to me, though Time's unflinching rigour,
    In mindless rote, has ruled from sight
The substance now, one phantom figure
        Remains on the slope, as when that night
            Saw us alight.

I look and see it there, shrinking, shrinking,
    I look back at it amid the rain
For the very last time; for my sand is sinking,
        And I shall traverse old love's domain
            Never again.

March 1913

189

The Phantom Horsewoman

QUEER are the ways of a man I know:
        He comes and stands
        In a careworn craze,
        And looks at the sands
        And the seaward haze
        With moveless hands
        And face and gaze,
        Then turns to go . . .
And what does he see when he gazes so?

II

They say he sees as an instant thing
        More clear than to-day,
        A sweet soft scene
        That was once in play
        By that briny green;
        Yes, notes alway
        Warm, real, and keen,
        What his back years bring—
A phantom of his own figuring.

III

Of this vision of his they might say more:
        Not only there
        Does he see this sight,
        But everywhere
        In his brain—day, night,
        As if on the air
        It were drawn rose-bright—
        Yea, far from that shore
Does he carry this vision of heretofore:

IV

A ghost-girl-rider. And though, toil-tried,
    He withers daily,
    Time touches her not,
    But she still rides gaily
    In his rapt thought
    On that shagged and shaly
    Atlantic spot,
    And as when first eyed
Draws rein and sings to the swing of the tide.

1913

The Prospect

THE twigs of the birch imprint the December sky
  Like branching veins upon a thin old hand;
I think of summer-time, yes, of last July,
  When she was beneath them, greeting a gathered band
    Of the urban and bland.

Iced airs wheeze through the skeletoned hedge from the north,
  With steady snores, and a numbing that threatens snow,
And skaters pass; and merry boys go forth
  To look for slides. But well, well do I know
    Whither I would go!

December 1912

'She Opened the Door'

SHE opened the door of the West to me,
    With its loud sea-lashings,
    And cliff-side clashings
Of waters rife with revelry.

She opened the door of Romance to me,
    The door from a cell
    I had known too well,
Too long, till then, and was fain to flee.

She opened the door of a Love to me,
    That passed the wry
    World-welters by
As far as the arching blue the lea.

She opens the door of the Past to me,
    Its magic lights,
    Its heavenly heights,
When forward little is to see!

    1913

'It Never Looks like Summer'

'IT never looks like summer here
    On Beeny by the sea.'
But though she saw its look as drear,
    Summer it seemed to me.

It never looks like summer now
    Whatever weather's there;
But ah, it cannot anyhow,
    On Beeny or elsewhere!

Boscastle, March 8, 1913

The Shadow on the Stone

I WENT by the Druid stone
That broods in the garden white and lone,
And I stopped and looked at the shifting shadows
That at some moments fall thereon
From the tree hard by with a rhythmic swing,
And they shaped in my imagining
To the shade that a well-known head and shoulders
Threw there when she was gardening.

I thought her behind my back,
Yea, her I long had learned to lack,
And I said: 'I am sure you are standing behind me,
Though how do you get into this old track?'
And there was no sound but the fall of a leaf
As a sad response; and to keep down grief
I would not turn my head to discover
That there was nothing in my belief.

Yet I wanted to look and see
That nobody stood at the back of me;
But I thought once more: 'Nay, I'll not unvision
A shape which, somehow, there may be.'
So I went on softly from the glade,
And left her behind me throwing her shade,
As she were indeed an apparition—
My head unturned lest my dream should fade.

Begun 1913: *finished* 1916

A Night in November

I MARKED when the weather changed,
And the panes began to quake,
And the winds rose up and ranged,
That night, lying half-awake.

Dead leaves blew into my room,
And alighted upon my bed,
And a tree declared to the gloom
Its sorrow that they were shed.

One leaf of them touched my hand,
And I thought that it was you
There stood as you used to stand,
And saying at last you knew!

[?] 1913

'The Curtains now are Drawn'

(SONG)

I

THE curtains now are drawn,
And the spindrift strikes the glass,
Blown up the jaggèd pass
By the surly salt sou'-west,
And the sneering glare is gone
Behind the yonder crest,
    While she sings to me:
'O the dream that thou art my Love, be it thine
And the dream that I am thy Love, be it mine
And death may come, but loving is divine.'

II

I stand here in the rain,
With its smite upon her stone,
And the grasses that have grown
Over women, children, men,
And their texts that 'Life is vain';
But I hear the notes as when
    Once she sang to me:
'O the dream that thou art my Love, be it thine,
And the dream that I am thy Love, be it mine,
And death may come, but loving is divine.'

1913

Albuera

The ghastly climax of the strife is reached; the combatants are seen to be firing grape and canister at speaking distance, and discharging musketry in each other's faces when so close that their complexions may be recognized. Hot corpses, their mouths blackened by cartridge-biting, and surrounded by cast-away knapsacks, firelocks, hats, stocks, flint-boxes, and priming-horns, together with red and blue rags of clothing, gaiters, epaulettes, limbs, and viscera, accumulate on the slopes, increasing from twos and threes to half-dozens, and from half-dozens to heaps, which steam with their own warmth as the spring rain falls gently upon them. . . .

SEMICHORUS I OF THE PITIES (aerial music)

They come, beset by riddling hail;
They sway like sedges in a gale;
They fail, and win, and win, and fail. Albuera!

SEMICHORUS II

They gain the ground there, yard by yard,
Their brows and hair and lashes charred,
Their blackened teeth set firm and hard.

SEMICHORUS I

Their mad assailants rave and reel,
And face, as men who scorn to feel,
The close-lined, three-edged prongs of steel.

SEMICHORUS II

Till faintness follows closing-in,
When, faltering headlong down, they spin
Like leaves. But those pay well who win Albuera.

SEMICHORUS I

Out of six thousand souls that sware
To hold the mount, or pass elsewhere,
But eighteen hundred muster there.

SEMICHORUS II

Pale Colonels, Captains, ranksmen lie,
Facing the earth or facing sky;—
They strove to live, they stretch to die.

SEMICHORUS I

Friends, foemen, mingle; heap and heap.—
Hide their hacked bones, Earth!—deep, deep, deep,
Where harmless worms caress and creep.

CHORUS

Hide their hacked bones, Earth;—deep, deep, deep,
Where harmless worms caress and creep.—
What man can grieve? what woman weep?
Better than waking is to sleep! Albuera!

The night comes on, and darkness covers the battle-field.

The Eve of Waterloo

SCENE VIII OF ACT SIX OF *The Dynasts*, PART THIRD

*The rising ground of Mont Saint-Jean, in front of Waterloo, is gained by
the English vanguard and main masses of foot, and by degrees they are
joined by the cavalry and artillery. The French are but little later in taking
up their position amid the cornfields around La Belle Alliance.*

*Fires begin to shine up from the English bivouacs. Camp kettles are
slung, and the men pile arms and stand round the blaze to dry themselves.
The French opposite lie down like dead men in the dripping green wheat
and rye, without supper and without fire.*

*By and by the English army also lies down, the men huddling together on
the ploughed mud in their wet blankets, while some sleep sitting round
the dying fires.*

CHORUS OF THE YEARS (aerial music)

The eyelids of eve fall together at last,
And the forms so foreign to field and tree
Lie down as though native, and slumber fast!

CHORUS OF THE PITIES

Sore are the thrills of misgiving we see
In the artless champaign at this harlequinade,
Distracting a vigil where calm should be!

The green seems opprest, and the Plain afraid
Of a Something to come, whereof these are the proofs,—
Neither earthquake, nor storm, nor eclipse's shade!

The Dynasts

Yea, the coneys are scared by the thud of hoofs,
And their white scuts flash at their vanishing heels,
And swallows abandon the hamlet-roofs.

The mole's tunnelled chambers are crushed by wheels,
The lark's eggs scattered, their owners fled;
And the hedgehog's household the sapper unseals.

The snail draws in at the terrible tread,
But in vain; he is crushed by the felloe-rim;
The worm asks what can be overhead,

And wriggles deep from a scene so grim,
And guesses him safe; for he does not know
What a foul red flood will be soaking him!

Beaten about by the heel and toe
Are butterflies, sick of the day's long rheum,
To die of a worse than the weather-foe.

Trodden and bruised to a miry tomb
Are ears that have greened but will never be gold,
And flowers in the bud that will never bloom.

CHORUS OF THE PITIES

So the season's intent, ere its fruit unfold,
Is frustrate, and mangled, and made succumb,
Like a youth of promise struck stark and cold! ...

And what of these who to-night have come?

CHORUS OF THE YEARS

The young sleep sound; but the weather awakes
In the veterans, pains from the past that numb;

Old stabs of Ind, old Peninsular aches,
Old Friedland chills, haunt their moist mud bed,
Cramps from Austerlitz; till their slumber breaks.

CHORUS OF SINISTER SPIRITS

And each soul shivers as sinks his head
On the loam he's to lease with the other dead
From to-morrow's mist-fall till Time be sped!

The fires of the English go out, and silence prevails, save for the soft hiss of the rain that falls impartially on both the sleeping armies.

197

San Sebastian

WITH THOUGHTS OF SERGEANT M—— (PENSIONER), WHO DIED 185–

'WHY, Sergeant, stray on the Ivel Way,
As though at home there were spectres rife?
From first to last 'twas a proud career!
And your sunny years with a gracious wife
    Have brought you a daughter dear.

'I watched her to-day; a more comely maid,
As she danced in her muslin bowed with blue,
Round a Hintock maypole never gayed.'
—'Aye, aye; I watched her this day, too,
    As it happens,' the Sergeant said.

'My daughter is now,' he again began,
'Of just such an age as one I knew
When we of the Line, the Forlorn-hope van,
On an August morning—a chosen few—
    Stormed San Sebastian.

'She's a score less three; so about was *she*—
The maiden I wronged in Peninsular days. . . .
You may prate of your prowess in lusty times,
But as years gnaw inward you blink your bays,
    And see too well your crimes!

'We'd stormed it at night, by the flapping light
Of burning towers, and the mortar's boom:
We'd topped the breach; but had failed to stay,
For our files were misled by the baffling gloom;
    And we said we'd storm by day.

'So, out of the trenches, with features set,
On that hot, still morning, in measured pace,
Our column climbed; climbed higher yet,
Past the fauss'bray, scarp, up the curtain-face,
    And along the parapet.

'From the battleried hornwork the cannoneers
Hove crashing balls of iron fire;
On the shaking gap mount the volunteers
In files, and as they mount expire
    Amid curses, groans, and cheers.

198

'Five hours did we storm, five hours re-form,
As Death cooled those hot blood pricked on;
Till our cause was helped by a woe within:
They were blown from the summit we'd leapt upon,
　　And madly we entered in.

'On end for plunder, 'mid rain and thunder
That burst with the lull of our cannonade,
We vamped the streets in the stifling air—
Our hunger unsoothed, our thirst unstayed—
　　And ransacked the buildings there.

'From the shady vaults of their walls of white
We rolled rich puncheons of Spanish grape,
Till at length, with the fire of the wine alight,
I saw at a doorway a fair fresh shape—
　　A woman, a sylph, or sprite.

'Afeard she fled, and with heated head
I pursued to the chamber she called her own;
—When might is right no qualms deter,
And having her helpless and alone
　　I wreaked my will on her.

'She raised her beseeching eyes to me,
And I heard the words of prayer she sent
In her own soft language. . . . Fatefully
I copied those eyes for my punishment
　　In begetting the girl you see!

'So, to-day I stand with a God-set brand
Like Cain's, when he wandered from kindred's ken. . . .
I served through the war that made Europe free;
I wived me in peace-year. But, hid from men,
　　I bear that mark on me.

'Maybe we shape our offspring's guise
From fancy, or we know not what,
And that no deep impression dies,—
For the mother of my child is not
　　The mother of her eyes.

'And I nightly stray on the Ivel Way
As though at home there were spectres rife;
I delight me not in my proud career;
And 'tis coals of fire that a gracious wife
　　Should have brought me a daughter dear!'

August 1813

Embarcation

(*Southampton Docks: October* 1899)

HERE, where Vespasian's legions struck the sands,
And Cerdic with his Saxons entered in,
And Henry's army leapt afloat to win
Convincing triumphs over neighbour lands,

Vaster battalions press for further strands,
To argue in the selfsame bloody mode
Which this late age of thought, and pact, and code,
Still fails to mend.—Now deckward tramp the bands,

Yellow as autumn leaves, alive as spring;
And as each host draws out upon the sea
Beyond which lies the tragical To-be,
None dubious of the cause, none murmuring,

Wives, sisters, parents, wave white hands and smile,
As if they knew not that they weep the while.

Drummer Hodge

I

THEY throw in Drummer Hodge, to rest
   Uncoffined—just as found:
His landmark is a kopje-crest
   That breaks the veldt around;
And foreign constellations west
   Each night above his mound.

II

Young Hodge the Drummer never knew—
   Fresh from his Wessex home—
The meaning of the broad Karoo,
   The Bush, the dusty loam,
And why uprose to nightly view
   Strange stars amid the gloam.

III

Yet portion of that unknown plain
    Will Hodge for ever be;
His homely Northern breast and brain
    Grow to some Southern tree,
And strange-eyed constellations reign
    His stars eternally.

[*First printed* 1899]

The Souls of the Slain

I

THE thick lids of Night closed upon me
    Alone at the Bill
    Of the Isle by the Race[1]—
Many-caverned, bald, wrinkled of face—
And with darkness and silence the spirit was on me
    To brood and be still.

II

No wind fanned the flats of the ocean,
    Or promontory sides,
    Or the ooze by the strand,
Or the bent-bearded slope of the land,
Whose base took its rest amid everlong motion
    Of criss-crossing tides.

III

Soon from out of the Southward seemed nearing
    A whirr, as of wings
    Waved by mighty-vanned flies,
Or by night-moths of measureless size,
And in softness and smoothness well-nigh beyond hearing
    Of corporal things.

IV

And they bore to the bluff, and alighted—
    A dim-discerned train
    Of sprites without mould,
Frameless souls none might touch or might hold—
On the ledge by the turreted lantern, far-sighted
    By men of the main.

[1] The 'Race' is the turbulent sea-area off the Bill of Portland, where contrary tides meet.

V

And I heard them say 'Home!' and I knew them
    For souls of the felled
    On the earth's nether bord
Under Capricorn, whither they'd warred,
And I neared in my awe, and gave heedfulness to them
    With breathings inheld.

VI

Then, it seemed, there approached from the northward
    A senior soul-flame
    Of the like filmy hue:
And he met them and spake: 'Is it you,
O my men?' Said they, 'Aye! We bear homeward and hearthward
    To feast on our fame!'

VII

'I've flown there before you,' he said then:
    'Your households are well;
    But—your kin linger less
On your glory and war-mightiness
Than on dearer things.'—'Dearer?' cried these from the dead
    then,
    'Of what do they tell?'

VIII

'Some mothers muse sadly, and murmur
    Your doings as boys—
    Recall the quaint ways
Of your babyhood's innocent days.
Some pray that, ere dying, your faith had grown firmer,
    And higher your joys.

IX

'A father broods: "Would I had set him
    To some humble trade,
    And so slacked his high fire,
And his passionate martial desire;
And told him no stories to woo him and whet him
    To this dire crusade!"'

The Souls of the Slain

X

'And, General, how hold out our sweethearts,
    Sworn loyal as doves?'
     —'Many mourn; many think
It is not unattractive to prink
Them in sables for heroes. Some fickle and fleet hearts
    Have found them new loves.'

XI

'And our wives?' quoth another resignedly,
    'Dwell they on our deeds?'
     —'Deeds of home; that live yet
Fresh as new—deeds of fondness or fret;
Ancient words that were kindly expressed or unkindly,
    These, these have their heeds.'

XII

—'Alas! then it seems that our glory
    Weighs less in their thought
    Than our old homely acts,
And the long-ago commonplace facts
Of our lives—held by us as scarce part of our story,
    And rated as nought!'

XIII

Then bitterly some: 'Was it wise now
    To raise the tomb-door
    For such knowledge? Away!'
But the rest: 'Fame we prized till to-day;
Yet that hearts keep us green for old kindness we prize now
    A thousand times more!'

XIV

Thus speaking, the trooped apparitions
    Began to disband
    And resolve them in two:
Those whose record was lovely and true
Bore to northward for home: those of bitter traditions
    Again left the land,

XV

And, towering to seaward in legions,
    They paused at a spot
    Overbending the Race—
That engulphing, ghast, sinister place—
Whither headlong they plunged, to the fathomless regions
    Of myriads forgot.

XVI

And the spirits of those who were homing
    Passed on, rushingly,
    Like the Pentecost Wind;
And the whirr of their wayfaring thinned
And surceased on the sky, and but left in the gloaming
    Sea-mutterings and me.

December 1899

The Man He Killed

'Had he and I but met
    By some old ancient inn,
We should have sat us down to wet
    Right many a nipperkin!

'But ranged as infantry,
    And staring face to face,
I shot at him as he at me,
    And killed him in his place.

'I shot him dead because—
    Because he was my foe,
Just so: my foe of course he was;
    That's clear enough; although

'He thought he'd 'list, perhaps,
    Off-hand like—just as I—
Was out of work—had sold his traps—
    No other reason why.

'Yes; quaint and curious war is!
    You shoot a fellow down
You'd treat if met where any bar is,
    Or help to half-a-crown.'

1902

Channel Firing

THAT night your great guns, unawares,
Shook all our coffins as we lay,
And broke the chancel window-squares,
We thought it was the Judgment-day

And sat upright. While drearisome
Arose the howl of wakened hounds:
The mouse let fall the altar-crumb,
The worms drew back into the mounds,

The glebe cow drooled. Till God called, 'No;
It's gunnery practice out at sea
Just as before you went below;
The world is as it used to be:

'All nations striving strong to make
Red war yet redder. Mad as hatters
They do no more for Christés sake
Than you who are helpless in such matters.

'That this is not the judgment-hour
For some of them's a blessed thing,
For if it were they'd have to scour
Hell's floor for so much threatening. . . .

'Ha, ha. It will be warmer when
I blow the trumpet (if indeed
I ever do; for you are men,
And rest eternal sorely need).'

So down we lay again. 'I wonder,
Will the world ever saner be,'
Said one, 'than when He sent us under
In our indifferent century!'

And many a skeleton shook his head.
'Instead of preaching forty years,'
My neighbour Parson Thirdly said,
'I wish I had stuck to pipes and beer.'

Again the guns disturbed the hour,
Roaring their readiness to avenge,
As far inland as Stourton Tower,
And Camelot, and starlit Stonehenge.

April 1914

In Time of 'The Breaking of Nations'[1]

I

ONLY a man harrowing clods
    In a slow silent walk
With an old horse that stumbles and nods
    Half asleep as they stalk.

II

Only thin smoke without flame
    From the heaps of couch-grass;
Yet this will go onward the same
    Though Dynasties pass.

III

Yonder a maid and her wight
    Come whispering by:
War's annals will cloud into night
    Ere their story die.

1915

[1] Jer. 51: 20.

'And there was a Great Calm'

(ON THE SIGNING OF THE ARMISTICE, NOV. 11, 1918)

I

THERE had been years of Passion—scorching, cold,
And much Despair, and Anger heaving high,
Care whitely watching, Sorrows manifold,
Among the young, among the weak and old,
And the pensive Spirit of Pity whispered, 'Why?'

206

'And there was a Great Calm'

II

Men had not paused to answer. Foes distraught
Pierced the thinned peoples in a brute-like blindness,
Philosophies that sages long had taught,
And Selflessness, were as an unknown thought,
And 'Hell!' and 'Shell!' were yapped at Lovingkindness.

III

The feeble folk at home had grown full-used
To 'dug-outs,' 'snipers,' 'Huns,' from the war-adept
In the mornings heard, and at evetides perused;
To day-dreamt men in millions, when they mused—
To nightmare-men in millions when they slept.

IV

Waking to wish existence timeless, null,
Sirius they watched above where armies fell;
He seemed to check his flapping when, in the lull
Of night a boom came thencewise, like the dull
Plunge of a stone dropped into some deep well.

V

So, when old hopes that earth was bettering slowly
Were dead and damned, there sounded 'War is done!'
One morrow. Said the bereft, and meek, and lowly,
'Will men some day be given to grace? yea, wholly,
And in good sooth, as our dreams used to run?'

VI

Breathless they paused. Out there men raised their glance
To where had stood those poplars lank and lopped,
As they had raised it through the four years' dance
Of Death in the now familiar flats of France;
And murmured, 'Strange, this! How? All firing stopped?'

VII

Aye; all was hushed. The about-to-fire fired not,
The aimed-at moved away in trance-lipped song.
One checkless regiment slung a clinching shot
And turned. The Spirit of Irony smirked out, 'What?
Spoil peradventures woven of Rage and Wrong?'

VIII

Thenceforth no flying fires inflamed the grey,
No hurtlings shook the dewdrop from the thorn,
No moan perplexed the mute bird on the spray;
Worn horses mused: 'We are not whipped to-day';
No weft-winged engines blurred the moon's thin horn.

IX

Calm fell. From Heaven distilled a clemency;
There was peace on earth, and silence in the sky;
Some could, some could not, shake off misery:
The Sinister Spirit sneered: 'It had to be!'
And again the Spirit of Pity whispered, 'Why?'

Domicilium

[The poem was written in *Early Life and Architecture* with the comment, 'The poem, written between 1857 and 1860, runs as follows: . . .]

It faces west, and round the back and sides
High beeches, bending, hang a veil of boughs,
And sweep against the roof. Wild honeysucks
Climb on the walls, and seem to sprout a wish
(If we may fancy wish of trees and plants)
To overtop the apple-trees hard by.

Red roses, lilacs, variegated box
Are there in plenty, and such hardy flowers
As flourish best untrained. Adjoining these
Are herbs and esculents; and farther still
A field; then cottages with trees, and last
The distant hills and sky.

Behind, the scene is wilder. Heath and furze
Are everything that seems to grow and thrive
Upon the uneven ground. A stunted thorn
Stands here and there, indeed; and from a pit
An oak uprises, springing from a seed
Dropped by some bird a hundred years ago.

       In days bygone—
Long gone—my father's mother, who is now
Blest with the blest, would take me out to walk.
At such a time I once inquired of her
How looked the spot when first she settled here.
The answer I remember. 'Fifty years
Have passed since then, my child, and change has marked
The face of all things. Yonder garden-plots
And orchards were uncultivated slopes
O'ergrown with bramble bushes, furze and thorn:
That road a narrow path shut in by ferns,
Which, almost trees, obscured the passer-by.

Domicilium

'Our house stood quite alone, and those tall firs
And beeches were not planted. Snakes and efts
Swarmed in the summer days, and nightly bats
Would fly about our bedrooms. Heathcroppers
Lived on the hills, and were our only friends;
So wild it was when first we settled here.'

A Bird-Scene at a Rural Dwelling

WHEN the inmate stirs, the birds retire discreetly
From the window-ledge, whereon they whistled sweetly
    And on the step of the door,
    In the misty morning hoar;
  But now the dweller is up they flee
  To the crooked neighbouring codlin-tree;
And when he comes fully forth they seek the garden,
And call from the lofty costard, as pleading pardon
    For shouting so near before
    In their joy at being alive:—
Meanwhile the hammering clock within goes five.

I know a domicile of brown and green,
Where for a hundred summers there have been
Just such enactments, just such daybreaks seen.

Shortening Days at the Homestead

THE first fire since the summer is lit, and is smoking into the room:
  The sun-rays thread it through, like woof-lines in a loom.
  Sparrows spurt from the hedge, whom misgivings appal
That winter did not leave last year for ever, after all.
    Like shock-headed urchins, spiny-haired,
    Stand pollard willows, their twigs just bared.

Who is this coming with pondering pace,
Black and ruddy, with white embossed,
His eyes being black, and ruddy his face
And the marge of his hair like morning frost?
    It's the cider-maker,
    And appletree-shaker,
And behind him on wheels, in readiness,
His mill, and tubs, and vat, and press.

Old Furniture

I KNOW not how it may be with others
    Who sit amid relics of householdry
That date from the days of their mothers' mothers,
    But well I know how it is with me
      Continually.

I see the hands of the generations
    That owned each shiny familiar thing
In play on its knobs and indentations,
    And with its ancient fashioning
      Still dallying:

Hands behind hands, growing paler and paler,
    As in a mirror a candle-flame
Shows images of itself, each frailer
    As it recedes, though the eye may frame
      Its shape the same.

On the clock's dull dial a foggy finger,
    Moving to set the minutes right
With tentative touches that lift and linger
    In the wont of a moth on a summer night,
      Creeps to my sight.

On this old viol, too, fingers are dancing—
    As whilom—just over the strings by the nut,
The tip of a bow receding, advancing
    In airy quivers, as if it would cut
      The plaintive gut.

And I see a face by that box for tinder,
    Glowing forth in fits from the dark,
And fading again, as the linten cinder
    Kindles to red at the flinty spark,
      Or goes out stark.

Well, well. It is best to be up and doing,
    The world has no use for one to-day
Who eyes things thus—no aim pursuing!
    He should not continue in this stay,
      But sink away.

Childhood among the Ferns

I SAT one sprinkling day upon the lea,
Where tall-stemmed ferns spread out luxuriantly,
And nothing but those tall ferns sheltered me.

The rain gained strength, and damped each lopping frond,
Ran down their stalks beside me and beyond,
And shaped slow-creeping rivulets as I conned,

With pride, my spray-roofed house. And though anon
Some drops pierced its green rafters, I sat on,
Making pretence I was not rained upon.

The sun then burst, and brought forth a sweet breath
From the limp ferns as they dried underneath:
I said: 'I could live on here thus till death';

And queried in the green rays as I sate:
'Why should I have to grow to man's estate,
And this afar-noised World perambulate?'

In Tenebris

I

'Percussus sum sicut foenum, et aruit cor meum.'—Ps. 101

WINTERTIME nighs;
But my bereavement-pain
It cannot bring again:
Twice no one dies.

Flower-petals flee;
But, since it once hath been,
No more that severing scene
Can harrow me.

Birds faint in dread:
I shall not lose old strength
In the lone frost's black length:
Strength long since fled!

In Tenebris

Leaves freeze to dun;
But friends can not turn cold
This season as of old
For him with none.

Tempests may scath;
But love can not make smart
Again this year his heart
Who no heart hath.

Black is night's cope;
But death will not appal
One who, past doubtings all,
Waits in unhope.

Transformations

PORTION of this yew
Is a man my grandsire knew,
Bosomed here at its foot:
This branch may be his wife,
A ruddy human life
Now turned to a green shoot.

These grasses must be made
Of her who often prayed,
Last century, for repose;
And the fair girl long ago
Whom I often tried to know
May be entering this rose.

So, they are not underground,
But as nerves and veins abound
In the growths of upper air,
And they feel the sun and rain,
And the energy again
That made them what they were!

Afterwards

WHEN the Present has latched its postern behind my tremulous
    stay,
  And the May month flaps its glad green leaves like wings,
Delicate-filmed as new-spun silk, will the neighbours say,
  'He was a man who used to notice such things'?

If it be in the dusk when, like an eyelid's soundless blink,
  The dewfall-hawk comes crossing the shades to alight
Upon the wind-warped upland thorn, a gazer may think,
  'To him this must have been a familiar sight.'

If I pass during some nocturnal blackness, mothy and warm,
  When the hedgehog travels furtively over the lawn,
One may say, 'He strove that such innocent creatures should
    come to no harm,
  But he could do little for them; and now he is gone.'

If, when hearing that I have been stilled at last, they stand at
    the door,
  Watching the full-starred heavens that winter sees,
Will this thought rise on those who will meet my face no more,
  'He was one who had an eye for such mysteries'?

And will any say when my bell of quittance is heard in the gloom,
  And a crossing breeze cuts a pause in its outrollings,
Till they rise again, as they were a new bell's boom,
  'He hears it not now, but used to notice such things'?

'We are Getting to the End'

WE are getting to the end of visioning
  The impossible within this universe,
  Such as that better whiles may follow worse,
And that our race may mend by reasoning.

We know that even as larks in cages sing
  Unthoughtful of deliverance from the curse
  That holds them lifelong in a latticed hearse,
We ply spasmodically our pleasuring.

And that when nations set them to lay waste
Their neighbours' heritage by foot and horse,
And hack their pleasant plains in festering seams,
They may again,—not warely, or from taste,
But tickled mad by some demonic force.—
Yes. We are getting to the end of dreams!

He Resolves To Say No More

O MY SOUL, keep the rest unknown!
It is too like a sound of moan
      When the charnel-eyed
  .   Pale Horse has nighed:
Yea, none shall gather what I hide!

Why load men's minds with more to bear
That bear already ails to spare?
      From now alway
      Till my last day
What I discern I will not say

Let Time roll backward if it will;
(Magians who drive the midnight quill
      With brain aglow
      Can see it so,)
What I have learnt no man shall know

And if my vision range beyond
The blinkered sight of souls in bond,
      —By truth made free—
      I'll let all be,
And show to no man what I see.

[1927]

The Darkling Thrush

I LEANT upon a coppice gate
    When Frost was spectre-grey,
And Winter's dregs made desolate
The weakening eye of day.
The tangled bine-stems scored the sky
    Like strings of broken lyres,
And all mankind that haunted nigh
    Had sought their household fires.

The land's sharp features seemed to be
    The Century's corpse outleant,
His crypt the cloudy canopy,
The wind his death-lament,
The ancient pulse of germ and birth
Was shrunken hard and dry,
And every spirit upon earth
    Seemed fervourless as I.

At once a voice arose among
The bleak twigs overhead
In a full-hearted evensong
Of joy illimited;
An aged thrush, frail, gaunt, and small,
    In blast-beruffled plume,
Had chosen thus to fling his soul
    Upon the growing gloom.

So little cause for carollings
    Of such ecstatic sound
Was written on terrestrial things
    Afar or nigh around,
That I could think there trembled through
    His happy good-night air
Some blessed Hope, whereof he knew
    And I was unaware.

31st December 1900

Index of titles of poems

Index of titles of poems

Index of titles of poems

Index of first lines of poems

Index of first lines of poems

221

Index of first lines of poems

222

EVERYMAN'S LIBRARY: A Selected List

This List covers a selection of volumes available in Everyman's Library.

BIOGRAPHY

ESSAYS AND CRITICISM

1

FICTION

REFERENCE

Reader's Guide to Everyman's Library. Compiled by *A. J. Hoppé.* This volume gives in one alphabetical sequence the names of all the authors, titles and subjects in Everyman's Library. (An Everyman Paperback only, 1889). *Many volumes formerly included in Everyman's Library reference section are now included in Everyman's Reference Library and are bound in larger format.*

RELIGION AND PHILOSOPHY

At Waking

WHEN night was lifting,
And dawn had crept under its shade,
Amid cold clouds drifting
Dead-white as a corpse outlaid,
With a sudden scare
I seemed to behold
My Love in bare
Hard lines unfold.

Yea, in a moment,
An insight that would not die
Killed her old endowment
Of charm that had capped all night
Which vanished to none
Like the gilt of a cloud,
And showed her but one
Of the common crowd.

She seemed but a sample
Of earth's poor average kind,
Lit up by no ample
Enrichments of mien or mind.
I covered my eyes
As to cover the thought,
And unrecognize
What the morn had taught.

O vision appalling
When the one believed-in thing
Is seen falling, falling,
With all to which hope can cling.
Off: it is not true;
For it cannot be
That the prize I drew
Is a blank to me!

Weymouth, 1869

She, to Him

I

WHEN you shall see me in the toils of Time,
My lauded beauties carried off from me,
My eyes no longer stars as in their prime,
My name forgot of Maiden Fair and Free;

When, in your being, heart concedes to mind,
And judgment, though you scarce its process know,
Recalls the excellencies I once enshrined,
And you are irked that they have withered so:

Remembering mine the loss is, not the blame,
That Sportsman Time but rears his brood to kill,
Knowing me in my soul the very same—
One who would die to spare you touch of ill!—
Will you not grant to old affection's claim
The hand of friendship down Life's sunless hill?

1866

On the Way

THE trees fret fitfully and twist,
Shutters rattle and carpets heave,
Slime is the dust of yestereve,
    And in the streaming mist
Fishes might seem to fin a passage if they list.

    But to his feet,
    Drawing nigh and nigher
    A hidden seat,
    The fog is sweet
    And the wind a lyre.

A vacant sameness greys the sky,
A moisture gathers on each knop
Of the bramble, rounding to a drop,
    That greets the goer-by
With the cold listless lustre of a dead man's eye

But to her sight,
Drawing nigh and nigher
Its deep delight,
The fog is bright
And the wind a lyre.

The Bride-Night Fire

(A WESSEX TRADITION)

THEY had long met o' Zundays—her true love and she—
 And at junketings, maypoles, and flings;
But she bode wi' a thirtover[1] uncle, and he
Swore by noon and by night that her goodman should be
Naibour Sweatley—a wight often weak at the knee
From taking o' sommat more cheerful than tea—
 Who tranted,[2] and moved people's things.

She cried, 'O pray pity me!' Nought would he hear;
 Then with wild rainy eyes she obeyed.
She chid when her Love was for clinking off wi' her:
The pa'son was told, as the season drew near,
To throw over pu'pit the names of the pair
 As fitting one flesh to be made.

The wedding-day dawned and the morning drew on;
 The couple stood bridegroom and bride;
The evening was passed, and when midnight had gone
The feasters horned,[3] 'God save the King,' and anon
 The pair took their homealong[4] ride.

---

[1] *thirtover*, cross.   [2] *tranted*, traded as carrier.
[3] *horned*, sang loudly.   [4] *homealong*, homeward.

The Bride-Night Fire

The lover Tim Tankens mourned heart-sick and leer[1]
   To be thus of his darling deprived:
He roamed in the dark ath'art field, mound, and mere,
And, a'most without knowing it, found himself near
The house of the tranter, and now of his Dear,
   Where the lantern-light showed 'em arrived.

The bride sought her chamber so calm and so pale
   That a Northern had thought her resigned;
But to eyes that had seen her in tidetimes[2] of weal,
Like the white cloud o' smoke, the red battlefield's vail,
   That look spak' of havoc behind.

The bridegroom yet laitered a beaker to drain,
   Then reeled to the linhay[3] for more,
When the candle-snoff kindled some chaff from his grain—
Flames spread, and red vlankers[4] wi' might and wi' main
   Around beams, thatch, and chimley-tun[5] roar.

Young Tim away yond, rafted[6] up by the light,
   Through brimbles and underwood tears,
Till he comes to the orchet, when crooping[7] from sight
In the lewth[8] of a codlin-tree, bivering[9] wi' fright,
Wi' on'y her night-rail to cover her plight,
   His lonesome young Barbree appears.

Her cwold little figure half-naked he views
   Played about by the frolicsome breeze,
Her light-tripping totties,[10] her ten little tooes,
All bare and besprinkled wi' Fall's[11] chilly dews,
While her great gallied[12] eyes through her hair hanging loose
   Shone as stars through a tardle[13] o' trees.

She eyed him; and, as when a weir-hatch is drawn,
   Her tears, penned by terror afore,
With a rushing of sobs in a shower were strawn,
Till her power to pour 'em seemed wasted and gone
   From the heft[14] o' misfortune she bore.

---

[1] *leer*, empty-stomached.
[3] *linhay*, lean-to building.
[5] *chimley-tun*, chimney stack.
[7] *crooping*, squatting down.
[9] *bivering*, with chattering teeth.
[11] *Fall*, autumn.
[13] *tardle*, entanglement.

[2] *tidetimes*, holidays.
[4] *vlankers*, fire-flakes.
[6] *rafted*, roused.
[8] *lewth*, shelter.
[10] *totties*, feet.
[12] *gallied*, frightened.
[14] *heft*, weight.